Before Spring
Came Summer

Michelle Hockley

First published in 2018

ISBN 9781 7201 7223 9

Dates used throughout this novel are in accordance with the
Calendar Act 1750. 1 January begins the New Year, and not, 25
March as was previously the case.

To the special people in my life
Mum, Dad, Anita and Ian

And my reader

CHAPTER ONE

Coronation of Charles II
23 APRIL 1661

A single dove flies high above. White wings span to power the clear blue sky. I watch it turn to take a different route: a sudden change of heart; a new idea; a new calling perhaps? Is this a planned escape or a chance taken? A forced release or a momentary separation? I shield my eyes with cupped hands to watch the flight unfold, soaring higher and higher until a static pause of contemplation. I hold my breath on a tacit beat then whoosh, gone beyond the sun.

Across the way I see the Banqueting House, where black cloth once draped; slung low to hide the severed head the axe struck to take away the good we had.

'Long live the King. Three cheers for our King...'

Michelle Hockley

Charles, your battle is won. You stuck your ground and made them see, a fine sovereign you will be. Make My Majesty proud - I implore you. Make your father proud - I beg you. Fill the world with colour. Don't waste time. Steer us from stagnation.

A feathered hat falls at my feet. Caps thrown high now fill the air to pledge the joy they feel. Maypoles swing as children dance. Woven threads entwine the load as pleasure makes afresh. Tankards rise and beer spills. Laughter sounds. Hope is here.

Yet, within the joyous crowds I stand alone, drowning in a flood of thoughts that postulate a dance inside my head; penetrating my mind, bellowing around me like cloth in a mellow breeze. Former times sealed in a bygone age, bound in a scrapbook of my past, unleash themselves upon me; unravelling their twisted coil. Without my taking part, for I feel week, our nation starts to heal its wounds, renewing its force.

I need to move away from all this merriment and rest on the side of the warm dusty road. I don't see hats fly towards the April sun. Cheers too, have all but disappeared. Heavy clouds form overhead as my foot scratches on a frosty ground beneath the long black skirt I wear. I pull my arms closer around my knees to hug away the bitter cold. I hear my mother's voice.

* * *

December 1617

'Come along Jane, darling. Please don't dally, not today.'

I hold my mother's hand to hurry from our home in Whitehall. My little legs, at five years old, go double time to keep her pace as we giggle and shiver in the December chill. We take a turn that leads us past the royal mews, where my father, William Ryder, a Harbinger, is responsible for making preparations during royal progress, providing adequate horses for hundreds of courtiers when they travel with King James.

'Mama, please can we take a peep into the mews to see papa?' I say, pulling at my mother's arm, distorting our harmonious gait.

'No Jane. Leave your father to his work, we are already late.'

Without question, I accept her demands of me, and we continue on our way to the royal laundry, where my mother is a Lavender within the royal household of Queen

Anne of Denmark. Today I am accompany her.

'Come along Jane. Oh please be careful of that frosty patch. Don't slip young lady,' she says, swinging me off the ground, transporting me safely over the ice, making me light of heart with our cordial stride.

The Laundry is unusually quiet; no chatter from the staff. Is this because my mother's late arrival, for which I am culpable? I can only hope that she is not berated for my disobedience. We stand in the doorway as a more senior Lavender approaches with an officious resolve, breaking the otherwise muted household.

'Madam Ryder.'

'Is there a problem?' enquires my mother.

'Madam Ryder. The Lord Steward has requested your attention.'

'Do we know why?' my mother enquires again.

'Please can you speak with him right away.'

I feel a little anxious, for a charge from the Lord Steward, who is responsible for all departments that concern below stairs, is an unusual occurrence. Without delay, we hurry to our calling.

Standing outside the office, my mother inhales deeply, squeezes my hand, and then knocks on the offending door.

'Come in,' replies Ludovic Stuart. 'Mrs Ryder and

Before Spring Came Summer

Miss Jane, please, take a seat.'

With no possibility of my reaching a chair, I choose instead, to lean against my mother's knee, watching the Lord Steward begin to move his lips.

'It is with regret Mrs Ryder, that I have to inform you, your husband, William Ryder, was taken ill this morning. Sadly, he has not survived. He was taken from us today, by Our Good Lord.'

My heart beats faster. The words hurl themselves into the air reaching us like ramrods of the heaviest force. I push against my mother's knee willing her to admonish the fate that struck my tender ears. She must stop the Lord Steward saying what cannot be true. Unable to breathe I loosen my collar but it doesn't help me. I need to get out of here. The door is shut. The latch is stiff. Both hands firmly grasped and it comes free.

'Jane. Please come back at once. Stand beside your mother,' she says.

I continue with my quest, running faster and faster down the corridor to find my way outside. I hear only my feet tapping loudly on the hard solid floor and then feel the harsh cold frozen air upon my face.

'Why? My Good Lord? Why my papa?' I scream.

I feel my mother's arms around me. Her warm tears rest upon my cheek.

'Jane. Please don't run away like that. Talk to me Jane.'

'Everything will change mother. It has to change.'

She crouches down before me, tidying my cap.

'Come darling. Please be strong. Together we shall find a way through this. I promise.'

'The royal household won't want us now, not without my father.'

'We have to wait and see Jane. First, let us mourn our loss.'

I stamp my feet and clench my hands to will away this torment. Pleading for the shattered pieces of our lives to be swept away. I want my feet to stamp so hard they take away the hurt I cannot see. Stomp. Stomp on the frosted cobbles.

'No Jane,' my mother pleads, scooping me in her arms to arrest my frantic gestures. My aching head finds comfort deep inside the folds of her cloak as we walk, but our morbid tread wins out the usual feathered step.

CHAPTER TWO

The Maxwell Household

October 1623

Today, our London home in Charing Cross, on the corner of Whitehall, is awash with excitement. With a moment to spare, I manage to avert a collision between my four year old sister Elizabeth, who gallops the wooden hobby horse she recently received from my grandmother Maria Paraides who lives in Antwerp, through the parlour, crashing into our servant Margaret who is busy making preparations for forthcoming celebrations.

'Got you,' I say, lifting up Elizabeth, swinging her onto my hip, almost stumbling over Diana who has crawled on the floor behind to join in; though of course at one year old, is quite content with the shuffle she makes and the gurgles she creates.

'Miss Jane,' says Margaret. 'You can see I'm busy here.'

'I'm sorry Margaret,' I reply, bending down to lift Diana onto my other hip. Hoping to fend off any tears by bouncing as I carry them towards the back of the house, from under Margaret's feet.

'Not you as well Anne,' shouts Margaret. That makes me giggle, because Anne, my younger sister by one year, at ten years old, should know better. To be fair, she usually does, but today has clearly embroiled herself in this heightened atmosphere.

My mother, Elizabeth Ryder, nee Elizabeth de Boussy, remarried in 1619, two years after my father's death, to a James Maxwell. A distinguished gentleman, not only amongst city merchants where he forms overseas trade links with the East India Company and the Levant, but also within the royal court, holding offices: Gentleman of the Bedchamber to Prince Charles; Gentleman Usher and Black Rod, placing our family firmly within the inner sanctum of the royal court.

My mother, whose position of Lavender dissolved when Queen Anne of Denmark died of dropsy in 1619, spends more time with her growing family: two Ryder girls; Anne and myself, and two new arrivals shortly after the marriage: Elizabeth and Diana.

Outside in the courtyard, away from under Margaret's feet, church bells make a thunderous sound, the ground vibrates from their manic tones. It's not unusual for us to hear the sound of bells. They chime often in celebration to commemorate the many saint days, or the accession of the late Queen Elizabeth, or the foiled attack upon King James' life on the 5 November, accompanied by fireworks to represent the gunpowder used by the traitors in 1605. However, today, there is more determination in the notes they play. Celebrations are felt more strongly, because our Protestant religion is safe after months of speculation that we could be forced to convert to a Papal church.

Religion is the backbone of our society, playing an enormous part in all our lives within the confines of our Protestant country. Early in our lives, rituals filter beneath our skin. We play with the carved letters of the Lord's Prayer on the wooden paddle of the Horn Book long before we can read. That is not to say that other religious factions do not exists in our society. Some folk choose to worship God under the Puritan faith. Others, though frowned upon, practise Catholicism. Inevitably, tension does prevail. No more so, than when religion is used as a political weapon, like we've experienced for the past six months.

This came about when King James, desperate for his

daughter Elizabeth to be restored to her lost lands of the Palatinate, sent Prince Charles with the Marquis of Buckingham, incognito and uninvited, to the Spanish court to restore good relations with Spain by proposing a marriage union with his son and the Infanta Maria Anna; sister of Philip IV, King of Spain. A match was indeed agreed, but accompanied with the impossible condition that Prince Charles was to convert to the Catholic faith. Whilst this union may satisfy land disputes, it has created untold anxiety for the Protestant people. An apprehension has furiously built-up over the past few months like a cauldron reaching boiling point with no sign of abating. That is until today.

From the moment the Privy Council issued word that Prince Charles will arrive into England without securing a union with the Spanish Infanta or forgoing his own beloved Protestant religion, the twisted antagonism amongst our people has been replaced with one of relief and happiness. The notice, attached to the door of St Margaret's church by the Lord Mayor confirming this important decision, has sent everyone into an almost state of hysteria.

'Girls,' calls out my mother, straining to be heard over the church bells. 'Please can you collect the lanterns so Margaret can dress the front windows.'

Whilst we would prefer to dance to the sound of the

bells, our eagerness to please our mother wins out and we immediately stop what we are doing to open the store in the courtyard, and return to the house with our arms laden, grappling to hold the lanterns, not wanting to spoil them. One by one we pass the lanterns to Margaret as she arranges them around the window to show those who pass our home, that the Maxwell household is also rejoicing in this celebrated news. Though, from what I see in the street beyond, I'm not convinced that our lanterns will make the slightest dent in that direction. Bonfires as tall as trees are being built outside.

'Margaret,' I say, standing beside her with my nose now pressed on the windowpane. 'If those mounds become any bigger, when they are lit, I am certain they will burn forever.'

She doesn't engage in conversation, slightly flustered by today's events. She ignores the trail of neighbours outside carrying large pieces of furniture from their homes to place on top of the biggest bonfires I have ever seen. She is not even distracted from her work when Elizabeth jumps up and down, calling out to her papa, seeing my stepfather arriving home from the royal court, coming towards the front door.

I lift Diana in my arms again and run to the front door to greet him, with Anne and Elizabeth in tow and

Diana gurgling over my shoulder, not knowing what is going on but loving the attention.

'Sorry Margaret,' I say. 'We shall be back soon.'

'Mind you do as well girls,' she says smiling, but knowing she is no contest for my stepfather's arrival home.

Standing in the hallway like obedient soldiers, expecting to receive a hug as is always the routine, we are surprised when instead, he enters quite breathless and heads straight through the drawing room in search of my mother. Perturbed, we run to follow after him and stand quite still as he holds council with my mother in the parlour. With his arms outstretched, he begins.

'You cannot imagine the excitement in the streets,' he says. 'More than 300 bonfires from Whitehall to Temple Bar all waiting to be lit the moment Prince Charles puts foot on English soil.'

Each of us, including my mother, stand with our eyes wide, jaws gaped as he pauses, leaving a moment for us to digest such an image.

'...fifteen prisoners were released today Jane,' he says, singling me out from the group. 'They were set free as they walked to Tyburn to be executed this morning. Our city is alive again and all because everyone is so over joyed by the news that we shall remain of a Protestant faith.'

I have never seen my stepfather consumed by such

elation that I'm seeing today. As he bends down to each of us girls then swings us around in his arms, I can't help but feel relief that my new papa couldn't love us anymore than he does.

Long into the early hours I lay awake in my bedchamber listening to the heavy chants from the crowds.

'We have him,' they shout in their heavy tones. 'We have him,' they repeat to the rhythm of their marching feet; never once faltering in their chorus.

I imagine the crowd walking behind Prince Charles, as he makes his way to Royston where King James, who is recuperating from a bout of gout, awaits the return of his son. King James will be proud of Charles' strength of mind against the persistent demands of the Spanish court to protect his faith. I feel comforted to know that Charles made such a popular decision for our people, even though he was unable to appease his father's wishes to restore lost lands for his sister Elizabeth.

CHAPTER THREE

Lammas
August 1626

The summer shine brings darkness, as plague runs wild through a tepid breeze, biting deeper and deeper into all our lives. A putrid, fetid trail of destruction reigns, forcing the hand of the royal court to surrender its seat in Whitehall for the safer, cleaner air of Hampton Court Palace, to distance itself from the diseased fleas and infested rats. I too am part of that expulsion, to escape infestation of the decrepit.

Taking a direct route through Chelsea with my sisters and mother, we make the twelve mile journey to Kingston-Upon-Thames to reside in our country home and be close to the royal court. Silence lies heavy inside our carriage as we adjust to the changes in our lives, forced upon us by rodents. I sit pressed against the window, hypnotised by the vast expanse of golden corn as we pass field after field where men, women and children reap what they have sown. Girls and boys, younger than me, stand astride haystacks as they grapple, twisting the corn to stand tall. Others, perhaps from different families are in the field wiping their brow. Faces worn from long hot days they jostle and cheer together. Feed and drink together. Spirits are high. Their labour is hard, though benefits come from their toil. They are not aimless, they have a purpose.

Inside the carriage expressions are motionless, as we are carried from the impending threat of death. My world is more like a play upon the London stage, with its flamboyant gestures bound in its everyday strict etiquette and unnatural protocol. Life for the labourer is far removed from my own existence, who appear untethered, in tune with nature, with a more godly purpose to feed their souls. I don't suppose I shall ever understand how life is for them, anymore than they will know what life is like for me. Though something must tie us together, fastening us across this great chasm in our society. We are all born as God's children. We each breath the air that God provides. We feel the same sun upon our cheeks. The same rain soaks our clothes and moistens our skin. Perhaps we can never know the answers and will always be devoid of any reconciliation to these questions.

Before Spring Came Summer

Fast approaching Kingston-Upon-Thames, catching site of the Great Bridge nearing, I see the ducking stool at the East end, where no doubt, some unfortunate woman who is totally misunderstood, will find herself during the course of our stay. For as long as I can remember there has always been a great urgency to eradicate women who seem to have unusual powers. Arrested because they are different, and what the courts recognise as being a witch. I don't think I've ever met such a woman, or even convinced such a person exists, but a guilty charge is real enough when strapped to a heavy chair, submerged deep into a river only to discover that if she drowns, she was in fact innocent. I am told, the best remedies for combating disease can be got from a witch, so perhaps they have their uses. Obviously we don't align ourselves with such recipes, even if it means we may save someone's life. Instead, the ladies at court take a more reserved approach by either visiting an apothecary or making their own remedies. We bind bunches of herbs such as rosemary, lavender, sage, mint, wormwood and for good measure, nutmeg. Each bunch is secured above doors, around the windows in our homes or used to fill the pomander we carry about our person. Our carriage continues past a row of shops and the gardens behind the river, before turning south into Thames Street, going beyond where the monthly Horse Fair is staged, before entering the back lanes. Silence is broken with Diana's chanting, 'clatter, clatter, clatter,' she sings as we approach Clattern Bridge, over the river Hogsmill. Elizabeth used to call out clatter when we crossed this bridge, but she is fast becoming too grown up to shout out such child's play; which, according to what we have been told, the bridge is named as such, to replicate the noise of horses hooves as they trundle and clatter over this small enchanting structure.

Arriving at the house, our servants, Sarah and William, who are employed to keep this home for my mother, welcome us to the country. Although Margaret is not with us because she is taking a break with her brother Jack, we do still have our tutors come to this house, except today, we shall forego our lessons of geography, French and letters, to celebrate Lammas; the beginning of Harvest.

Anne and I help Diana and Elizabeth from the carriage, with their spinning top and hobby horse. We all stand briefly to say hello to our servants at the request of our mother. Once formalities are finished, we each break away quickly to our rooms to be reunited with our possessions that were sent ahead of our arrival.

Running to the second floor and entering my bedchamber, I see my room is laid out in an orderly fashion. My favourite pastimes of needle point and tapestry are placed on the trunk below my bed. Samplers that I've made to emulate those pieces made at Mortlake, not far from here, that my stepfather showed me two years ago being made for the palaces, are stretched on frames. A small vase of cut flowers adorns the fireplace. A silver framed looking glass, that has been placed on the wall above my dressing table, makes me feel quite grown-up. I sit on the edge of the freshly laundered bed with my feet skimming the ornate rug that decorates the waxed parquet floor, and begin to study my new surroundings. On the bedside table, covered in a white lace cloth with a fresh candle and a brass snuffer, I add a small charcoal sketch to remind me of my dear horse Rayleigh who is housed at the royal mews.

It is impossible to ignore the excitement about the house as everyone familiarises themselves. Elizabeth and Diana share a room on the third floor and Anne is on the second floor, adjacent to me. From the vantage point of my window, I can see the chimney stacks of Hampton Court Palace rising into the sky through the trees, where untold responsibilities are now firmly pressed upon King Charles' shoulders, after King James was taken from us on 27 March 1625. A lifetime of preparation in kingship whilst a prince, is now unleashed upon our shores as virgin territories are navigated at the royal court for all the world to see. I smile to myself as I look out beyond, thinking how life has a habit of righting itself. All that fuss about Prince Charles marrying a Catholic princess for fear of losing our right to be Protestants. Yet here we are, our king is now married to Henrietta Maria, who herself is a Catholic, and as far as I can see, the world has not come to an end. The crops still grow to feed us and our religion proceeds as Protestants the way we always hoped it would.

Sarah tries to calm the excitement to bring order to her household, calling us to come and eat. I am always hungry, so of course am happy to attend obediently. Anne is the same, not always hungry, but always obedient. We arrive promptly to take our places in the distinguished dining room, with freshly polished wainscot, overlooking the pretty formal gardens with neatly trimmed borders. I recognise the tableware and linen that has been transported from London as we settle into our mid-day meal of chicken, mullet, game pie and manchette.

When our meal is complete, we tidy ourselves in readiness to attend the service for Lammas at All Saints Church. We follow my mother's lead out of the house where we file in behind, or beside her, walking to the church, close to the Town Hall on the Market Square. I take a deep breath to savour the fresh, clean breeze, distinct from the smoke of London. The air is calm, motionless and quiet. I welcome the August heat that gently warms my face, seeping through my whole body as birds fly freely through the trees, rustling the sweet smell of Lavender as they flutter through the sky. The path we tread is dry. Dust balloons from bouncing shingle as my feet crunch through loose chippings. Every step I take is reassurance that the commotion and dangers of London are far behind us.

'Are you alright Jane?' enquires my mother, turning around to check we are all keeping up with her. 'You seem a little reticent today and somewhat thoughtful.'

'I am quite content, thank you, Mama.' I reply, though she is quite right, I am a little subdued.

'That's fine then Jane. Good girl.'

The piper's harvest song greets us from inside the church calling us to take our pew. We sit alongside other courtiers from London who also reside close to the royal court, taking this moment as an opportunity to compare notes about: their journey; the speed at which they were expected to leave the city; their servants and the state of their lodgings. Whilst on the opposite side of the church, are the locals from the village, who themselves, last year, suffered a devastating outbreak of the plague, where hundreds lost their lives as disease burrowed itself into the tapestry of their very being.

Sir John Finet, Master of Ceremonies at the royal court, arrives from the palace and walks swiftly past us in his usual efficient manner, always appearing busy even when he cannot possibly be so, always with a sense of purpose in his stride. He politely acknowledges my mother as my stepfather follows closely behind, accompanied by Mr Maule, Gentleman of the Bedchamber and Mr William Smithsby, Keeper of the Standing Wardrobe and Privy Lodgings at Hampton Court; who rarely leaves his post, being responsible for looking after that palace, even when the sovereign is not in residence.

Repose quickly descends on the congregation as if thrown a blanket of calm, when freshly baked bread, made from the first ripe grain, is carried aloft to be sanctified upon the altar. Prayers for a prosperous harvest are made and song is sung. I sing the hymns in full voice, so the angels can hear and answer my prayers as the labourers, that I saw in the fields this morning, dance inside my head.

* * *

Having settled quickly into life in the country, Sarah has requested we accompany her to the Saturday market; promising us a sight to see. However, on waking this morning, I don't feel quite as I should noticing some unusual aches, causing me a delayed rise which doesn't go unnoticed by Sarah when I finally arrive downstairs.

'Miss Jane, I thought you were going to neglect your breakfast this morning,' she says. 'It's not like you.'

Before Spring Came Summer

'I was not feeling quite my usual self this morning Sarah. Is my mother here?'

'She's at court today with your father,' replies Sarah, mistakenly addressing my stepfather as my father, to which I am quick to correct, pointing out that he is Elizabeth and Diana's father, not mine or Anne's. I know I sound obnoxious whenever I correct this mistake, but I never want the memory of my father, William Ryder, to be forgotten, even though I do still carry his name. Already I recognise the difference between these two men. James Maxwell, if I dare to say, appears more intelligent than my father and with that, is more scheming as he strives to make bold business decisions with the courtiers and his vast network of London city merchants, and those within the East India and the Levant Companies. Whereas my father, rightly or wrongly, always focused entirely on his duties at court, even on the day he died. God rest his soul.

When we arrive at the market, I find it a little overwhelming as the blaze of colour and multitude of aromas waft towards me: fish; shell fish; leather; herbs; spices; flowers; hardware; cloth; wool; chickens and dogs. I almost jump out of my skin when the meat stall, beside where we are standing, slaps down an enormous carcass.

'Best price today ladies. Mutton chops. Come and get your Mutton chops.'

Michelle Hockley

Sarah moves towards the counter holding a basket over her arm.

'My lady. What can I do for you today?' asks the stall-holder as he stands confidently in his long apron and open neck shirt, with a carcass slung over his shoulder, gripped only by the animal's protracting bone.

'Six chops of mutton,' replies Sarah. 'At your best price mind,' she quickly adds, obviously used to dealing with the vendors.

I watch with interest as the chops are cut, weighed, wrapped and placed into her basket, until I start to feel terribly nauseous. Every produce exhumes an intense aroma, multiplied by the summer heat of the day. I try to ignore this feeling and ask Anne if she will accompany me to the herb stall where I think, if I hold a bunch of mint beneath my nose, I shall feel better. But the words won't come out and everything around me is blurred and the sounds are muffled. I fold my arms and grip my body tightly. What is happening to me? Why do I feel heavy; my legs and my head, oppressed. Now I feel more pain; intense pain in my back and now my head. I unfold my arms from their tight grip about my body to move them towards my face, putting my hands over my eyes to stop the banging in my head. Barrels of orange carnations that once adorned the flower stall, start to quiver, taking a swipe at my cheek as they come closer and closer, until building momentum, spinning faster and faster about my person. I clench the pain in my back. I am confused. I'm hot. So hot. Should I try to go back to the house? I can't stop the market spinning and the pain in my head and back is worsening. I am falling. Unable to catch myself. The cobbled stones come ever nearer. My hands go out to break my fall. I can't stop what is happening and hit the ground hard. I let go. Everything is silent. Everything stops.

* * *

Eyes open wide. Body tensed beneath the lightly draped white sheet. Hands grip the linen. Scrunch the bedclothes, tighter and tighter. Frightened. Head throbs, pounding, clamping down on me. The cuckoo calls outside my chamber, I try to answer his cry. A red shiny apple is proud upon my bedside table. Rayleigh looks back at me from the charcoal sketch. I see my hands clenched beneath my chin covered in papules; blisters filled. Immediately I know, I've fallen prey to smallpox.

I feel my mother's presence as the strong beer swells against my lips, numbing me, causing me to sink into the soft plump feather pillow where my eyes close to enter an orderly, pristine garden, where the sun shines. Sisters small, young again, play chase with each other. Their laughter pleases me as I observe them. They don't see me. I want to join in and run through the aroma of almond and lavender that floats about me - but there is no time for me to play. A stranger takes my hand. I must follow. He is strong, all knowing, perhaps he can help me. Voices in the distance come closer and louder, much louder.

'Jane. Jane. Miss Jane. How are we today young lady?' Doctor Langdon holds my hand. I cannot smile. My face is stiff. The skin is tight. Mama peers over his shoulder waiting eagerly for me to respond.

'Am I alive sir?'

'You are very much alive Miss,' replies Langdon. I remember the market and the cobbled ground.

'Did you find me at the market yesterday, doctor?'

'Miss, that wasn't yesterday. It was almost one week ago. Your mother and Sarah have been helping you to recover and have doused your arms, legs and face, in Lavender and Almond oil. I am pleased to say, that in one or two days, the infection will have absolved itself. Once the last scabs have fallen away from your face....' I interject, cutting off his sentence. I look at my mother, scared.

'My face Mama. What of my face?'

I've never been vain. Never too prim and lady like. But I've seen some awful disfigurements about the court and streets of London as a result of this disease. Although I'm not pretty, not like Diana and Elizabeth, more plain like Anne, I don't want to look ugly, I'm only fourteen years old. I am feeling sorry for myself, but only for a brief moment. I know how destructive this disease can be, leaving one blind or worse, fatal. I am alive and getting back to health. On the wall directly over my bed is a crucifix. I lean my head back, 'thank you God. Thank you.'

* * *

I have remained, as instructed, in my bedchamber for a further week, until the last scab left my limbs and face, and the infection left my body, ensuring my sisters are safe from the smallpox disease. The girl in the mirror, above my dressing table, looking back at me, is unfamiliar. A pocked marked girl about her cheeks is someone new to me. With hair lank and ringlets flat, I open the bedchamber door for the first time in what seems like an awfully long time. Making my way down the stairs I am soon greeted with a loving smile from Sarah.

'Welcome back Miss Jane,' says Sarah. 'You gave us all a fright there, Miss,' she adds.

'Thank you for helping me Sarah. I am sorry to have caused so much trouble. Where are my sisters? They are not ill too are they?' I enquire.

'They are in the garden waiting for you. We've set

out your favourite food on the table in the garden. Go on Jane. Go and see them,' encourages Sarah.

But I have so many questions. After being absent for so long, and in and out of consciousness, I barely know what is fact from dream.

'What happened to the red apple beside my bed?' I ask.

Sarah takes both my hands in hers, crouches to my level, and begins to explain this curiosity. 'Elizabeth insisted we put that apple inside your room. When she explained the reason, we couldn't argue with her so we did as she requested,' replies Sarah.

'What does it mean? Did she want me to eat it?' I enquire

'Apparently, the spots and scabs get drawn into the apple away from your pretty face,' Sarah explains.

'Elizabeth thought of this?' I ask.

'She did. I don't know where she hears these things, but she is quite clever that one,' Sarah says.

'So where is the apple now?'

'Buried in the garden with all your spots,' she replies. 'William buried it for us one night and looking at you Miss, I'd say there is some truth in what Elizabeth has heard, for you are still such a pretty little thing.'

I smile, still clutching her hands, for although she is

heartening, there is no getting away from the fact, I am pockmarked and shall forever carry the scars of a once diseased child.

'Now please Jane, go into the garden, there's a good girl. They are all waiting and I doubt we can keep Diana amused for much longer,' says Sarah.

I walk towards the door leading to the garden. Elizabeth runs to me first, wrapping her arms around my leg. I hug each of my sisters before taking my seat on the wooden bench beside the table filled with pies, cakes and fruit. Mama smiles as she places a blanket over my legs before we eat and talk incessantly about the recent journey I endured alone.

* * *

Time is a good healer and the next four days seem to prove that point. Today, at the front of the house where the sun shines, I watch my sisters playing nine pins, whilst the shackles of the past two weeks slowly unleash themselves and I can join in some of their laughter. In the distance, we hear the piper playing the Harvest song and throw the pins to the ground to see a stream of corn laden carts being led away from the fields. The reapers, each adorned with a crown of golden corn strewn with fluttering ribbons, fill the street with joy and hope. The strenuous activity of their labour seems far behind them, knowing they will feast as honoured guests at the Lord of the Manor's table.

I lift Diana so she can see more clearly, bouncing her to the rhythm of the bells, whistles, cheers and pipes. A girl, about my age, smiles at me from a passing cart. I stop the bounce to fix my gaze upon her friendly bright eyes, framed by her coronet of corn, and return the smile. In that moment, the great divide that society has placed between us is at once negated. For it is not about our status, making us different, it's that we already have the most valuable possession that makes us equal; the gift of life. If the smallpox disease I had was fatal, then this young girl would own far more than I was ever able to receive. I wave my hand to seal our union and watch the carts until they turn out of sight.

When I turn back towards the house I see my stepfather has returned from the royal court.

'Welcome back Jane,' he says, handing me a small, silver spoon tied with a delicate, light-blue bow, engraved with the words, *Thank you Lord for keeping our brave, precious Jane, safe.*

'Thank you papa,' I whisper, recognising how blessed we are to have a life to live and the opportunity to make it all worthwhile.

CHAPTER FOUR

Come and Meet the Whorwoods

1634

A new decade, 1630, arrived safely, though needed to steady itself to accommodate recent political changes after the assassination of the Duke of Buckingham in 1628, and dissolution of parliament in 1629; where our monarch took the decision to lead his country via personal rule. Out of these changes have come a more satisfactory union between Charles and Henrietta Maria, who together, without the intervention of Buckingham, are working towards a more stable future for our country. Already in our sight is the promise of a peace agreement with Spain to bring an end to war, and on the 29 May 1630, we were blessed with the arrival of an heir to the throne. As time rolls forward, I too am finding myself being challenged by change.

This afternoon, I sit alone in the sitting room of our London home, with body rigid and mouth gaped wide as my entire childhood flashes before me. My stepfather, who seemingly did not require a response to the statement he delivered, leaving the room after announcing I shall l be meeting my future intended in precisely one hour. Feeling the numbness start to subside in my feet, I too leave the room to prepare myself for such an occasion.

Without applying any obvious system to my approach, I pull one garment after another from my wooden chest, throwing them on the floor beside me until eventually, I am surrounded in utter chaos; slamming down the lid and shouting for assistance. I accept that marriage is an arranged affair, but what I don't understand, is why the meeting is without prior notice. Catching a glimpse of myself in the dressing table mirror, the pockmark scars look back at me.

'Mama. Margaret. Anne. Elizabeth. Diana. Anyone,' 'Is anyone there? Please.'

'What is the commotion, Jane?' my mother enquires.

'Haven't you heard? I ask, staring up at her from the pile of clothes that surrounds me.

'About what Jane? What's happened?'

'My stepfather has requested I make myself available to meet my future intended in the drawing room by 3 o'clock today.'

'I am sorry Jane, I know nothing about this.'

Seeing fear in my eyes she produces a small wooden pot of lotion and starts to apply to my scars.

'There Jane, take a look,' instructs my mother.

'That's perfect, thank you.'

'My sweet Jane. I am proud of you my darling,' she replies.

Both of us taking a seat on the edge of my bed, where my mother takes my hands in hers to impart her motherly advice upon her eldest.

'Jane. We can trust your stepfather's choice. He will always have your best interest in mind.'

'I hope so Mama.'

Interrupted by a knock at the front door, my mother goes to accompany my stepfather. When I arrive in the hallway, the dining room door is slightly ajar allowing me to catch a glimpse of what lies behind before knocking to enter. Seated by the front window is my mother and stepfather with an obvious vacant chair between them. I don't recognise the family sitting along the back wall and my spying is disturbed when the door swings open wide and my stepfather grabs my hand, leading me further inside the room.

'Please may I introduce to you, my eldest stepdaughter, Jane Ryder,' he announces with sweeping aplomb, which, quite frankly, has ignited no interest from his audience, causing me to blush with embarrassment as the room remains quiet and the air thick with tension. It is at times like this, that Sir John Finet, Master of Ceremonies, would be most useful, taking control of this awkward situation. Still, my stepfather, who doesn't give up easily, is far from defeated and encourages me to engage with our guests.

'Jane. Jane. Come please. This is Sir Thomas Whorwood and his wife, Lady Ursula Brome-Whorwood.'

Holding out my hand I make a small bob with my head and smile. They don't respond, instead, remain cold and vacant towards me. I decide to give them the benefit of the doubt, for they are perhaps nervous, and move towards my intended, Master Brome Whorwood. He doesn't hold out his hand to me, so I bob my head before moving away to take my seat on the other side of the room, adjacent to my mother, with my back to the front window.

Margaret enters the room with goblets of small beer and dishes of sweetmeats, handing them to us individually. When she comes to me, her kind face is a blessing to see, thankful for the warm, reassuring glances she shows me.

Before Spring Came Summer

The chatter between our guest and my parents is general, allowing me time to soak up the future that is being presented to me. Sir Thomas Whorwood is stout, greying and clearly suffering gout, whilst Lady Whorwood is lean, slender, wiry and proud. I would describe her as elegant if she smiled, but as yet, we've not been given the pleasure of such an expression.

Master Brome is so young, boy like in fact. Sir Thomas seems proud of his son's achievements, eager for us to know that Brome is currently reading Law at Trinity college, Oxford, graduating in two years. The family, it would seem, own properties in Holton Park, Oxfordshire and Sandwell Hall, West Bromwich, neither of which am I familiar. Anyway, since these properties are owned by Sir Thomas, I suspect I can live with Brome in either Oxford, close to his studies, or hopefully in London, near to my family.

'Master Brome, do you have siblings?' I ask, hoping to make him feel a little less uneasy.

'Yes. William and Thomas,' he replies with minimal effort, unable to look directly at me.

The brief encounter does serve its purpose though, for I'm at least able to hear his voice, which seems distinguished enough. When he looks away, I fix my gaze firmly upon my future husband, wanting to bore into his soul to understand him. But I'm soon forced to lower my eyes to save his embarrassment, as he drops sweetmeat into his beer, currently attempting to fish out with his spoon.

'What age is Jane?' enquires Lady Ursula, turning to my stepfather, ignoring my mother.

'Twenty two y...' replies my stepfather, with barely a chance to finish what he is saying before Sir Thomas interjects to tell us that Brome is nineteen years.

I am immediately relieved, for I know he is too young to marry, but equally curious as to why my stepfather has left it until now, to learn that this boy is too young to wed. Of course my stepfather, not one to allow a business deal to turn sour, appears completely unruffled by this fact. He instructs Sir Thomas to make an application to the Start Chamber to request a marriage licence confirming his consent for this union to go ahead. Sir Thomas agrees to do as my stepfather requests, though I can't decide if he does so willing, or reluctantly as conversation moves on swiftly to discuss my dowry.

My stepfather takes the lead on financial matters, offering money, jewellery and plate, to the sum of £2,600 and Whorwoods will provide me with an allowance of £667 per year. The two sides of the room seem in combat so all we can do is wait until our opponents are ready to reply. Lady Ursula is unmoved, but Sir Thomas is more than accepting, agreeing to the sums offered. Oh jolly good, I think sarcastically. That is me sold. I wonder if that was to the highest bidder?

As the adults at last shake hands, producing documents to be signed, I turn to the window, where my attention is consumed by a gentleman walking by the house with a small monkey on a lead. The man doesn't look at me, but the monkey does. Is it laughing at me? It twists about its leash on tip toes, with his lip turned up to show its sharp, white teeth. I snigger to myself. I feel the room falls silent behind me and eyes upon me. I turn back into the room. I feel berated as Sir Thomas and Lady Ursula, with stern faces alike, hold their stare. My body runs cold. I turn to Brome if only to break the fixed glare, hoping for support, but he quickly drops his head. My body stiffens knowing that ownership will soon pass from my stepfather to these strangers that I see before me. Whether out of fear, or to safeguard my own dignity, something rages inside me. Without thought I stand to my feet.

'If you have no more questions for me, I shall bid you all farewell,' I announce in a rather priggish manner, which even surprises me.

No one responds. No one is remotely interested in me now the deal has been settled, which stabs me deep inside. To give my stepfather time to object to my leaving I hover for a second, suspended in this moment. Of course, to retract my intention to leave, and return to my seat, would appear awfully lame, so on hearing no protest, continue to walk slowly to the door. It is my mother's sweet voice I hear, bravely standing out from the pack, thanking me for my time. I don't need to acknowledge her, she will know what I am thinking, and continue outside to the hallway, where I remain for a moment, drenched in frustration at not having any say in my own future or being able to protect the liberty I once had; which on waking this morning, I believed was somewhat in tact.

CHAPTER FIVE

Enlightened
September 1634

Our seamstress, Mrs Fountain, has me standing on a stool in the parlour of our London home for the final fitting of my wedding dress.

'Miss Jane. Please stop fidgeting. If you don't, I can assure you the hem on this dress will be all out of line,' she blasts.

'I'm sorry Mrs Fountain. Will you be much longer?'

'Not long now Jane. Not long.'

I let out a small sigh to compose myself, for I know however long I am expected to be patient, it will be too long.

Unfortunately, the Star Chamber have sanctioned a marriage licence. Sir Thomas Whorwood has given his consent for the marriage to go ahead to overcome that Brome is under age. As a consequence, the wedding arrangements have quickly followed, gathering speed, taking on a life of their own. The date of the ceremony is set for Sunday 22 September at St Faith's Crypt, beneath the east end of St Paul's Cathedral, with a wedding breakfast to follow at the Guild Hall in the City of London; a short carriage ride from the church.

Since the marriage licence negates the need for banns to be read in church prior to the ceremony, I haven't seen Brome since our first meeting. At times, I struggle to picture him in my mind's eye, which is somewhat unsettling given that he will soon own my whole being when I'm flung into the arms of my in-laws to embark upon married life at Holton Park estate in Oxfordshire, and live amongst virtual strangers.

Every second of this past month with my family, especially my mother, has been most precious. Cherishing every moment together. Preparing my trousseau. Listening to my mother's wisdom, helping me come to terms with the next chapter in my life.

'There we are Jane,' says Mrs Fountain. 'All done. The hem is finally complete,' she says, standing back to admire her work as she removes the last two unwanted pins from her crumpled mouth.

'Oh, thank you Mrs Fountain,' I say with utter relief. 'Mother,' I shout. 'Please come and see my dress, Mrs

Fountain has finished her work.'

I watch my proud mother circle the stool I stand, glowing with admiration for her eldest child, making me smile at her affection for me. Mrs Fountain moves the large looking glass, leaning it against the wall directly opposite me. The cream lace skirt falls gently away from the cut-in waist skimming my toes all the way down from the high majestic neck line, where my tiny physique is framed elegantly with flowing bellowing sleeves of gentle silk.

In the reflection I see my mother carrying the long veil towards me. I bend a little to help her reach my head where she fixes yards and yards of Chantilly lace to the back of my hair. Mrs Fountain moves away from the mirror to help her. Together they lift the top of the veil to cover my face.

'What do you think Jane?' my mother ask.

In that instant, I don't know what I think. It's not Jane Ryder looking back at me. It's no one I recognise. Feeling cold and spare, I wonder if a bride should feel like this?

'Thank you Mama. The dress is beautiful,' I respond, not wanting to upset her but at the same time, determined to shut out these unfamiliar feelings which I don't understand. I remove the veil quickly to reveal myself, before jumping from the stool. Enough already. Enough. I have to get out of this dress; out of the parlour. I hand the costume to Mrs Fountain and the veil to my mother, returning quickly to my workaday garb.

On reaching the hallway, I hear Margaret at the front door. The removal men, who were expected to collect the last of my belongings ahead of my arrival to Holton House, are already here.

I can't bear this fiasco a moment longer. I'm determined not to stay and witness my possessions leave this happy home, as trades men strip away my things, chipping away, bit by bit at the memories of the past twenty two years. I feel like the axle of a revolving wheel watching the spokes of commotion spinning without me because I'm too ill-equipped to step out and save myself from this debacle. I am saddened by the abundance of ill-defined noise that surrounds me.

'Excuse me Margaret. Can I reach my coat please,' I say hurriedly, squeezing between her and the removals, determined more than ever to have the outside breeze upon my skin to cool off my tangled emotions.

'Sorry Jane,' replies Margaret, moving aside, providing me with enough room for my arm to reach the stand where I see my coat hanging.

'Thank you Margaret.'

Bundling my coat in my arms and placing on my cap as I rush down the front steps, I look towards the royal mews, where I intend to air my woes to my beloved Rayleigh; who I know won't judge me, but will listen knowingly.

'Don't go far Miss Jane,' Margaret shouts after me. 'You will be eating with your sisters in a little while.'

Of course I hear her, but I don't reply. I don't look back. My eyes are fixed firmly in the direction of the mews and my intent quickens with each step. My breath is heavy. I feel suffocated. My soul is asphyxiated. I can't breathe even though I hear my breath. I'm trapped. Everyone around me is occupied with helping me move forward, but what I see is only darkness and erosion.   Arriving at the mews I'm surprised by how desolate it is. No one is here to ask permission to enter. I break the stillness as I walk across the dampened cobbled stones, moving ever closer towards Rayleigh's stable, passing the harness room, looking all the while for anyone to show themselves. I see Rayleigh leaning his head over his stable door, my concern for etiquette diminishes. I make my way towards him regardless of permission.

'Rayleigh. Hello boy,' I whisper, patting his neck as I open the gate, encouraging him to the centre of his stable to give me room to remove the blanket from his back. As I hold his cloth outstretched ready to fold, I hear voices. My immediate reaction is to call out and let them know I'm here, but I stop myself when I hear the head footman, Mr Shipman, mention my stepfather's name.

'Mr Maxwell has requested three large carriages polished and prepared for this Sunday at 10 o'clock. I want you Mr Graham and you Mr Robert to make a start on that today please,' he demands before retreating to his office, closing the door shut behind him.

I start to imagine a procession of three polished carriages with me in my dress and veil. I smile to myself as I pat Rayleigh. Then stop in my tracks when I hear my name.

'What do you make of this marriage of Jane Ryder?' says Mr Robert

'I don't know much about it other than it's happened in a rush. Seems to have come out of nowhere,' replies Mr Graham.

'You've not heard then?'

'Heard what? Mr Robert,' says Mr Graham.

'Mr Maxwell made a pact, a deal if you like, with Sir Thomas Whorwood. Maxwell, in his role as Black Rod has agreed to ignore a charge brought against Sir Thomas, in exchange for him agreeing for his son, Brome Whorwood, to take Jane Ryder's hand in marriage. I suspect Maxwell wants to get her off his hands.'

'Crafty Maxwell,' replies Mr Graham.

My heart races, banging on my chest. My breathing

is heavy and laboured. I need to undo my coat to free my throat, but dare not move, they mustn't know I'm here. If they hear me, they will stop talking and I am at that stage where I don't want to know anymore but I do want to know more. Oh my Lord.

'What was the crime then?' asks Mr Graham. 'Was it attempted treason?'

'No, I doubt Maxwell would save anyone from that crime, he's very close to the king. This was pretty bad though. Sir Thomas was in a land dispute with a man in Kings Norton and arranged for his bailiff to kill this man to ensure the land remain part of the Whorwood estate.'

'Caught for arranging a murder? That is bloody awful,' says Mr Graham.

'Yes. Carries a heavy sentence, unless you got something you can trade, like a pockmarked maiden.'

'Oh don't say that. It sounds bad for Miss Ryder. She's been used as part of the conspiracy.'

'It does sound bad but that is what Maxwell has done and Sir Thomas has agreed.'

'Blimey. Those toffs stop at nothing. Ain't they got no morals?'

'You know how it goes Mr Graham. You scratch my back and I shall scratch yours,' says Mr Robert.

'I'd rather not, thank you.'

'Back to work you two,' shouts Mr Shipman from his office. 'Have I not given you enough work to do?'

Nausea takes hold of me with the realisation that the stepfather, who I trust with all my heart, a pater like my own, has defended a known criminal, using me as his fine. Mr Robert is right, it's my pockmarked skin. That's it. My stepfather thought no one would marry me because of my scars. This crime was the ideal opportunity to relieve himself of my charge. How could he? Why would he use me in this way?

My mind remains as busy as ever, throwing about ideas to justify this absurdity. Although Sir Thomas didn't kill with his own hands, he ordered the killing via his bailiff. In my book, that is as good as murder. In return for his evil doings, his son will have me as his wife and his crime, that should lead to severe punishment, is duly overlooked. This is quite unbelievable.

For the first time in four weeks the image of Brome's face appears in my mind. I see a young, unresponsive boy sitting in our drawing room, determined not to engage with me. I now understand why; because he didn't want this marriage anymore than I did and was at the meeting under duress. I then see the stern image of Lady Ursula and realise her disregard for me, for she perhaps knew why she was forced into that situation. This whole state of affairs is far worse than I could ever have imagined. It's no longer about me moving into the next chapter of my life. It's about a pact between two men to satisfy their needs by using the innocence of Brome and myself. We are but pawns in their despicable game. Foot soldiers in their battle. Damnatio ad bestias; where the criminal is set free and the exculpated are thrown to the lions to suppress their hunger.

I stumble backwards, falling against the wooden stable wall where my body sinks lower and lower until it settles on the warm hay with my hands clutching the buttons on my collar. Rayleigh's hoof moves forwards and backwards without making a sound. Both Brome and I are trapped inside this match. I have no power to stop this union. I am but a woman. I have no rights to my future. It is not my decision who will own me. My mother must never know, for this will break her heart. She will never learn of this loathsome transaction.

Pulling myself to my feet, I pat my beloved horse and open the stable door with my heavy body bound in chains of hopelessness. The free spirit I had in childhood that I was reluctant to surrender, is now firmly behind me, enabling me to take that leap into adulthood, to mingle with the dammed.

I see Mr Robert standing beside the gleaming black carriage turning over a cloth in his hands, agog by the sight of me, looking like he's seen a ghost.

'Miss,' he says, 'I didn't know...'

His voice is distant to me. I make no effort to reply. My aim is to leave the royal mews. I keep moving. Shuffling my way towards the exit, shoulders high around my ears to block out anyone or anything, until I see daylight outside.

My body doubles. I grab a railing on the side of a building to halt me falling down any further. Taking a moment to digest the worthlessness I feel, I register the revolt thrust upon me, realising I am but a token to aid the freedom from wrong doings in this unfair, dismal world in which we live. I scorn every man today who cannot recognise and respect the needs I have as a woman and the value that females bring to this blighted, feeble world.

Loosening the grip I hold on the railings, peeling away my fingers, I try to stand up straight, but remain so fragile. Come on Jane, I say to myself. Please, you must be strong. Remember, no one helps the enervated, there is no place in our society for the weak. Tears start to fill my eyes. I look up to stop them fall; determined to hold them back and not surrender to this feeling of uselessness. At this juncture, with what lies before me, I have two choices; allow this cruelty to crush me, or strive above it and play a role.

Approaching my house, I see Margaret at the front door.

Before Spring Came Summer

'There you are young lady. Where have you been? Your sisters are all waiting to take supper.'

'Do forgive me Margaret,' I say, passing her my coat to hurry into the dining room where each of my sisters sit at the table, turning towards me as I enter the room.

How will their lives pursue? Elizabeth, kind and good-natured, never seeing the bad in anyone; how will she cope? Diana will make a stand if it's ever possible, whilst Anne, a Ryder, will remain steady and loyal to the cause, never wanting to break free from the reins put on her, to toe the line in whatever is expected of her. It will remain to be seen who will win out in the end, who will come good in this short and precarious life we are expected to endure.

CHAPTER SIX

Sunday 22 September 1634

September sun streams inside my bedchamber when I wake. All is good with my world until I catch site of the wedding dress draped across the chair and remember, today is the day. *Marry in September's shine, your living will be rich and fine.*

When I arrive downstairs, the flowers have already been delivered. I take bunches of lavender to a seat in the parlour, where my mother begins to dress my hair. One by one, she fixes the pretty petals to my curls and threads the buds onto the veil. The sweet smell begins to fill the room, making me feel relaxed, more able to yield my fate.

'Your hair is perfect Jane,' says my mother encouragingly.

'Thank you Mama,' I reply, reaching to give her a big kiss, flinging my arms around her waist as I sit on the stool, holding her tight, not wanting ever to let her go.

'I have something for you Jane. Hold out your hand for me please,' says my mother as she gently takes my right hand to place a tiny gold ring, encrusted with sapphire and diamonds on my little finger.

'Thank you Mama, this is beautiful.'

'I visited the astrologer last week. Sapphire is the birth stone of September and will bring you good fortune in your marriage.'

'I hope the astrologer is right Mama,' I say, with a wry look that she will understand, without me needing to say anything. 'I shall always treasure this, keeping it about my person. Thank you.'

Our quietness is soon disturbed on hearing my stepfather return home from court, having been away this past week with King Charles at Nonsuch Palace. My mother gathers up my train as I walk into the hallway, where my stepfather places the veil of delicate lace, to cover my face. I don't speak to him, struggling to make eye contact, rejecting the arm he offers to lead me to the waiting carriage.

Margaret is already standing outside beside the carriage, crying, mopping the tears with her apron. She holds my flowers as I enter the coach to take my seat.

'Good bye Miss Jane,' she says, peering inside. 'You take care of you, won't you,' snuffling, barely able to speak.

'Thank you Margaret, I shall,' pointing to the flowers she is holding, beckoning her to pass them to me, a task she's been assigned, but somehow today, has lost complete control of her emotions, poor thing.

Although Margaret has less monetary wealth than me, she has nonetheless found her purpose in life. I am sure she too will marry one day. It is possible she will engage with someone whom her family have known for many years; perhaps even someone she has been acquainted all her life. Whereas I, with the royal court at my feet, question if my life is more blessed. From nowhere, my mind is alerted to an image of the little girl who smiled at me from the corn cart all those years ago. I see her waving, reminding me that as long as we have the gift of life, we are all blessed with nothing to fear.

My stepfather makes himself comfortable in the carriage, taking the seat beside me, tapping the roof with his rod.

'Now Jane,' he says looking down on me. 'Are we all set?'

'Yes, I do believe we are, stepfather. Yes, I do believe we are,' keeping my gaze straight ahead unable to look at him.

The journey remains contemplative and frosty, but eventually we arrive at the east end of St Paul's Cathedral, close to the entrance of St Faith's Crypt, which is already busy, bustling with people who have attended their Sunday church service in neighbouring chapels. My stepfather offers his arm once more. In deference to his wishes, I cannot help myself but concede to his outstretched hand to move forward on his terms, where my security must reign.

The church is in full bloom with an abundance of; rosemary, myrtle and orange blossom, complimenting the bouquet I carry. In the distance, on the right- hand side of the chapel, I can see Brome Whorwood wearing a long, cream and white doublet with a gleaming sword by his side. He looks handsome enough. Sir Thomas Whorwood, alongside Lady Ursula who is wearing an overly large floral arrangement upon her head, sit in the pew behind their son, where I deduce from Ursula's body language, is still not smiling, continuing instead to remain strict and stern. On the left hand side, sitting behind my mother, I see Mrs Stanton with her grown-up children and dear Edward Sackville, now Lord Chamberlain to Henrietta Maria's household, with his kind wife Mary, who is now governess to the royal children.

A telling note, sung by the choir dressed in dark blue robes, standing proudly in the quire stalls, tells me there is no turning back. Elizabeth and Diana take their cue to walk down the aisle, scattering petals from their flower baskets as they proceed. I take my first step towards the altar, where I come shoulder to shoulder with Brome Whorwood, as I'm placed before the priest to begin the service.

'...Will you have this woman to thy wedded wife, live together after God's ordinance in the holy estate of Matrimony? Wilt thou love her, comfort her, honour and keep her in sickness and in health and forsaking all other, keep thee only unto her so long as ye both shall live?'

Ceremoniously, Brome presents me with a silver poesy ring, and a cream leather draw string pouch containing gold and silver coins, that he slips over over my wrist, as we listen to the reading from Hebrews 13:4 of the King James Bible.

'Marriage honourable in all and the bed undefiled: but whoremongers and adulterers God will judge.'

A shiver transcends down my spine, even though I am not cold. I see Anne looking at me. She smiles. I don't.

In the vestry we are all quiet as we wait to sign the register. I am somewhat numbed by all that is going on about me until Brome starts to turn back my veil with such gentleness, showing me warmth and tenderness that makes me sigh a heavy breath of relief.

I catch sight of Sir Thomas and Lady Ursula as we start to leave the church, surprised when Sir Thomas waves to me, smiling kindly. I bow my head to acknowledge him graciously; accepting the civility that appears between us. Perhaps we are doing each other a good turn. Only time will tell. Ursula, standing by his side, continues to give nothing of herself. I don't see my mother as we make our way up the aisle, but I know she will be following my every move, willing for this partnership to work peacefully, remaining blissfully unaware of the circumstance at which I've arrived here.

Outside the church I stand beside Brome. A group of onlookers throw wheat over our heads whilst we wait for the congregation to join us. A broad smile sits across my face as I'm swept up in this special moment with the sun shining upon us. I squeeze Brome's arm, because the happiness of our future is surely in both our hands. *Married in September's golden glow, smooth and serene your life will go,* and ponder a moment on the adventures that lie ahead of us.

An enormous clatter comes from inside the church, followed by a scuffle of commotion after a ferocious scream. Letting go of Brome's arm I look inside the chapel. Everyone is scrambling towards the right-hand side of the nave at the front of the church. I instantly throw down my bouquet, lift my skirt from my ankles and sprint back inside, running straight for the huddled crowd.

'Move back Jane. Move away,' says my mother.

The ushers lean over Sir Thomas Whorwood who is laid full length on the floor with his clothes loosened to give him air.

'Brome,' I shout as loud as I can, 'come quickly, it's your father, he's been taken ill.'

A doctor, one of our guests, attends Sir Thomas, doing all he can to help. Brome eventually arrives. Without a moments hesitation, he pushes me away to kneel beside his father willing for a miracle, until the doctor turns to Lady Ursula and shakes his head.

'I'm sorry Lady Whorwood, your husband has passed.'

Ursula catches my eye, giving me the most horrid glare as she orders everyone, except her family, to leave the church; pointing to the doorway for us to make our exist. Brome and his two brothers, William and Thomas, poor souls, wail as they kneel beside their father's body. Echoes of their grief resounds the stone walls. I walk away leaving behind a wedding ceremony in tatters and a marriage torn apart before it's even had a chance to begin.

CHAPTER SEVEN

Holton House, Oxfordshire
Monday 27 October 1634

Arriving at Holton House after the wedding ceremony was under a heavy cloud. The wedding breakfast cancelled, my pretty dress replaced with a dull black frock, and the honeymoon; a time of indulgence in mead and honey to encourage fertility, has morphed itself into a month of mourning whilst we await preparations by the College of Arms, for the funeral of Sir Thomas Whorwood.

The turreted manor house is entirely befitting for the plight I find myself. A decrepit pile stands isolated on a raised 'island' surrounded by an intense blackened moat. The dark, stark décor, echoes lost love within, where the stagnant sentiment forbidding new growth, fashioned with ancient possessions of another era, make for empty hollow veins running through the corridors. Luggage trunks, that arrived before me, still line the gloomy walls of our marriage quarters; nothing prepared in advance that would make me feel welcome or special. My spirit for life drains away with the weight of this heavy, decaying milieu, as my soul is absorbed into the tapestry of this crippled and disfigured dwelling.

Amongst the acres of land, is a deer park, where white deer, a breed unknown to me, are tethered by a high wall surrounding the estate, ensuring no other breed enters to disrupt the heritage of this long preserved herd, incarcerating the white deer, governing their liberty. I liken myself to at least one of those deer, wanting to break free, but stalled by the soaring walls, too high to make the necessary leap. Acres upon acres of land lie before me. When I am bold enough to ask, I shall request a horse and take it upon myself to gallop away the cobwebs that hang inside my head, obstructing my ability to find happiness and contentment within my mind. Oh, how I yearn for the light hearted pleasures of Whitehall, longing for the shallow, incessant, pointless chatter of the royal court.

God showed his hand on my wedding day; exploited to protect Brome's father from imprisonment, only for him to be taken from this world almost minutes from my betrothal. If God had taken Sir Thomas, as He intended, ten minutes earlier, I could have walked away unscathed by this rotten mess. Though with the marriage now consummated, there is no going back. The vows I promised before my Lord on that sunny September day, must be ever honoured and fulfilled.

Lady Ursula Whorwood left for London yesterday morning, for it's her wish to re-enter Oxford with the body of her deceased husband. We are expecting the cortège to arrive at Holton House any moment, for today is Sir Thomas Whorwood's funeral.

Whilst we wait their return I have been charged with covering the mirrors in our private quarters, with black fabric. A task I am willing to oblige, to ensure Sir Thomas' spirit does not become trapped inside the glass and remain forever in this world without moving beyond. The same concern applies to the windows, but for now, I wait delivery of additional black cloth from downstairs. Other rooms in the house have already been dressed. The first drawing room adorns hangings of the family's coat of arms, shields and banners, for it is here, where Sir Thomas will lie in State before the funeral, allowing a quiet period for thought and remembrance.

On removing my jewellery, since the sparkle is also forbidden because it may attract the spirit, I take a moment to ponder the sapphire and diamond ring bestowed upon

61

my little finger by my mother on the wedding morning. Memories of happier times seep into my mind. My vision immediately becomes brighter, though to remain strong, I force myself to shut those happier times out, continuing to banish the jewellery inside a small onyx box, suitably placed on my dressing table. I catch a glimpse of my tired, white drawn visage in the mirror before throwing the black cloth over the looking glass, tying it down securely.

'Madam Whorwood. Madam Whorwood,' says Mary Hurles, my maid servant, as she raps abruptly, on the bedchamber door.

'Come in Mary. The door is open,' I respond pleasantly.

Mary makes no eye contact when she hurries into the room, also dressed in black regalia fitting for at least the next many months, carrying a heaped up pile of black cloth.

'I've been asked to leave this fabric with you Madam. I assume you know what it's for,' she says coldly.

I stand to acknowledge her attendance. Quickly taking the cloths from her arms. Thanking her for her efforts.

Mary Hurles is young, with a pretty pleasant face, but is unsure of me after I entered the scullery room, unannounced, soon after my arrival, where I found her and some of the other servants joyous at the demise of their master; describing Sir Thomas as a, 'brutal, greedy, penurious and savage man to both the servants and the tenants of the estate.' Mary was full of rant as an obvious ring leader; fuelling the fire as she acted out Sir Thomas' drunken behaviour, before falling into the arms of the footman. I was shocked to hear such disloyalty of their recently departed employer. In turn they were stunned into silence when they saw me at the doorway. I didn't judge them or repeat my findings to Brome or Lady Ursula, but they don't know me, and for now, remain wary of what I shall do with the information. Mary and her army will naturally be on their guard with me. The coldness she and the other servants afford me, will remain until we gain trust for each other. I therefore, forgive Mary for her apparent disregard for me and accept that the present situation will play out until I build bridges with the staff to prove I am allied with them and assure them my lips are sealed. Something I intend to do, only, when I have the energy or desire to do so. As Mary starts to leave the room, we both hear a carriage draw up beside the moat beneath my window. Mary momentarily freezes in her tracks.

'Please don't look out of the window Madam, the cortège has arrived,' she says in a panicked, flustered fashion, turning about her heel in confusion, heading for the door to make her way down the stone steps.

'Thank you,' I reply but speaking only to the closed chamber door, after her leaving without pleasantries.

As my curiosity overtakes my sanity, I move with some trepidation to the window to take a peek at the arrival below. Leaning tight against the open black drapes to hide my shape, standing firmly on the edge of the chamber wall, I can see the small bridge that leads from the road across the moat to the main entrance, where the procession has driven to a halt. Paused on the bridge is a large glass carriage drawn by six tall, black horses protecting the chested body within, draped in a black pal, adorned with the crest and arms of the Whorwood family. Heralds, dressed in long black hooded cloaks, each carry a black staff with one Herald wearing a red tabard, embroidered with the gold crests of the King-of-Arms, standing each side of the coach. A parade of carriages stand waiting behind, carrying mourners. I don't expect to know any of the guests, because the Whorwoods do not attend the royal court and my parents will not be present. My stepfather is carrying out business transactions to finalise trade deals with the recently formed African Trading Company; the wrangles and details of which, I know nothing about.

Consumed by what I am seeing, I venture a little closer to the window to watch the chested body be removed from the carriage and carried aloft towards the house, where

Before Spring Came Summer

Sir Thomas will lie until he is carried to the solemnisation before his final interment, later today.

I jump back quickly from the window when I see Emmanuel, Lady Ursula's coachman, staring up at the house. I don't know if he was looking at this window, but he was certainly looking upwards. Pressing my back tight against the wall, I try to think logically. How could Emmanuel, who is ageing, possibly see me high up through this small dark window? He doesn't even wear spectacles. Maybe he doesn't need spectacles?

'Sorry my Lord. Please protect me from Sir Thomas' spirit.'

Busying myself to forget the sin I have committed, I complete the task in hand, covering all the windows in our quarters, wasting no more time, aware that the family are expecting me to stand by their side to pay my respects. I smooth down my red ringlets about my shoulders, still somewhat flustered by what I have done, feeling if my hat is on straight, for I am taking no more risks by looking in the glass. Grabbing my cloak from the chair, I leave the chamber to walk down the cold staircase towards the first drawing room, conscious that everyone present at this ritual will be unknown to me, taking my first real step into the Whorwood's world and Holton Park estate.

Reluctantly, I push the large, heavily carved oak door

onto the dimly candle lit room, where a prayer is already in progress by the priest poised over the body of Sir Thomas Whorwood. Someone moves aside from the doorway as I enter, allowing me to slip into the space provided. Once my eyes adjust to the shadowy light, I see that it was Brome who made room for me. I smile, but he doesn't respond. In fact, he hasn't responded to me since we walked up the aisle, out of the church, on our wedding day.

The family move forward to pay their respects, gathering around the closed casket, which stands on a raised trestle, still bound by the black velvet pal thrown over the chest. Brome's brothers, Master Thomas and Master William, small in stature since they are so young, being only fifteen and ten years respectively, peer over the casket with tears streaming down their young pale cheeks, but make not a sound. Next is Field Whorwood, Sir Thomas' younger brother. Sir John Curson, a friend of the Whorwood family from Water Perry, seven miles from Oxford, is next in line to pay his respects to Sir Thomas, making up the four mourners who will assist Brome in his role as Chief mourner.

Lady Ursula stands close to the casket directing the mourners towards the body of this sombre, darkened, temporary mausoleum. I glance over to her, for she must be suffering and feeling emotional pain. But it's impossible to read her thoughts and her stoicism holds strong, exuding little, if any, emotion. Whatever she is feeling, she keeps tight inside, for to know her would be to pry, something Lady Ursula Whorwood would regard as unacceptable.

I am the final person of the immediate family to pay my respects. As I move closer to the casket and bow my head, I accidentally brush against the black velvet pal. At once, I see an image of Sir Thomas smiling at me as I left the church on my wedding day and momentarily question what was going through his mind. Once my respects are paid, I step away from the chest and stand in silence beside my newly acquired family, with my head lowered.

The Herald, selected by the College of Arms in London; John Philipot Somerset, King-of-Arms of the Provence, will direct the solemnities. George Owen, York Herald, who stands with the four assistant mourners, will raise the Standard and Pennon, bearing the arms of the Whorwood family and forming a solemn vignette. Dr George Seaton, Rector of Bushey in Hertfordshire, also appointed by the College of Arms, will take the service. He quietly moves to shake each of our hands; Brome first, before Lady Ursula, then myself. As he clasps both my hands with the utmost care, I look up at his soft face where immediately I sense a rush of emotion gather up through my body. These feelings, I'm ashamed to say, are not for Sir

Thomas, but selfishly, for myself.

'God be with you Madam Whorwood,' with which he places his hand upon my shoulder, where I stand quite still to appreciate the peaceful moment. Mourners continually arrive at the house entering the first drawing room to pay their respects. Lady Ursula, Brome and his brothers, break away to the withdrawing room, a space reserved for those persons who come up to ranking or meet the social grade expected of the family.

Mourners such as; tenants, villagers, teachers, tailors are admitted to the house to honour the body of Sir Thomas, but are designated a separate room for refreshments, ensuring they mix with their own kind. A protocol that is rarely challenged in society making me angry that rank and file cannot be disbanded on sad occasions such as this. I follow them into this more intimate room, that is equally adorned with dark drapes, black velvet wall hangings and the wispy candle light. We are ushered to a long table at the back wall, to help ourselves to comfits of sugar coated nuts and seeds as the servants hand each of us a goblet of Hippocras where the first sip of sweet spiced wine, warms my body.

A slight muttering comes from mourners as they enter the room, but most are quiet in their own deep thoughts. I smile politely to the brothers, Thomas and

Before Spring Came Summer

William, on catching site of their tired, red, frightened eyes. The table is also laid with platters of sponge fingers, filled with seeds and spices delicately wrapped in a fine paper, edged with black. Without considering my position, because someone needs to show these young boys some tenderness, I take it upon myself to offer them the platter of funeral biscuits; delicacies that signify the resurrection or renewed life. They take a biscuit, and I return the platter to the table without engaging in conversation.

As a wife, I must be seen to support Brome, so will make every effort and close in on the family group to act out this role. Ursula begins the ring-giving ritual, handing her sons their mourning rings of black onyx, blatantly ignoring my presence. Having highlighted my obvious exclusion from such a symbolic gesture, I take my leave, stepping away from the cluster, to give them the space they need.

It is not long before a couple of local folk, who clearly do not worry themselves about segregation, make their way into the withdrawing room, seemingly heading in my direction. Yes. Here they come. This will get me into so much trouble. I can't ignore them. That would be too rude.

'You must be Madam Whorwood,' says an elderly man, eager to take his place beside me. 'Madam Whorwood,' he repeats, taking off his hat, tucking it under his armpit whilst trying, at the same time, to balance a goblet of sweet wine and a funeral biscuit.

'Hello sir. You are?' I ask politely, shaking his outstretched hand, raising a curious smile.

'Mr Almond, Madam. My name is Mr John Almond. I am the Miller at the Water Mill of Lyehill quarry on the Whorwood's estate,' he explains.

'Then I am pleased to meet you sir,' I reply.

Mr Almond turns quickly to his more unsettled companion, who is clearly conscious of being in the withdrawing room. A gesture from Mr Almond encourages his haste.

'Madam, this is my friend, Mr John Stampe,' he says enthusiastically looking at me to ensure I am seeing his friend in the middle distance, whilst he fidgets from one foot to the other with excitement. 'Look John, its Madam Whorwood. Come on Mr Stampe, meet Madam Whorewood.'

Eventually, a somewhat more polite Mr Stampe finds the courage to move forward, overcoming his embarrassment of Mr Almond's enthusiasm on this solemn meeting; fully aware of my alarm and confusion.

'Stampe,' says Mr Almond. 'Look, it's Madam who recently wed Master Brome, Jane Ryder, who we hear is quite well-to-do within the royal court of our majesty, with her father being a Groom of the Bedchamber.' Turning to me, 'isn't that right Madam Whorwood?' he says with an expression of accomplishment as if waiting for an applause to his outstanding knowledge of my personal life.

I begin to smile. It was difficult not to, though somewhat surprised by his grasp of my credentials.

'Mr Stampe. I am pleased to meet you,' I say, offering my hand as he swiftly removes his hat.

'Welcome to Holton miss. Sorry, I mean Madam', says Stampe.

'Do you live in the village, Mr Stampe?' I ask, recognising he feels rather uncomfortable with the whole encounter.

'I lease Holton Farm, a mile from the estate. I have leased for many years, seen many comings and goings about Holton.'

I smile again, certain that those stories could only make for interesting listening. The conversation takes a sudden halt whilst my new companions appear fixated on my gaze until Mr Almond breaks the silence to explain his intentions for today.

'We want to pay our respects to Sir Thomas, but we won't go inside the church for the service,' he adds.

'Oh, why is that Mr Almond?'

Mr Stampe quickly interjects to explain further. 'We don't follow the Protestant faith Marm, we are Catholics.'

71

Michelle Hockley

A shiver runs through my body. I wasn't expecting to hear that. I remain expressionless on the outside whilst crumbling beneath my soul. They will not be persecuted, not anymore, those days are thankfully behind us. However, to be a recusant is to be marked out by the Privy Council, who will fine them heavily for not attending the Anglican church meaning it is far from acceptable in our society. I have never heard anyone in London be so overt about their leanings, especially to a young woman who they barely know. Though, that said, I have to admire their honesty, respecting their doggedness in wanting to stay true to themselves. After all, who am I to judge? Surely that is for God to decide. I shall take them as I find them. For now they are two kind, country folk.

The first of the nine church bells, to signify that the deceased is a man, starts to toll, giving me the perfect opportunity to take my official place at the ceremony in the grounds outside the house. We start our gait to the rhythm of the fifty-two bells; the number of years Sir Thomas spent upon this mortal coil.

On the other side of the bridge, across the moat, stands about twenty people from the village, those of the poorest and most in need. Each dressed in their best mourning clothes, they are here to show their appreciation for the anticipated endowments they might receive on the death of their Lord of Holton Manor. As part of any funeral procession, they will take their places, two-by-two, directly behind the Yeoman of the Guard, who leads us all to St Bartholomew's, the chapel on the estate.

The choir, dressed in red surplus, are next in line and the procession gathers momentum with the noble esquires, gentlemen and knights; wearing long black hooded robes, file in behind before the ladies of noble guests. The chaplain of St Bartholomew's, Reverend John Normansell, is followed by John Philipot, Somerset, King-of-Arms. The Heralds, who carry Sir Thomas Whorwood's sword, hilt and scabbard, lead on next. Myself and Lady Whorwood, accompany each other in a pair, follow on in sequence in front of the covered chest drawn by six horses, since fed and watered after their earlier journey from London. As I look back, the bend in the road allows me the opportunity to see the magnificence of the procession. For the first time, I feel myself wanting to reach out to Brome which I probably would, but protocol will not allow for such emotion. Instead, I hold my ground, continuing to walk forward towards the church.

Ursula and myself are ushered to our pew. The chest is placed beneath the arches of the chancel, within the nave, on a raised trestle, where Brome kneels on a black velvet cushion beside his late father, with the Pennon and Standard held either side. Looking towards the stained glass window, where the light is starting to fade, I recall my own father, wondering what he would now be like if he had not died so young, all those years ago, and how completely different my life would be if he had stayed alive.

Formalities of the ceremony continue to unfold before God, as the York Herald takes hold of Brome's long black train as he stands to receive Sir Thomas' noble achievements from the King-of-Arms. The chapel remains silent as we witness the passage of his father's sword, pommel, family Standard and Pennon. From the corner of my eye I try to gauge Ursula's reaction to this transition. She remains strong and unflinching, until she gives out the tiniest of gasps, when Sir Thomas' embalmed body, within the chest, is lifted towards his final interment to the majestic tomb inside Brome Chapel, in the South transept of St Bartholomew's church, signalling the end of the service. I instinctively go to hold her gloved hand, but she quickly pulls it away before I am able to hold a reassuring grasp.

We pause at the church door to be handed an already lit lantern to help guide us as dusk falls. On the mound, outside the chapel, are gathered the poor who take their rightful places once more, to walk, two-by-two, towards the house, before continuing their return to the village. I pull my black cloak tighter around me, holding the lantern asunder for maximum light. The mist is falling around us, but I can make out the figures of Mr Stampe and Mr Almond, leant against the outside wall of the church, watching as we leave. Mr Almond waves his hand to me but the best I can do is lift my head in acknowledgement, for Ursula, who walks with me in procession, would view any response as undignified behaviour.

The chill of the house, when we return, hits me hard as we enter the vestibule; a sensation I fear will never leave me in this daunting, uninviting environment. Protocol erodes as the procession disbands. Guests re-focus their intent and move swiftly towards the Great Hall to take the Arvel funeral supper. Distracted by the open door to the first drawing room, I stand to observe the now empty trestle, framed by the remaining velvet hangings, reminding me what once was and what now is. Although I've never known Holton House with the living presence of Sir Thomas Whorwood, I definitely feel someone is missing, which leaves me unwittingly heavy hearted as I enter the Hall to take my seat amongst strangers.

CHAPTER EIGHT

Inheritance

'What is the problem, Brome?' I enquire as he rushes into our quarters, banging the door behind him. 'You look flustered,' I add, hoping for a response to his anxious behaviour.

'The testament from my father is being read and mother is waiting for us both in the drawing room. Come quickly,' he replies with his eyes wider and darker than I've ever seen them before.

'Are you sure she wants to see us both?' I enquire, since I am rarely included in anything, let alone family business.

'Yes. Yes, hurry now. My mother is waiting, and she doesn't wait,' he barks, raising his voice in what I assume is, frustration.

'I'm not obliged to a minutes' peace in this house,' I mutter, pushing away the tapestry frame, annoyed by the ever presence of tension in this house, caused by someone's reviling of another.

'Pardon Jane. What did you say?' snaps Brome.

'I was saying...' but I stop myself. I'm aware he's terrified most of the time and to start an argument with him is unfair.

'Then come along Jane as I ask of you.'

In the drawing room, Lady Whorwood is seated behind the large oak table with Field Whorwood and another person, whom I deduce is the solicitor.

'Come along you two,' requests Ursula impatiently.

We take a seat at the table, opposite the already gathered party and listen to what Ursula has to say.

'I have called an audience with you, so Mr Davies can inform Brome, of his late father's wishes,' explains Ursula, taking control of the meeting.

'Thank you Lady Whorwood,' replies Davies. 'It's your late father's wish, Brome, that you inherit Sandwell Hall, in Staffordshire.'

'...That's correct,' interjects Ursula, eager to hasten proceedings. 'You will leave Holton at the end of the week to manage the property at your late father's wish.'

Brome is ashen, stuttering a response, '..um, um. Are you asking me to manage the house at Sandwell and be responsible for timber production, land and property? A

Before Spring Came Summer

Lord of the Manor?'

'No Brome,' starts Ursula. 'We are not asking you, young man. We are telling you.'

My reaction is to lean across to Brome to take his hand, to tell him it will be alright, but I don't, being always uncertain of what response I might receive from him, causing me embarrassment in front of Ursula. I too am scared about managing a large house and estate, living so far from London, but I'm determined to rise to the occasion. Someone as unfeeling as Ursula, should never see your weaknesses. I begin with practicalities.

'Lady Whorwood,' I address. 'Will servants already be in situation at Sandwell Hall?'

Ursula, unable to hide her total disregard for me, looks amiss by my confidant demeanour. 'Jane. Servants are already in place at Sandwell Hall, residing there when the Whorwood's are away, but you will need to find your own maid servant. I have enquired if the servants here wish to go with you, but I'm afraid, no one is keen to be permanently by your side.'

I am so taken aback to hear confirmation on how unpopular I am with the servants and at the same time, annoyed by how much Ursula has relished in telling me that fact.

'If that is all the questions you have Jane, please leave

the meeting now as you will understand, I have rather important matters to discuss with my son.'

Thinking on my feet, I decide, 'I would like to visit my family, alone, in London, prior to my moving to Sandwell please. I shall make arrangements to leave tomorrow if that is convenient for you all,' I announce, turning to Brome, who nods in agreement, accepting that I'm the least of his problems.

I close the heavy door behind me and lean against the solid wood, taking a moment in the stark oppressive corridor. Everything the Whorwoods do, is done in a hurry. Nothing is ever planned properly in advance. Nevertheless, Sandwell Hall must be more pleasant than Holton House. If nothing else, to be away from Lady Ursula will be a blessing. Mary Hurles, my so called maid servant, disturbs my thoughts as she comes out of the withdrawing room, carrying a tray of used glasses.

'Are you alright Madame Whorwood,' she enquires, as I straighten my head from the oak door.

'Yes Mary. Thank you. I am fine.'

Such a pretty girl yet harbouring so much dislike for me.

'Mary. Please can I have your attention for a minute?' I say abruptly, nettled by her apparent refusal to continue in my service. 'As you are already aware, Brome and I shall be residing at Sandwell Hall from the end of the week. Please make the necessary arrangements for our belongings to be packed and sent in advance of our arrival on Sunday'

'Yes, Marm.' she replies, walking away towards the kitchen then stopping before she gets to the door.

'Marm, apologies if I'm speaking out of turn, but are you alright?'

'Yes thank you Mary. Now off you go please.'

I see a chink of winter-sun making its way inside, diluting the stagnant air that surrounds me. Like a moth, I'm drawn towards the light and stand on the steps outside to inhale the fresh air. Without even thinking, I stretch out my arms, lean back my head and close my eyes to enjoy the cordial winter air brush my skin; willing for this warm feeling to never end.

It's not long before a dog barks about my feet. I quickly resume a posture more fitting to my position. Across the moat walks Mr Stampe. I smirk at the thought of him seeing my display of an outstretched pose, which must have appeared shockingly undignified. I make a fuss of the small terrier jumping excitedly about my ankles, as I walk to greet Mr Stampe on the bridge. His tunic and breeches are well worn, but he dons a clean crisp white collar for the occasion of coming to the house, and sports a black scarf around the crown of his floppy hat, reminding us that we are still in mourning.

'Good afternoon Miss Whorwood. Sorry, I mean, Madam Whorwood,' says Mr Stampe.

'Hello Mr Stampe, how are you?' I enquire as the terrier dog leaves me, to return to his master.

'What a fine day it is today,' he says.

'Yes, the winter sun is warm and the sky is clear, which is more than can be said for the inhabitants of Holton House,' I say, taking Mr Stampe into my confidence with a familiarity I probably shouldn't. He doesn't react; I guess from years of knowing his place in this world.

'Are you going into the house?' I ask.

'Yes, I have to see Lady Whorwood to reconcile business of my tenancy to the farm after Sir Thomas Whorwood's demise. I understand the solicitor is at the house today.'

I move aside to allow Mr Stampe the opportunity to go about his business, for I know he will be too polite to take his leave and arrive late for his meeting.

'I shall let you get along Mr Stampe.'

'Oh that's alright, they don't know I'm coming. I thought I'd make an appointment with Lady Ursula. They are probably busy today,' he says, continuing to chatter. 'I hope you were not too embarrassed by Mr Almond's approach at the funeral. He means well, wanting to welcome you to the estate, even though he is a little over excitable.'

'I enjoyed meeting you both. I was a little taken aback at first, but it was kind of you both to show such pleasantries. Thank you.'

Mr Stampe becomes distracted by his dog, showing his affection before returning to me.

'Do you ride, Madam?'

'Indeed I do. I love to ride, though it seems they have only the two horses at Holton House, which Emmanuel uses for the coach.'

'No Miss. They have the stables around the back of the house, that's where they keep the horses. Oh Madam, you have been cooped up in the house, haven't you. Has no one showed you around the estate?'

'No. I am only familiar with the walk from the house to St Bartholomew's chapel and back again,' smirking at the realisation that I've allowed such lethargy in myself.

It seems refreshing to hear my titter, especially when Mr Stampe joins in; an emotion I remember from my past life. It's clear that I have lost my true spirit for life and wonder if King Charles and the courtiers would even recognise me these days if I were to enter the royal court again, having now become so dull.

'Would you like me to show you Madam?' asks Mr Stampe.

'Yes please. Though not if it will cause you trouble with the estate and the Whorwood family.'

'I'm not afraid of them and nor should you be my dear,' advises Mr Stampe, taking me off guard by his frankness. 'Would you like me to show you around the grounds?' he enquires once more.

'I would like that Mr Stampe, thank you. I would like that very much indeed.'

CHAPTER NINE

Happy Reunions

'Almost there Madam Whorwood,' shouts the driver as he pulls the carriage around the corner to the top of Whitehall.

The joy of seeing my mother standing on the steps when I arrive, her face beaming with genuine love for me, makes my heart want to burst. She is quickly joined by my sisters who each greet me until I am breathless, huddled inside their embrace, breaking free only with the help from Margaret, as she takes my luggage.

'Thank you Margaret. I have only this one piece.'

'Oh. Madam Jane,' she says looking awfully shocked.

'What is it Margaret? What's the matter?'

'Pardon me Madam, but you look so thin and pale.'

'A little tired from the journey I suspect. I shall soon bounce back after one of your fine feasts, I am sure.'

Margaret smiles but I can see she is unconvinced,

knowing me too well, recognising when I am unhappy. She doesn't say anything more. The drawing room is alive with the voices of my sisters - something I took for granted. My mother soon identifies that I am a little overwhelmed and takes control of the commotion.

'At least let Jane into the drawing room and take off her cloak,' says my mother.

'But please mother,' replies Elizabeth, 'she is only here for a short time before going to live so far away in Staffordshire.'

My sisters have so many questions. Clearly nothing is going to halt their interest.

'So what is it like to be married?' asks Diana kneeling beside me, looking up, eyes wide with intrigue.

'To be honest, it's pretty dull.' At which point my family draw a little closer offering me their full attention. Without interruption, each of them await eagerly to hear my news of the past few months.

'The Whorwoods are understandably sad by the sudden loss of Sir Thomas Whorwood. The servants do not like me and few people, if any, talk to me each day. Brome seems scared all the time and his mother, Lady Ursula, is strict. The house is huge. They have stables, but no one rides for pleasure. William and Thomas are quiet, not like you lovely girls who have more energy than I have seen for months.'

Diana, who seems awfully disappointed by what she is hearing of my married life, speaks first.

'You are right Jane, that does sound dull. When I marry, I hope there will be more glamour than at Holton House. You poor thing Jane.'

Anne on the other hand is more practical in her views.

'That is married life,' she says, 'your position is to help Lady Ursula until you have children.'

In theory, Anne is of course quite correct, but I would also like to add one more item to her list of my responsibilities; to save Sir Thomas from severe punishment. But what would be the point of exposing my stepfather to those who have no reason to distrust him? They would never believe me over him and any contest would result in me losing those who I do believe love me.

Whilst we are talking, I can't help but notice Margaret paused in time, standing perfectly still, holding a jug of beer, gazing at me.

'I'm so sorry Margaret, are you wanting to serve the meal?' I enquire.

'No Madam. Pardon me, but I couldn't help overhearing you say the servants are unfriendly towards you.'

'Yes, and quite rightly so. It was all my own doing. I entered the scullery unannounced soon after my arrival and overheard the servants speaking ill of Sir Thomas Whorwood. They are now very unsure of what I propose to do with that information,' I explain.

'My brother Jack knows Mary Hurles,' says Margaret, not sure if she should speak out, but does anyway.

'Your brother knows Mary? Well, she is, or should I say, was my maid. We also have: Margery Bower, the cook and Joan Miller, dairy maid. Then there's Emmanuel the coachman and Mr Truman, the footman. Sarah the scullery maid, the groundsman and gardener and we have a journeyman...' I recite until my mother takes my hand, recognising that I am fretting.

'That's enough Jane,' says my mother. It's not important for us to know the names and positions of the entire household staff at Holton.'

Margaret, still holding the jug, not having moved, appears keen to continue.

'According to my Jack,' she says, 'all the servants were embarrassed by what you heard Jane, but Mary is most upset that you've refused to take her with you to Sandwell Hall, not wanting her to be by your side. I'm sorry Miss Jane, but I thought you should know.'

'Yes, Margaret, you have done the right thing, thank

you.'

Determined not to dwell on Ursula's deviants towards me, I accept what Margaret has told me and take action.

'Wonderful Margaret. If that's what Mary wishes, then I shall write immediately and engage her to Madam Jane Whorwood's household.'

'I think we should eat,' says my mother, gathering up her precious fold, 'for we need to rise early tomorrow, so Anne, Jane and myself, will be in good shape when we go to Hampton Court Palace for the French Ambassador's public audience.'

At which there is a resounding cheer throughout our happy home and I once more feel safe, secure and content.

* * *

The public audience for an ambassador is most often a colourful affair and today is no exception. We join the entourage of eight coaches to drive us to the steps of Lambeth Bridge, where we board the royal barges for the flamboyant journey to Hampton Court Palace. Our barge follows that of Jean d' Angennes, Marquis de Pougny, ambassador ordinary of France, who travels in Our Majesty's barge with a canopy and twelve oarsmen. Although a common occurrence, such a ceremony draws the crowds, and already a gathering has formed along the river bank to watch the sail. Our journey progresses along the River Thames as the early morning mist is clearing. Clouds begin to part as cold air touches our breath. I am happy to have Anne and my mother seated in the barge alongside me, knowing we shall be together for an entire day and Holton House is but a distant memory.

Arriving at Hampton Court Palace, we disembark at the Privy Stairs and walk behind the ambassador and his entourage. We follow the route to his first public audience through the Privy Gardens, on to Close Walk, then forwards to Black Cloister Court, where we wait for Sir John Finet, Master of Ceremonies. He will make the final adjustments in diplomacy to ensure correct protocol, to avoid a direct slight on the King of France through any mistakes we make to his representative. Courtiers wait in their correct places until the Heralds call us to proceed through the Guard Chamber and into the Presence Chamber where we all see King Charles seated beneath the canopy of State upon the dais.

The bugle sounds, bringing us courtiers to attention. The Presence Chamber door flies open and with great aplomb the ambassador, carrying his documents for the king, bound by a red ribbon, enters with his entourage, swinging his cape over his shoulder. As is normal, Sir John

Before Spring Came Summer

Finet continues to fuss, shuffling between the ambassador and his entourage, hurrying them along, pushing them forward into position where the Marquis de Pougny takes his important steps towards the throne. Having watched so many diplomatic ceremonies over the years, I'm fully aware that the slightest ill gesture made by either parties will be interpreted as an offence to, in this case, the King of France. For this reason, the courtiers watch with immense intrigue. You can hear a pin drop. Everyone is holding their breath in anticipation, waiting for Charles to offer his hand to the ambassador to symbolise a satisfactory audience. These ceremonies may appear somewhat unnecessarily flamboyant, but they are far from inconsequential. Finet is possibly more relieved than we are when the Marquis de Pougny accepts Charles' hand. A private audience can now take place, where confidential, diplomatic business can be discussed behind closed doors of the Withdrawing Chamber. We too are grateful to be ushered from the Presence Chamber that has become rather stuffy and stale.

The Great Hall, where we shall take refreshments, is today flanked either side by scaffold with a stage at the far end in readiness for the performance by The Queen Henrietta Maria's Men, the most celebrated group of players, after the King's Men. Although the seating plan is in strict order, I decided to swap my place with Anne so I can sit

91

between my sister and mother. Sitting opposite is Countess of Kent and the Duchess of Richmond, who whilst I usually enjoy their company, am conscious they are a little too eager to learn of my first months of married life, with my having been away from court for sometime. None of which, do I care to discuss. We talk. I am polite with my carefully constructed replies to provide them with minimum of details, refusing to fuel any gossip. I am relieved when the Marshals of the Hall announce the arrival of their Majesties and I can make my excuses to cease our meaningless discourse.

We all rise and remain standing until Charles and Henrietta take their seats at their table and the ambassador and his entourage take their seats nearby. The Cupbearers, Sewers and Carvers enter the room to wait on the head table. Throughout this ritual my attention is drawn to Charles who smiles in my direction before proceeding to move his hand backwards and forwards. The moment I realise he is directing himself at me, I try to make sense of what he is suggesting but am forced to stop short when I see the Duchess of Richmond staring up from her plate. That doesn't seem to stop Charles who continues to move his hand from side to side and then pointing over in my direction. I have no idea what he means and smile politely, though remain curious.

Before Spring Came Summer

After the banquet, when Charles and Henrietta leave the Hall, the Revelers arrive to make their final modifications to the stage, ensuring the scaffold is secure. The Usher Waiter arrives to clear our table. When he lifts Anne's plate, I see tucked beneath on the cloth, a tiny folded note and quickly grab it before anyone has a chance to notice; tucking it casually into the palm of my hand as I walk to join my sister and mother to mingle with the other courtiers. The note has no addressee on the outside and may be of no great interest, but Anne was sitting in my original seat, and maybe that was the reason why Charles was frantically trying to gain my attention. I shall be most disappointed if I find it's an old recipe for home-made game pie. Either way, I make my excuses to leave the Hall and decide to head for Base Court, where I shall find some solace to read the note in private.

On leaving the Great Hall, I run into Mary Curzon, Edward Sackville's wife and guardian to the royal children, on her way to the Watching chamber. Not wishing to ignore her, I put my business on hold for a few moments longer.

'Jane, darling, how lovely to see you. Is your mother here too?'

'Yes she is, and so is Anne.'

'How are you finding Holton House, and how is married life treating you?'

'It's different from the life I've known before, and on Sunday, I move with Brome to take charge of Sandwell Park Estate,' I reply, knowing she enquires after genuine concern, not court gossip.

'How are the royal children?' I ask. 'You certainly have your hands full with: Prince Charles, James and Princess Mary,'

'They are delightful. No trouble at all.'

'How is Edward Sackville? Is he enjoying his role as Lord Chamberlain to Henrietta Maria?'

'Absolutely. I shall pass on your good wishes to him.'

Mary starts to edge towards the private chambers, clearly conscious of her awaiting duties. I say my goodbyes and continue down the passage towards the Privy Stairs, too excited to go all the way to Base Court.

Once I am confident the coast is clear, I open the tiny folds. My hands are shaking as I start to read the note. 'Sweet J. Meet me in Paradise. Yours, C.' I want to cheer at the top of my voice but that would be foolish. Instead, I quickly gather myself rushing past the Page of the Privy Stairs, acknowledging him with a smile as I negotiate in my own mind the most favourable route to Paradise. I could take the backstairs to lead me directly inside, but in case I've misinterpreted the letter, I should take the route down the Long Gallery to enter that way. Quickening my pace along the Gallery, noticing the huge grin I am wearing across my face, I reach the door of Paradise Chamber. Without hesitation, I knock four times.

'Come in,' replies Charles.

I open the door slowly until I see Charles sitting alone, surrounded in the opulence to which this chamber provides. A special room. A secret world beyond, where the best of everything and most playful objects imaginable are held; each with their own secrets, dating back hundreds of years, left behind by previous monarchs. A lightness within the room is immediately breathtaking, as if within its walls, is the faintest sound of wind chimes welcoming you inside this treasure trove. The head of a unicorn looks down on me from the wall beside the tapestries laden with silver, so bright, they twinkle. Delicately positioned drapes of gold and light blue edged with exquisite pearls frame either side of the windows that overlook the park beyond. I step inside, as if I am walking on air, floating like a feather.

'Jane. Come in. Or should that be, Madam Whorwood?' says Charles seated on the long splendid couch encrusted with gold thread.

'Sir. Thank you for inviting me. I did eventually find your note. No one saw me arrive. I was most discreet.'

'I would expect no less from you Jane, always discreet.'

'This room is still as splendid as ever I remember,' I say, continuing to look around, with my eyes wide in amazement, trying to take in the wonder that never fails to overwhelm.

'This room will never change Jane. It will always be a special place for special things.'

'I can't begin to tell you how good it is to see you, Your Majesty.'

'Likewise Jane. You have been absent from court for sometime, though you've had good reasons I hear.'

'Yes sir, much of my time has been spent in Oxfordshire.'

'Your stepfather tells me he chose well for you, though I'm somewhat intrigued as to why he chose the Whorwoods who have no connection to the royal court, entirely outside your neighbouring circle.'

Determined not to be forced to lie to My Majesty or be disloyal to my stepfather, I panic a little trying to change the conversation, finding myself walking towards the life-sized violin made entirely of glass; lifting it carefully to place beneath my chin to pluck gently at the fragile strings.

'Still pitch perfect,' I say, taking a closer step towards Charles so he can hear the sound it makes, distracting him from my marriage arrangements.

'Of course. It will always be so. Never falters. Play it

properly Jane, take the glass bow and play.'

'I would rather not sir, for fear it will snap in my clumsy hands.'

'Oh Jane, you are not so clumsy.'

'You know I am a little boisterous sir, I always have been.'

'Well you don't look so boisterous today. Though yes, you are quite right, you were rather hedonistic and full of life.'

I smile. 'I am not sure I was ever hedonistic sir, but I shall be strong again one day,' I say, putting down the violin carefully on its stand to sit on the couch opposite Charles.

I lean back to enjoy the pleasures and gaze at the delicious ceiling draped in dark blue pleated silk, adorned with silver jewels, as if witnessing the most perfect night sky that could take me to a promised land.

'I could stay here forever sir.'

'I could too Jane, but we must be on our way to watch the players who have arrived to entertain us. Duty, I'm afraid, does call,' he says.

In the Great Hall, I sit alongside Anne, in time for the Revellers to announce the arrival of Our Majesties, whose thrones have been placed at the edge of the stage from where they will watch the play.

I feel Anne slowly lean towards me. 'Where have you

been?' she whispers.

'To see Mary Curzon,' I reply

'No you haven't. I recognise that glint in your eye. Besides, I've spoken with Mary and you weren't with her then.'

'Shh. We must listen to the Lord Chamberlain making his announcement. I shall tell you later, promise,' hoping for now at least, to satisfy her intrigue.

'...Queen Henrietta Maria's Men,' begins the Lord Chamberlain, 'are proud to perform for you today, The Wedding, by James Shirley,' to which I immediately let out a gentle snort, being familiar with the comedy, knowing that this play is even more farcical than my own wedding day, if that's possible.

As the screens open to expose the first scene, everyone applauds, but I can still feel Anne's curiosity breathing down my neck, right up to the point where we all eventually settle down to be entertained. Not for a moment are we disappointed, the audience are finding the play extremely amusing as the actors work through the farce comedy and misdemeanours until true love is allowed to blossom and each character, after a good deal of brawling and duelling, marry their love. The play ends with not one, but three weddings. I channel my attention towards the character named Jane, played by John Page, who marries

Before Spring Came Summer

Haver, her true love, played by John Young. The gentleman of the audience heartedly shout Bravo to show their appreciation to the players, whilst the ladies, including myself, politely clap and smile, possibly aware, as I am, of the irony that a woman doesn't even get the opportunity to play a happy wife on a stage of make believe.

With the final curtain call, our day is sadly coming to a close. On leaving the palace we board our carriage accompanied by my stepfather having completed his duties with the court. Moving slowly down the long drive towards the iron gates, leaving Hampton Court in the distance, I thank my family for this splendid day. I know Anne still wants to know where I went, but not wanting to lie to my sister, I mouth the words, 'not now.' She smiles in an accepting way, for I am sure she is satisfied to see me happier than when I arrived at the house yesterday.

.

CHAPTER TEN

September 1635

'It's a boy Mr Whorwood. It's a boy. You have a beautiful baby boy,' screams Mary Hurles, as she runs from the bedchamber, here at Sandwell Hall, to fetch Brome who I imagine is waiting in the parlour, pacing up and down on the polished flagstone tiles.

'Mr Brome. Madam Whorwood is ready for you now. Quickly, quickly. Please follow me.'

I don't hear Brome's voice, but I hear footsteps gather pace, getting closer and louder as they climb the wooden steps to my room.

Brome opens the door of the bedchamber and stands struck, unable to speak a word. The mid-wife walks towards him and places in his arms, our first born wrapped in swaddling clothes. I watch Brome as he gazes proudly upon our baby's resting face with little red curls peeping above the cloth.

'Thank you Jane. He is beautiful,' Brome whispers as he sits down gently beside me on the bed with tears of joy in his eyes. 'Shall we give him the name, Brome?' he enquires.

'Yes. I think that is most appropriate for such a strong boy and our first born', I reply obligingly, pleased he is taking such an interest in our cherished gift.

The past year has been quite rewarding. On arriving at Sandwell Hall, Brome and I have grown closer. He appears much less anxious away from his stern, officious mother. Sandwell Hall, whilst another large house, is definitely less austere than the house at Holton. Ironically, although I am many hundreds of miles from London and my family, I feel settled here, making this our home. Mary Hurles is happy too, getting used to being so far from Oxford; making new friends in the village.

Our travels to London have been few this year. On one occasion, which I do believe was the turning point in my relationship with my husband, Brome was summonsed to make a statement at the Star Chamber on grounds he'd broken the law by marrying so young, without his father's consent. I insisted on accompanying him to the hearing, witnessing his statement that was presented eloquently and true. Yet the court were insistent that a crime had been committed because Sir Thomas Whorwood died prior to consummation of our marriage. At the death of the guarantor, the licence was deemed null and void and according to the law, a felony was committed. Brome was understandably terribly annoyed, feeling the court hadn't listened to his statement, that the crime was completely unintentional, being unaware that the licence of consent was valid only whilst the guarantor was alive, even though consent had been given. Ironically, when this licence was requested, we married to save a criminal, only to be found guilty ourselves.

The sentiments my husband delivered to the court, though honest, were unfounded and we were forced to pay a fine of five hundred pounds. Brome took me into his trust that day, saying it was uncanny that his father continued to cause him distress even from the grave. At once, the barriers between us began to recede. It was clear that I was not the only casualty of Sir Thomas' crimes. The play acting performed by Mary Hurles in the kitchen at Holton when I arrived, if not a little brazen, was indeed true. It now transpires that Sir Thomas' behaviour was not restricted to his servants and tenants, but also to his sons. Brome was subjected to his father's bile made worse by heavy drinking. To which end, his son is left insecure and defeated. On that day, when he confided in me, he was not forth coming with knowledge of why our marriage was arranged in such haste, so I chose not to divulge what I knew, for fear it would be too much for him to bear; compounding belief that his father was in fact brutal and savage. After the court hearing, I promised to protect Brome from such harm ensuring

him that together, we would be strong. The situation we now find ourselves, the path that life has chosen for us, is neither of our doing. We are simply the product of such aberration.

The mid-wife helps me sit upright in bed and when comfortable, Brome gentle places our baby boy into my arms. 'Hello Brome junior,' I say, peering into his little face, adjusting his cloth, 'you are a gorgeous little boy.'

'We shall make him a strong and happy boy, Jane,' says Brome. 'He is blessed to have such a kind mother,' he adds.

'Thank you Brome. He is blessed with a good father too,' I say, holding out my hand to him, which he takes, entwining my fingers.

In the coming days I shall be churched by Reverend Thomas Johnson, at All Saint's, the nearby chapel. It houses many of the Whorwood ancestry beneath the Vestry here in Sandwell. However, we have decided that Brome junior will be baptised at St Bartholomew's on the Holton estate, 29 October. This decision pleases me because my family will have the opportunity to see for themselves, how beautiful is our first born.

CHAPTER ELEVEN

April 1637

With the onset of spring comes anticipated hope, but as lambs frolic in fresh green grass the bracken fungus protrudes the ailing trees, swelling and bulging, taking hold of wrinkled trunks.

I look out from my stepfather's apartment, here in Windsor Castle, holding my second born close to me, as I have since his premature birth here at Windsor, on 27 December 1636, giving us a terrible fright. I've been stubborn in my quest to save my baby's life by staying close to the royal apothecaries, refusing to return with Brome to Staffordshire, instead everyday hoping for a treatment to heal his malaise. Unfortunately, I have failed to stem the tide that befalls my son. I know our battle is as much as lost; unable to romp as the young I see, losing fast the sap that should be his.

The Garter procession approaches Windsor today. I

watch the knights, but I don't see colours of white plumes or blue velvet mantels, only a blur of light through tears forever drawn. My mother sits in the corner of the room, willing for the tide to turn, hurting with every pain baby James feels, and my pain too. Brome junior, excited by the ceremony, as I once was, clambers on a stool for a better view, breaking the heavy silence.

'Grand papa. Grand papa,' he shouts, watching the procession meandering its way into St George's chapel for prayers.

'Can you see your Grand papa?' my mother asks. 'Can you see King Charles and all his Knights?'

He turns to her briefly and nods, but soon returns back to the window taking in the splendour, beholding the rich vibrancy of this extraordinary ceremony, where my stepfather has paraded the Knights of the Garter from Whitehall to Windsor on carriage and by foot. I recoil from the window to sit beside my mother, cradling my feather weight baby as he struggles to breathe as each breath rattles.

'Mama, what more can I do?'

'Nothing more, I'm afraid Jane. Nothing more.'

We know the rattle is summoning his end. The warmth from his tiny body is no more. The bones I feel, never forming the bouncing flesh of a new born, are so cold. He his limp now. He has gone. I don't know what to do.

Before Spring Came Summer

My mother takes him from me and leaves the room. Mary Hurles takes hold of Brome junior's hand to lead him outside. James has renounced his gift from God, his to own for such a short while.

As night begins to fall, we take the short, solemn walk to St George's chapel. A tiny casket carried in my stepfather's arm with my mother following behind on this cold, dark, barren journey carrying torches to light the church. No pomp or ceremony, regalia or Herald for this unremarkable life spent.

On opening the chapel door, leaving the night behind, I couldn't have been more wrong. Candles lit, stand tall to light the chapel. Silence does not greet us, but instead the tones of a choir that fills our hearts. Is this for us? Who did this for us? I squeeze my mother's hand to steady my wonderment as the delicacy of song transports me effortlessly towards the altar, giving me the courage to send my baby to a place beyond. Who has brought such ritual to our deserted prayers? The warmth of the candles encase me. The sweet, sensitive, soft sounds, saturate my soul; releasing me from my injured mind, taking me out of my imperfect body.

The priest draws a cross in the air, liberating my little boy from the ties of his decaying existence in this cruel land. Blessing and cleansing his soul before entering a better world beyond. But as the choir reaches a crescendo, I feel the energy rise within me. Instinctively I move towards my baby, wanting one last attempt to save him. It must be me who shoulders his burden so I plough forward with every determination. My mother takes my hand in hers to halt my charge. The choir descends and plateaus into a muffled hum. Emotions reflect the flattened tones.

'Let him go Jane,' my mother whispers. 'Free him from the treachery that has befallen his saddened pitiful existence.'

'I don't know that I can Mama.'

'You have done everything, Jane.'

My gut turns over. Anxiety reigns once more, but I shall let him rest his weary, tired, defunct body away from this tainted, diseased ridden world.

The candles, tall like organ pipes surrounding the chapel, flicker in the draft of the cold night air. The blackened, stained glass window bares down upon me with exposed hues, from the faint light catching the leaded glass. I take hold of the heavy church door with my mother as I watch the priest and my stepfather proceed into the distant darkness away from the light inside. Before the door closes completely, there is movement at the back of the nave, an outline of someone crouched in prayer, but I cannot see a face with any clarity. Has someone been watching us throughout the service? I don't call out. It's a private moment. A quiet time. My mother pulls my black shawl closer around me to provide warmth and comfort as we leave the church, letting me know as always, she is there for me.

CHAPTER TWELVE

22 September 1637

Over the course of the past five months, grief within my heavy heart is more muted; enabling me to open up once more to those people who are still living and to embrace the tenderness my husband, everyday, shows towards me.

On waking this morning, I snuggle closer to Brome, who is still sleeping, feeling enormous pleasure to be resting by his side. Today is our wedding anniversary. Although I'm barely able to comprehend that we have accomplished three years of marriage, this fact does fill me with such joy. My mind turns back to the day we first met, having nothing to say, never wanting to spend time in each others' company. I titter to myself, recalling the amusement I felt, on seeing a monkey being walked on a lead outside my London home, aptly diverting my attention from the stark internal atmosphere of that first encounter with the Whorwoods;

believing for so long that Brome and I would never be an appropriate match. Yet here we are all grown up. Brome has graduated from Oxford with his Law degree and we have produced our beautiful boy, Brome junior, who everyday helps us to create our own respectable family unit.

September's shine floods in as I open the curtains. Resting my chin in cupped hands upon the sill, I gaze out beyond, remembering how important those rays of sunlight were to me on that fateful wedding day.

'Oh we have come a long way. Oh we truly have.'

'Jane, dear,' says Brome, sitting up, startling me. 'Are you talking to yourself?'

'I think I was Brome, but I am happy, feeling so contended.'

'As long as you're not going quite mad,' he says letting his head fall back down on the pillow.

I tease him, throwing myself upon the bed, encouraging him to get up. We've promised to spend the whole day together at Sandwell. Any business commitments, however pressing, will be put on hold until tomorrow.

After an intimate breakfast, Brome and I take a stroll in the grounds making time to admire the view around us, being reminded how the seasons change the appearance of what we see. Nature, going about its own business, regardless of any political or emotional upheaval; knows exactly what to do, and does it well. The landscape here, is extraordinary, with acres upon acres of fields protecting us from any changes that society imposes. Falling deeper into our thoughts, Brome shakes us from this contemplative mood, by making the perfect suggestion.

'Jane. Would you like to take the horses out?'

'You bet I would Brome,' taking off immediately, running back towards the stables, causing great excitement as we try to out-strip each other's pace.

Arriving at the stable first, I turn to Brome to hurry him forth, laughing as I go. Without hesitation he sweeps me up in his arms; caressing purposefully at the stable door. I let it happen, enjoying every second, feeling limp and free, giving up my body to the man I love. The warm wooden slats of the barn press against my back as I enjoy the closeness we have together, wanting this moment to linger on forever.

'Is that you sir,' calls out Derek, the Stable boy, from inside.

We quickly jump out of our embrace, giggling without making a sound. Brome continues to lean over me with one hand resting on the stable wall above my head, looking at me, panting his reply.

'Yes Derek. Madam Whorwood and I would like to

take out the horses. Please can you have them ready immediately, without delay.'

Brome resumes his fondness for me, kissing my forehead, enjoying the trepidation we find ourselves. He smiles as Derek replies from the back of the stables who is, completely unaware of the frolicking taking place by his employer outside.

Mounted happily on my horse, Sandy, we go into the grounds until clear of the house when Brome, without warning, begins to open up his stride, taking his horse into a canter, before a fast gallop. I compete, stopping for the time it takes to cock over my leg to sit more comfortably astride my horse.

'No time for ladylike gestures at this juncture, we have a race to win. Come on Sandy. Good boy.'

As I pick up pace to gain for lost time, my skirt flings back, as does my hair. Sandy beats the ground over and over again in search of triumph; drawing ever closer until we nudge a nose past Brome's horse.

'We've done it. Good boy Sandy. We've done it.'

'Come back Madam Whorwood and that's an order,' cries out Brome, in a playful manner, attempting to show his manly demeanour.

I smile with such elation, as I slow down my stride,

for today I have my husband's full attention, and am loving every minute of it.

'Whoa, Sandy, whoa, there's a good boy,' I say, pulling on the reigns to wait for Brome to catch up with me.

'Come on old man, what are you waiting for?' I shout, turning back to watch as he comes up behind me.

'My goodness you can ride Jane. Where did you learn to do that? You've lived in London all your life. Who rides like that in the City?'

'Me Brome Whorwood. Me,' feeling pretty pleased with myself, that I have been able to impress my husband.

I have never spoken to Brome about Rayleigh or of my father, William Ryder in his role at the royal mews, never believing he would be interested. As I take in the open countryside, I believe Rayleigh would love it here, to live out his latter years on all this land. Maybe I shall move him, especially as we are now more settled.

We resume our ride, taking us to the edge of the coppice, beyond many acres of land, forgetting about past troubles and our responsibilities of the estate. We ride until we can ride no more, defeated only by dusk as it starts to fall across the fields. Neither of us wanting to let go of this day to be shackled once more by duty. We take one last outburst of exuberance, galloping faster and faster, without slowing for a second. Today, my carefree spirit that I once knew, revisited me. Before I send her away, I'm thankful that she still remembers me.

Supper is informal in our bedchamber, eaten rather hurriedly as the passion we have for each other rules victorious, spilling over as we make love more sensually than ever before, feeling the respect we have for each other. Feeling as one.

'Good night Brome, my love,' I whisper.

'Good night my love, my pretty one,' he replies, kissing me on my forehead as we fall asleep.

CHAPTER THIRTEEN

Royal Court Sunday
7 January 1638

There is much excitement about Whitehall as our carriage moves swiftly and majestically through the court gate, opening up into the expanse of palace grounds. Our invitation arrived before Christmas, requesting the Maxwell family to partake in a court masque on Twelfth Night. According to Brome, the masque has been rushed through for political reasons. He and he may be correct, for it's certainly unprecedented to hold a masque on the Sabbath Day.

The apartment in the centre of the palace, where we shall stay for the next two days, is prepared pristinely. Brome junior is met by a royal nursemaid to whom he responds joyfully, as she leads him to join the other courtly children.

'You know Jane,' begins Brome as we enter our rooms, 'there is so much tension about the court.'

'Would that be political tension to which you refer?' I ask, knowing full well what he means, because recently, he's spoken of very little else.

'Yes, without Parliament, there is so much tension in London and the whole country,' he replies.

'Oh Brome, please let it rest. This should be a happy occasion,' I reply, determined to enjoy the rapturous atmosphere of the court.

He raises his eyebrows much to say, you are a woman, why would you care or even understand. I let that silent remark slide, determined not to quarrel. Moreover, I am not entirely sure if the tension he feels is perhaps only brought about by his unfamiliar surroundings.

With a knock at the bedchamber door, Brome immediately sits up straight in his chair; aware of his lack of protocol. When he sees it's my beautiful, precious sister Elizabeth, he relaxes.

'Elizabeth, my dear, how lovely to see you,' I say, wanting to scoop her up in my arms. 'Please come in.'

'Hello Jane. Hello Brome,' she says politely with a dainty, eloquent voice, as she slowly enters the room.

'Let me take a good look at you in the light. I haven't seen you for quite sometime. My, how you have grown.' Quite the young lady I always thought she would be.

'Isn't she lovely Brome,' I say as I turn to him.

'Yes, welcome Elizabeth. I shall leave you and Jane to chat a while,' he says, knowing he's no match for the love I have for her. Though perhaps on balance, more keen to attempt a resolve of the sentiments he has earlier observed at court.

'Jane, I have some news for you,' says Elizabeth excitedly, with a huge smile across her face.

'Tell me Elizabeth. Tell me all.'

Taking both her hands, I guide her to the table in the window where we sit in the grandest of salon chairs and give her my full attention.

'A rumour is circulating the court,' begins Elizabeth, 'that I am to wed William Hamilton. His brother James, Marquis of Hamilton, has suggested me a good match for marriage.'

'That's wonderful Elizabeth. If you are happy, then I am happy. Are you happy?' I ask, recognising my stepfather has come good this time, for William Hamilton's brother James, is third in line to the Scottish throne.

'I believe I am. I think I rather like him,' says Elizabeth. 'You will see him tonight in the masque, he is one of the fourteen Lords. A masquer.'

'Then we shall sit together so I can give you my opinion on his singing and dancing,' making her giggle as I once did with my mother when I was young, without responsibilities.

Much too soon we are disturbed with the maid-in-waiting arriving to prepare me for the evening. Elizabeth leaves the apartment to also dress for the impending court entertainment.

The maid begins with my hair, which I wear up, with the usual red ringlets covering my ears and pockmarked scars. The dress I step into is more colourful than of late, being now rid of the dowdy black garb, a constant reminder of surrounding morbidity. As the clasps are tied, the dress clings closer to my body. I smoother my hands over the tiny protruding bump to let my little one know they are safe inside.

'All done, My Lady,' she announces efficiently.

'Thank you,' I reply, still holding gently, my baby within.

Tonight's performance is the first court masque for three years, which further adds to the courtiers' excitement with their chatter bellowing in the Great Hall as we wait enthusiastically to be ushered through the palace. In that time, Peter Paul Rubens has painted the ceiling of the

Before Spring Came Summer

Banqueting House and a proclamation passed forbidding any masque to be performed in this building, for fear of damaging the masterpiece with an abundance of candle smoke. Instead, this masque will take place in a newly erected structure and it is to here, that we make our way.

Arriving to take our seats, Sir John Finet, Master of Ceremonies, is already inside running from one ambassador to another, ensuring diplomatic protocol is present amongst our foreign visitors. Elizabeth sits excitedly beside me waiting for the masque to begin as I scan the audience to see who has been invited. I notice the French Ambassador, Pierre de Bellievre, is absent, but do spy the Spanish Ambassador, Villa Mediana; concluding, rightly or wrongly, that either the two countries have come to blows in recent times, or the French Ambassador is feeling slighted by the hospitality we have shown towards him. Something, I'm certain, will have kept Sir John Finet awake at night in attempting to resolve. The Moroccan Ambassador Extraordinary, Indar ben Abdullah, on the other hand, is quite unmissable in his flamboyant dress and flowing headdress; smiling as he's shown to his appointed seat in one of the more prominent places reserved for special guests. A satisfying thought that we are in Morocco's favour and them in ours. Queen Henrietta Maria has already made her entrance and is seated beneath a golden canopy at a vantage point in the far end of the room, surrounded by courtiers of immense importance. I don't expect to see Charles for a while, for he will be amongst the players, waiting to perform a role specifically written for him, which is so often the case.

'Lords, Ladies and Gentlemen,' announces the Lord Chamberlain as the room falls silent. 'I am delighted to introduce, *Britannia Triumphans*, a new masque, by the eminent playwright, Mr. William Davenant.'

All eyes turn to the stage as the curtain opens to expose the first scene. A gasp ripples across the audience absorbing the magnificence of the set before us, observing the ingenuity of Inigo Jones, Surveyor of the King's Works. We all know how fortunate we are to have Jones within the royal household, responsible not only for the scenery and mechanical stage-sets, but also the rich, splendid architecture he has created throughout our city. Buildings such as: the Banqueting House;Queen Henrietta's Chapel at St James' and the Queen's House at Greenwich, bringing a modernity we might never have seen if not for his expertise.

The large stage is raised, flanked either side by a cascading staircase. On one side stands a lady dressed in a blue and white costume wearing a glorious golden navel crown, representing, maritime victory. On the opposite side is a gentleman holding a book, with his foot pressed upon a serpent's head to symbolise a good and rightful government.

The actors who play Action and Imposture arrive on stage against a backdrop of a London street depicting rows of houses along the River Thames. Both characters tell us about a world lived in accordance to their beliefs. Action, representing citizens of virtue and reason, whilst the Imposture purports an antitheses of these ideals, by deceiving our society with its falsehoods. We listen intently, knowing the lines they deliver are of the utmost importance to the message of the masque.

Without warning, a loud bang sounds, accompanied by a flashing light, causing me to jump out of my seat; not good in my condition. We watch as the smoke clears to reveal Merlin, King Arthur's magician wearing a purple silk gown, trimmed with ermine, standing astride with outstretched arms, holding a silver rod. He quickly sets about casting a spell, turning the scene into the Imposture's tainted world, so the audience can view how London will fair under his rotten beliefs.

I look across at Brome who is concentrating on the message being performed. He acknowledges me and mouths the words, 'I told you.' I know he's referring to the political tension to which he is currently obsessed. Whether

Michelle Hockley

Brome believes it or not, I am fully aware that the purpose of a court masque is to provide a platform for Charles to deliver a message to his courtiers, usually one of deep concern when Parliament is no longer sitting to make decisions with the king. It's apparent from the scene, there is a problem at sea with our ships being under attack from pirates, which in turn, is threatening the wealth of our country.

With another loud bang, this time managing to hold my stomach without too much of a jolt, the scene transforms into a flaming precipice against images of sea ports, representing Hell. The stage is quickly crowded with anti-masquers played by professional actors, because members of the court would never be associated with the evil message they bring to our attention. They generate a grotesque sound, playing mock music on: knackers; keys; bells and tongs until it is unbearable, creating a scene of horrific chaos and upset. The audience is enthralled by the action having clearly engaged themselves in the message being told. Personally, I want all this noise and commotion to stop, but tension is instead further heightened by a group of deceivers arriving on the stage led by a mountebank in a habit, accompanied by two wenches holding bottles of water for inspection. As they stand about the front row of the audience, three more actors, accompanied by a group of soldiers, boldly enter the stage representing; Jack Cade, Robert Kett and Jack Straw, each of whom we recognise for the troubles they caused society of yesteryear with their failed rebellions against their kings. The noise and mayhem swells about the stage, culminating into utter despair, until the courtiers in the audience take control by booing and hissing at the treacherous bile that is set before us.

Our charge is at last answered when Bellerophan, a hero from heaven, is winched across the stage, wearing a headdress of tall plumes, holding a lengthy javelin, astraddle of Pegasus with a broad expanse of outstretched wings, landing centre stage. The anti-masquers immediately run for cover, expurgating Hell from our sights.

As if like magic, though of course it's the mechanical prowess of our genius Inigo Jones, the stage pulls apart, making room for a jewelled encrusted palace that sparkles throughout the entire room, elevating to fill the void. Fame, the Roman Goddess of rumours, enters on a wire, swinging high above our heads; her long flaxen hair floating as she hovers. Suspended mid-air, she plays her golden trumpet, commanding us to listen before being hoisted off stage and replaced by a backdrop of Doric and Ionic column orders, that realises a sense of calm and reason; banishing the path previously purported by the Imposture.

Elizabeth gently tugs at my sleeve. 'Jane. Jane,' she

whispers.

'Are you alright Elizabeth?' conscious that the scenes have been somewhat breathtaking. 'Here he comes. It's William Hamilton.'

I immediately stretch up to ensure a clear view over the heads in front of me. Fourteen of the king's Lords take their places either side of the staged palace and begin their carefully choreographed dance and chorus.

'I see him Elizabeth,' I whisper, without taking my eyes off William for one second as he makes each precise step, poised gracefully to support a headdress of tall white plumes.

At exactly the correct moment, the masquers glide smoothly to one side and reveal King Charles, playing Britanocles.

'Hurrah hurrah,' we all cheer. Applauding not only for Our Majesty's entrance to the stage in his finely tailored costume, but in knowing that under Britanocles's leadership, order comes out of discord to save us all.

Maintaining the momentum of this fantastical performance, a strong gust of wind whips up, which I can feel from where I'm sitting, and in enters Galantea, a sea-nymph, flying through the air, singing on the back of a dolphin, trailing ahead of a perfect fleet of ships.

At last, and with some relief, we finally hear the

valediction, confirming that Britanocles, played so magnificently by King Charles, is the glory of the Western World and under his rule, we will be saved from the horrors professed by the Imposture.

'Hurrah. Hurrah. Bravo, Bravo.'

I sit back in my chair holding my belly, clutching Elizabeth's hand, to take a moment. I'm exhausted by the wonderment of this whole experience. William Hamilton resumes his fabulous dancing without missing a step, whilst his gaze is fixed firmly on Elizabeth. My heart melts to see her little face beam such pleasure, knowing she will marry without the discord or impairment that I once had to bear. Courtiers rush to the stage, eager to congratulate Charles on a successful masque and to take their places to join the masquers in dance.

'Jane, are you coming too?' says Elizabeth excitedly.

'I won't join you tonight my dear,' protective of my unborn, signalling to Brome to take our leave, content with the spectacle I have witnessed.

Once inside the apartment, with the door closed behind us, Brome begins.

'I said there was tension in the court didn't I?'

'You did my dear, you are quite right.'

Indeed he is. The message of the court masque, though shrouded in a huge spectacle, is nonetheless clear, that within our nation lies a growing fervour of individual thought outside those of our sovereign.

However, with being so tired from a long day, I try not to encourage his rant. Instead, prepare myself to retire inside the luxury of the linen that awaits my dreams. I bolster my pillow to watch Brome pace the floor with a glass of port, and relent.

'I am listening Brome.'

'You won't understand.'

'Try me. You may be surprised, but please speak in a whisper my love, the walls of Whitehall Palace have ears, and I don't want us spending the night in the Tower when I have this comfy bed,' I say, patting the clean laundered crisp white sheets.

'The Masque', whispers Brome, so quietly, forcing me to draw closer to strain my ears.

'That performance,' he continues, 'shows just how worried the king is about people rebelling against his demands on people's finances with the insistence of requesting ship money. Some men have already rebelled, refusing to pay this taxation. His Majesty is worried that he is losing control of his people.'

'Ship money? Taxes? The masque didn't mention taxes or ship money.'

'There you are. You don't understand.'

'Tell me what you mean Brome. What is this ship money?'

'Ship money, we are told, will protect our seas from pirates. That whole performance out there,' he says pointing to the door, 'is to justify the increase by showing us an alternative world when people rebel against their sovereign's request.'

'So the king is right then. This so called tax or ship money will be used to defend our shores from those reckless pirates we saw on stage.'

'We are not under threat from pirates today, anymore than before the tax was imposed. We are certainly not in danger of pirates along our inland waters, where tax is also being added.'

'So what is the money for then?'

'To fill the King's coffers. The royal court is running out of money.'

'Surely not. A king without money? I've never heard such a thing.'

'Whenever the king needs more money, he calls upon us to pay through our taxes. We fund his luxuries, his obsession with collecting art, along with his so called court entertainment and extravagance.'

'Brome, stop it. It is harsh what you are saying.'

'I'm right though. Tension is being pressed upon

tension; layer upon layer, bubbling just below the surface. King Charles is fully aware of it, which is why he shows how life will be, if we rebel against his demands.'

'Well in that case, I hope everyone pays this tax, rather than rebel, because I don't want to live in the Imposture's world of grotesque chaos.'

Brome pours himself another large port from the decanter and sits next to me on the bed, stroking my hair.

'No Jane, I don't want to live in that world either, but I'm afraid people are already starting to resent the king's stubborn and selfish means.'

'Brome, how dare you say such a thing?' pushing him away from me.

'I'm sorry Jane it's how I view it. People are obliged to question, at what price to their own financial demise, is the king doing right by his subjects?'

'But the alternative is so grim. You heard the noise. You saw the commotion brought about by past rebels as they entered the stage; those who'd fought and lost against their rulers. It doesn't bear thinking about. I don't want our children to see those atrocities.'

'Oh my pretty one,' he says, smoothing over our unborn child.

'No Brome. The masque reminds us to maintain our virtues.'

'Yes, but are they the right ones, Jane? Is there not some truth in what the Imposture was saying?'

'No.' I quickly retort.

'You would think like that Jane.'

'What is that remark supposed to mean?'

'Your vision is clouded by your love for the king and the royal court.'

'Oh Brome, don't be ridiculous. Any member of the audience would agree that those horrid scenes were of a country depraved, full of deceit, not of order and calm shown us by Britanocles, when King Charles, emerged from the golden palace.'

'Yes, you are quite correct; any member of the audience indeed. Though, that audience is made up entirely of courtiers who will always bow to the one that feeds them. Take your stepfather for instance. In his role, so closely linked to the king, he will do and say anything to save the royal court. So, I ask again,' continues Brome, 'is this the right virtue to have?'

'Of course it's the right one. Why would anyone choose hell over the sublime. Are you trying to live the rest of your life in the Tower for your treasonable thoughts?'

'I'm not against the king or my country, you know that. But politically, nothing makes sense to me anymore.'

'Why does everything have to be about politics?

131

Couldn't you enjoy the masque for the spectacle?'

'Well that would be treason.'

'Why? How can you say that to me Brome?'

'Because the king expects you to listen to his message, not look at the scenery.'

'Yes, you are quite right Brome,' I say sniggering, hurling a pillow towards him as he walks away to refill his glass.

'Oh Jane, my love. What will become of us all?'

'You could drink less of His Majesty's port, so he won't have to replenish the stocks this week and raise everyone's taxes to pay for it,' I suggest.

'I've already paid for this,' he says, smiling, holding up the glass before drinking it straight back. 'I've paid for this through taxes on our land, the taxes on our...'

'Yes, yes. Tax, tax tax,' I interject, as Brome clambers onto the bed beside me in a much lighter mood.

'Come on then, Madam Whorwood, tell me about the flying dolphin you were so transfixed by and the gust of wind that almost knocked you off your seat before a fine fleet of ships arrived on stage. I saw you swaying in the gale. I saw you holding our little one when Merlin came on stage with an almighty loud bang,' he continues as he wraps me in his arms for safe keeping.

'Oh Brome. Imagine. All the courtiers will be

dancing and singing with our king and queen now, whilst we are here talking about awfully depressing things.'

'Yes, we are my love. I'm sorry. Though I am worried by what I see and hear.'

'I know you are my dear,' I reply, patting his arms that hold me. 'Oh but, the costumes. Weren't they simply glorious?'

'They were indeed Jane. You are quite right, King Charles, couldn't have looked more charming in his garb upon the stage.'

'Enough now my love,' I say, feeling awfully drowsy. 'Please can you blow out the candles, so I can dream of the golden palace?'

As the light fades and the room fills with the last burnt out smoke, I feel my head sink further and further into the plump feather pillow as my thoughts at last turn to *Britannia Triumphans*. A Flying horse, a fantastical dolphin and the courtly atmosphere, soon send me off to sleep, leaving Brome in peace to analyse the political situation of the day.

CHAPTER FOURTEEN

A Difference of Opinion
1642

The formal gardens, here at Sandwell Hall, are in full bloom. The scented periwinkles intermingle with the sweet smelling honeysuckles, whilst the mature herbaceous borders move gently in the late summer breeze, creating delicate aromas amongst the proud, lofty, pink and blue lupins, as they nudge against the perfumed stocks. For a moment, as I sit on the terrace, the undertones of political unrest and tiresome polemics are obliterated. I watch my children as they play without a care in the world; a world that is changing in every way. As a family and a nation, we attempt to cling to a hint of normality within the turbulence of this ever increasing discord of our society, as we fail to halt the tide of a Civil War.

Change is upon everyone. All my sisters have now

flown the bosom of our family home in Charing Cross. Elizabeth did indeed wed William Hamilton in 1638, who almost immediately rose to Secretary of State for Scotland and was bestowed the title, Earl of Lanark. When Elizabeth is not residing in Scotland, she lives in London, Spurr Alley, St Martin's in the Fields.

Diana, my youngest sister, married soon after Elizabeth in 1639, to Charles Cecil, Viscount Cranborne of the Salisbury family, MP for Hertfordshire. When not on the country estate of Hatfield House in Hertfordshire, which I'm told often by Diana, is ten times larger than Holton House, she resides in the grandeur of Salisbury House, close to the River Thames. I always predicted she would marry well, and she appears to be rather enjoying a lifestyle of high society.

Anne, who did not marry until last year, 1641, is wedded to Sir Thomas Bowyer, MP for Bramber. They live in Charing Cross when not living simply in Leighthorne, Sussex, where Anne, having inherited twelve children from Sir Thomas Bowyer's previous two marriages, is clearly enjoying the domesticity of married life.

Mary, my faithful maid continues to keep close to me, joining in play on the terrace with Brome junior, now a boisterous seven year old and my youngest, Diana, three years old, for I am still somewhat fragile from losing my baby Elizabeth, at four years old, last year, in 1641. As we sit together in the delectable formal gardens, contemplating our future amongst the threats imposed on our society, I gaze at Brome junior and Diana before they run excitedly towards me with a ladybird they've found. I thank them for being there, holding them closer than ever.

'Good children. How thoughtful to bring Mama your finds.'

'Are you sad, mother?' enquires Brome junior.

'No, darling. I am fine thank you,' I reply, hoping to put his mind at ease for at least the time being.

Yet I am not fine. Instead, quite morose. The conflict of war is not only on the battlefield, but runs through the arteries of every family home. Our house, here in Sandwell, is to be confiscated by Parliament when they sequestrate our estate as punishment for the help Brome recently gave to the Royalists, when he sent arms to the Earl of Northampton to help fight at Warwick. As a consequence, we are forced to pay a hefty fine for the return of our own property, which we can ill afford. The conditions which Parliament place upon us, weigh heavy. I try hard to hide my true feelings from the children whilst the destruction of war cuts deep into all our souls.

London, especially Whitehall, is but a shell of its former self as our sovereign takes refuge in Oxford, making

Christ Church College the safer headquarters for the royal court. The courtiers have distanced themselves from the unruly unrest of Parliament who is forcing Charles to forego his strong belief in the divine right of kings, to open the way for Parliament to have a greater stake in the decisions of our country. The turmoil from the determined efforts of Parliament, to take away power from the king, has resulted in families being torn apart, becoming fractured in our beliefs, on whose side to support. It's a perplexing time in which we find ourselves. Our country has lost all sense of reality, and Brome has lost all patience. He has taking the drastic decision to remove himself from these complexities and go into exile, to live in Holland, leaving myself and our children, to reside at Holton House.

I am furious by his determination to take refuge away from our British shores rather than stay to fight the Royalist cause; turning his back on both his family and his country. Brome and I have spoken at length to resolve our issues, but this, it would seem, is his way of dealing with the situation, by, 'not minding to have to do the unhappy differences between king and parliament,' he said. It is certainly not my way. I can only view his actions as cowardly which I can barely stomach. As we close down the house here in Sandwell, leaving what was becoming a family home, my mind is swimming with thoughts of Brome's

138

thoughtlessness. I accept that Parliament has the upper hand presenting us with a difficult, if not impossible situation; that if we help the Royalist cause, we lose our possessions and yet to side with Parliament would be morally unacceptable and thus unthinkable. But my ethos is always to fight for what you believe, not run away from the problem leaving everyone else to clear up the mess. It's a great shock that Brome is leaving. Though I shall confront and do my best to survive the heartache of being thrust into the arms of Holton Park, Lady Ursula Whorwood, and those awful servants, who, as we know, detest the sight of me.

Brome is firm in his decision. No amount of my persuading has so far changed his mind to bring about a resolve. Today, I am to make the long journey south, without my husband. I grieve as I walk the children from their play on the sunny terrace to the waiting carriage where they board obediently, sitting close to Mary Hurles. Brome at least comes to peck them on their cheeks as they scramble to the window, bouncing on the carriage bench.

'Goodbye Brome,' I say, still completely aghast at the situation we find ourselves.

'Take care Jane. Look after the children,' Brome says as he closes the carriage door firmly.

The carriage pulls away slowly but purposefully, to journey once again into the unknown. My heart sinks.

Michelle Hockley

* * *

Our journey from Staffordshire to Oxfordshire is relentless. At every turn there are groups of standing soldiers poised in readiness with muskets held. Scattered across the country we see farm buildings taking on a different guise. No longer shelters for animals to care for their young, but bulging with ammunition within and cannon balls waiting to commit their murderous act on command of fire. God must be watching over us, for this is one journey Brome should never have allowed us to travel alone.

When, eventually, Holton House appears in the distance, we know our journey is almost complete, but this provides me no solace, as images of past visits grip at my soul. Mary smiles at me, as she places her hand on my knee. 'Marm, I think it will be different this time. I am sure of that.'

Our carriage crosses the moat, greeting me with utter despair as I come face to face with the sullied black, dense water that barricades this charmless building inside its own cell, sucking me deeper and deeper inside its unpleasant muse. Reluctantly, we alight the coach. I take Diana in my arms while Mary holds Brome junior's hand, to help him down. Both children look daunted. Which, I can only assume, are mimicking my emotions, which I am finding difficult to hide.

'Welcome back Madam Whorwood,' says Emmanuel the coachman, as he removes the bridal from the horses.

'Thank you Emmanuel. Thank you,' I reply, somewhat surprised, given the coldness he has previously shown towards me.

With the utmost military precision from the servants, our trunks are quickly unloaded. They stand in line to greet me and the children. Mary stays close by nudging as she whispers, 'I told you Marm.'

'What is going on Mary? Why is everyone so different towards me?'

'With the help of your servant Margaret, her Jack and my frantic letter writing to explain the misunderstanding, we've managed at long last to make everything right with the servants here at Holton,' purports Mary.

I am so touched to learn of Mary's efforts to reconcile an awful situation with the servants; relieved that this is one conflict, at least, I don't have to fight.

'Thank you Mary,' I reply as she hurries along to join the servants in the kitchen.

Abruptly shaken out of this warm kindness, when Ursula comes out from the withdrawing chamber.

'Hello, Lady Ursula.'

I offer her my hand which she takes unwilling as our trunks continue to be carried through the hall and up the stairs. Aware that Ursula would rather not engage in conversation with me, I make my excuse to leave her company.

'I shall go to our rooms to settle the children if you are in accordance,' I enquire.

'Yes, you are in the same quarters, at the front of the house,' Ursula informs me with her usual clipped tongue.

On entering the accommodation, I could be forgiven for thinking the rooms are in fact not the same, as a dainty aroma of fresh flowers greets me. All our belongings sent ahead of our arrival, are neatly arranged in a kindly fashion. I dare myself to surrender to the quietness and permit my body and mind a reprieve to slump in a nearby chair. Diana climbs on my lap. Brome junior leans against me, putting his arms around my waist as we sit close to each other. Though of course, I understand too well, that fresh flowers and neatly arranged personal belongings can only mask the true situation I find myself. Whilst a nation struggles in conflict; ripped apart, snatched from its core, I see reflections of my own battles weighing so heavily around me.

CHAPTER FIFTEEN

New Acquaintances

As the days and weeks roll forward here at Holton, nothing is ever spoken between myself and Ursula of her son's decision to take himself into exile. I therefore, am unable to establish if she agrees or disagrees with his choice. Instead, I take each day without ever broaching that sensitive subject.

With Brome's brothers, William and Thomas, no longer living at home, it is just myself, the children, the servants and Ursula who reside at this country pile. Mary Hurles soon settles back into a routine, resuming her gossip network in the kitchen; though I am always sure to knock before entering their domain, not wanting to make that mistake again. Margery Bower, our cook, does her best, but everyday it's proving more difficult to enter Oxford to buy provisions with the ever increasing garrison stationed to protect the king. I've suggested we create a kitchen garden with our own vegetables, fruit and herbs so something of nourishment is always on hand. Whether this idea will ever materialise or if indeed Lady Ursula, as the Lady of the household, will give me consent for such a change, is something I shall have to wait and see.

A horse has been assigned for my own use. We are becoming close associates as we ride out on most days, though no replacement for the love I still have for Rayleigh. I have reached the high wall at the edge of the estate that encloses the household to entrap the white deer. However, I no longer hold the notion I had on my arrival in 1634, to free myself and jump the rampart that harboured me. It is about more than me now, I have my children to consider.

On my ride out today, I see in the distance, Mr John Stampe, who I often look for when about the estate. As I ride towards him, it's clear he is now more aged; well it is ten years since we first met and he wasn't that young then.

'Mr Stampe. Mr Stampe,' I call quietly, not wanting to alarm him with my sudden presence.

'Madam Whorwood. Hello. I heard you were back in Holton whilst your husband has taken to the Continent.'

Of course I am not surprised that Mr Stampe already knows as much about my private life as I do.

'How are you Mr Stampe?' I enquire still mounted, looking down from my horse as he walks beside me.

144

'Oh you know,' he says, 'trying to make the best of the troubles that hang around us,' sounding somewhat defeated.

'I too am willing for the unrest to be over so we can get back to normal. It's already becoming more difficult to get into Oxford and impossible to gain passage to London without a pass.'

'Yes, everything has changed Madam. The king and his entourage at nearby Oxford will, no doubt, mean that taxes will rise to ensure enough coffers are available to support their luxuries.'

That's not going to happen. Parliament are raising funds, but for their own ends, not for the king. However, Mr Stampe does have a point about the royal court expenses. That is a major gripe of Parliament and certainly mentioned on more than one occasion by Brome. I take a moment to ponder if Mr Stampe is for or against the king, remembering he is a recusant, so anything is possible.

'Would you like to meet your neighbours who live nearby, Madam? What about seeing our village of Holton?' asks Mr Stampe, clearly recalling how isolated I was the last time I lived here.

'Yes please. That would be lovely, thank you. I would like that.'

'That's good Madam. I shall send word to the house

when I have the arrangements. You take your ride now, for it's good to see you've found the stables,' he adds as he looks up at me on this strapping tall horse.

'That's down to you Mr Stampe. You showed me the stables all those years ago. Do you remember?'

'I remember Madam. I remember'. He shouts, chuckling as he doffs his cap whilst I gallop into the distance, smiling at Mr Stampe's dry sense of humour.

* * *

The next morning a letter arrives post haste, brought to me in the breakfast room by the footman, David Truman.

'Madam. Will there be a reply or shall I dismiss the post boy?'

I read the note quickly as Mr Truman stands aside waiting for an answer. It's an invitation from John Stampe, having wasted no time in arranging a gathering at the house of a William Elliot and a widow, Elizabeth Ball, in Holton village.

'Mr Truman. Please let the post boy go. No reply.'

Lady Ursula, seated opposite me at breakfast, peers across the table as I fold the letter back into its creases before placing it securely inside my pocket. Wanting to distract her from my personal business, I comment on the pleasant weather we are having for November, for I have no intention of revealing my social life, if you can call it that, to someone who barely acknowledges my existence. However, I do ask permission to use Emmanuel's time, for I want to take the carriage on my first visit, even though, from the directions in the letter and according to John Stampe, the house is but a short distance from Holton House.

On ensuring the children are happy with Mary, I dress in my best and make my way to the carriage waiting outside the main front door. As we start to pull away, Margery Bower appears with a box, outstretched in her arms, tied with string.

'Madam. I've baked biscuits for you to take to the house.'

'Oh thank you Mrs Bower, that is kind.'

'I didn't want you to arrive empty handed. Please call me Margery.'

'Why thank you Mrs...Margery.'

'They are good biscuits. Made with fresh milk that Joan Miller, dairymaid, fetched for you this morning,' adds Mrs Bower.

'Thank her too for me. Please thank Joan Miller too,' I say as I wave through the carriage window feeling warm from her thoughtfulness.

Michelle Hockley

The distance to the meeting is indeed a short ride. On arrival I let Emmanuel return to Holton House as I can easily walk back after my visit. He is accepting of my orders with the horses and carriage soon moving away.

Standing outside the small whitewashed stone cottage, situated slightly off the narrow country lane, I absorb the charm of such a pretty home. Pushing open the small wooden gate, flanked either side by a low stone wall, tangled in ivy across the base, I walk down the narrow path towards the door and knock gently. The door is unlatched and opens immediately. I call out, not wanting to be too presumptuous by walking straight inside.

'Ms Ball. Mr Elliot. Is anyone at home?'

I can hear several voices coming from one of the rooms, but unable to make myself heard. Tentatively, I continue, still clutching my box of biscuits, to creep further inside the house, calling as I go. I come to an open door, from where I hear voices. When I peer inside, I'm surprised to find a throng of people sitting huddled by the hearth. Once I enter, all their heads turn towards their awaiting guest. One by one they stand to acknowledge my presence, whilst one lady comes immediately to greet me at the living room door.

'Madam Whorwood. How lovely to see you. We are so pleased you accepted our invitation. Please let me take your cloak Madam. I am Elizabeth Ball and very pleased to meet you at long last.'

Smiling at her welcoming manner, still keeping one eye on the many faces staring at me from the hearth, I thank Elizabeth for the invitation as I present her with the box of biscuits, informing her they were baked this morning by Mrs Bower.

The sitting room is small, housing large pieces of dark wooden furniture; chairs, wooden chests and cabinets. The ceiling is low making the room a cosy affair which seems to be drawn inwards by the many rows of books on the shelves, stretched across the whole of the back wall.

Elizabeth Ball wastes no time to introduce me to her waiting guests.

'This is Elizabeth Towersey, she is from nearby Vent Farm. Richard and Lena Parker, who you may already know from Holton. This is my William Elliot, who is a tailor. Together, we share this house. Finally, but by no means least, Jane and George Ball from Forest Hill up the road, near Shotover village'.

I shake the hands of each of them, who are clearly pleased to meet me.

'Take a seat Madam,' says William Elliot.

'Thank you. It's a pleasure to meet you all,' quickly feeling enormously at ease in their company, happy to partake in cakes and wine.

As the conversation develops, not a single person mentions Brome or Lady Ursula, but they ask after Diana and Brome junior, requesting I bring them along on my next visit. They enquire after my mother, stepfather and sisters. It comes as no surprise by now, that they already know my background and connections to the royal court, as did Mr Stampe and Mr Almond when we first met at Sir Thomas' funeral. As they stare at me, I wonder if I am but a novelty, with my coming from London and having lived in Whitehall with my connections so close to the king. I hope not. I hope they like me for who I am, not for who I know.

Thankfully, there is no talk of the current war, which is a light relief. With all my news out of the way and introductions over, I sit back to listen to their lives, forgetting about the disturbances we all have to endure, spending the most delightful day in their company.

As light starts to fall in, concious that the day is drawing to a close, I stand to take my leave. Through the latticed windows, I see mist already forming over the fields and wish Emmanuel had stayed. Fortunately, Richard and Lena Parker insist on driving me in their carriage, which I willingly accept.

On arriving back at Holton House I see Lady Ursula walking through the corridor. I wish her a good evening, but she doesn't speak to me. Instead, walks into the drawing room closing the door behind her. I ignore her rudeness, going straight upstairs to the nursery to look in on my children and catch up with Mary Hurles.

'You know Mary, Lady Ursula doesn't like me in the slightest.'

'Ignore her Marm. Once Brome starts to miss you and the children, realising he needs to be with his family, you will soon, I'm sure, return to your own home in Sandwell. Oh sorry, Marm. I've spoken out of turn. I am so sorry.'

'No Mary, what you say is quite true. I don't mind what you say if you stick close to the truth,' I reply, knowing I do have a close companion in Mary.

I collect the post that arrived late this afternoon to read in my bedchamber. Brome writes weekly to tell us of his movements. He is currently living in the Hague amongst other like minded people, who also distance themselves from the war in England, yet, recognise themselves as Royalists. How one can claim to be a Royalist whilst doing nothing to help the king, still remains a mystery to me.

The letters I receive are pleasant enough. He always asks after the children; requesting reassurance that Brome is engaged in his school work. Whenever he visits the royal court of the Prince of Orange, where Queen Henrietta is lodged, I am furnished with a full account of what he ate and who he met. Needless to say, he has overlooked the fact that Henrietta Maria is there to rally extra troops and gather funds, by selling the crown jewels in the most ruthless of ways, to bring back to our shores. We are expecting Henrietta's return quite soon, bringing with her extra help. Brome, on the other hand, fails once again, to disclose when he might return.

CHAPTER SIXTEEN

A Maxwell Reunion
Spring 1644

As a Royalist, and no longer living in London, safe passage to and from the capital is increasingly difficult. Whilst the royal court is forbidden to leave Oxford, a request to exit, is treated with the utmost suspicion. As a consequence, I have not returned to London for such a long time but today, this is about to change. In my hand I hold a legitimate travel pass, sent to me by my stepfather, summoning myself and my sisters to a meeting at our home in Charing Cross.

My passage to London is without problem, but not without scrutiny. The pass and papers are checked at every step of the way and my small hand luggage is searched on several occasions throughout the journey. Whitehall, without the royal seat, displays its wounds of war unable to hide the atrocity from its people. Parliamentary soldiers stand on guard at the Banqueting House, where once stood ladies of the royal court in their finery. People go about their business encased in a harshness. A city, barren, without life, brought about by uncertainties as we lack the leadership of our sovereign. Expressionless faces appear to be worn by all. Heads held low. Anonymity.

With my nose pressed up to the window of the carriage, I attempt to process what war and conflict has brought upon this city. Though of course, at a loss to answer how it came to this. Question after question without adequate response. How long can this go on for? How will it all end? Why do people have to fight so much? Why does religion always play its part in conflict, when religion is about love and peace? If disease is not enough to keep us constantly on our guard, then war is certainly a reminder of the perils in which we find ourselves.

'Here we are Madam Whorwood,' announces the driver, jolting me from my solitude.

'Thank you. I appreciate you being conscious to maintain my safety,' I reply.

'That's no problem Madam. Your Ma and Pa would have it no other way. You take care now. I understand Mr Maxwell is inside, so you should be fine from here,' he explains.

Before Spring Came Summer

No one greets me on the steps as they once did. Everyone more subdued, sombre. No smiles. No pleasure. I enter the house calling out to my parents as I stand in the hallway, putting my bag on the floor beside me, not wanting to rush inside with my usual energy until I have some idea, why this meeting has been requested. Hoping it is nothing serious.

'Miss Jane. Madam,' calls out Margaret.

'Hello Margaret. Is everything alright? Is my mother here?'

'She's in Chelsea today Miss, helping her brother whose wife has come down with the pox.'

'Oh, thank you Margaret,' I reply, certain this is an excuse, knowing my mother wouldn't miss an opportunity to see me at any cost. I don't quiz Margaret any further, these are strange times. Instead, I follow her lead and enter the drawing room, where drapes are tightly closed adding to my suspicion, that this encounter is for something quite grave.

My sisters; Anne, Diana and lovely Elizabeth, are already seated at the large wooden table with my stepfather opposite.

'Come along Jane,' Anne barks, 'where have you been? We are waiting for you.'

'Oh I'm sorry. Were you worried about me?' I reply

155

with a hint of sarcasm, confident that Anne, even though she is my blood sister, would probably never truly worry about me.

I smile pleasantly to my stepfather as I pull out the tall backed wooden chair. He acknowledges me with a nod, encouraging me to take a seat as quickly as possible.

'I thank you for coming so promptly,' says my stepfather as we lean forward to hear what he has to say, hoping all the time that nothing has happened to my mother, that something awful is not about to pass his lips. I clasp my hands beneath the table, wringing the cloth of my dress, believing that if I were to relax at this juncture, something terrible will result.

'As you girls are fully aware,' he begins, 'we are in the throws of a major conflict.'

'And don't we know it,' Diana interjects.

'Thank you Diana. If you could wait for me to finish,' replies my stepfather.

'I apologise father,' throwing herself back in her chair with the usual air of self-assurance about her.

'The Crown is in trouble,' my stepfather continues, 'we are losing a grip on the situation. The royal court is sinking into oblivion. Without access to its funds or royal plate, the court will undoubtedly enter into obscurity, unable to fight the cause or reclaim London as its ruling position,' he explains.

At first, I sigh with relief to hear it's not bad news about my family. Nevertheless, soon feel helpless that My Majesty is losing a stronghold against the Parliamentarians. I ask a question.

'What about the efforts made by Queen Henrietta that she secured and brought back to our shores? Have these been in vain?' I ask.

'Not at all, but we need more funds, plus Henrietta Maria is requesting leave abroad and to do so, will require financial help to aid her escape.'

We remain silent as my stepfather shuffles papers on the table laid out in front of him. He scans each of us to be sure he has our full attention before continuing.

'The city merchants of the Levant and East India Company, along with my good associates in the city, have agreed their support to help the court by offering gold that can be minted at New Hall College, in Oxford.'

'Bravo to the city merchants,' claims Diana flippantly, as she claps her hands in slow motion. 'It seems the whole problem is solved then.'

'Well it's not as simple as that,' says my stepfather.

'No, it rarely is,' says Anne, indignant of the plight we find ourselves, wondering, no doubt, why everyone, especially merchants, are not as organised or as clear thinking as she is. I watch her poised upright as she speaks, not in a flighty way, but self assured of herself. The same manner I am sure she presents, when organising her battalion of children in her domestic bliss.

'So, what do you want us to do?' I ask, recognising that my stepfather finds himself in the eye of a storm, confident he has already conjured a disgraceful plot, ensuring someone pays for his own ideals.

'The problem lies in moving the gold from London to the royal court in Oxford. I believe, that with careful planning amongst ourselves, we can achieve this for the king. What do you think?'

My mind returns to the earlier journey littered with constant scrutiny. Moving gold out of the City would of course be an enormous problem. Yet, with knowledge that my stepfather believes each of us is capable, it does perhaps present the perfect opportunity to make a concerted effort to outwit the Parliamentarians to restore King Charles to his seat here in London. The idea of making this happen starts to fill me with excitement. I'm ready to shoot my hand straight in the air to commit participation in this exciting proposition. An opportunity to add another dimension to my mundane life at dreary Holton House by assisting My Majesty to prove his beliefs, as he navigates us out of this mess to save our nation. Halted by my sisters' eagerness to make their contribution to the meeting I have to sit on my hands and wait my turn.

Elizabeth lets out a gasp, surprised that anyone could even imagine her involvement in such deceit, regardless of the reason. Anne, on the other hand is silent. By the look of her anguished brow, she is clearly giving some thought to my stepfather's request. Possibly even flattered. Possibly thinking she has been singled out at long-last for the diligence she would show in carrying out such a task. Diana doesn't hold back in making her feelings known.

'Father, do I have to remind you that my loyalties lie firmly with my husband and their family who now hold little compassion for the Royalist cause?'

She certainly has a fair point, for her father-in-law, William, Earl of Salisbury's property in Cranborne, was plundered not once but twice, in the most severe manner by the Royalists. By all accounts, it was indeed a brutal attack, leaving murdered sheep strewn across the land. The Salisbury family managed to save their finest furniture before the second plunder, by moving it safely to Carisbrooke Castle, on the Isle of Wight. Diana, thankfully, was safe, residing at Hatfield House. Parliament are so disgusted by the carnage that befell that home, they have offered to pay for the repairs. Sitting beside Diana, I can feel her rage; a white tautness forming around her lips in anger

159

as she relays the event, contemplating the audacity of her father for even suggesting she would help to act against her family after such barbarity. My stepfather holds out his hand across the table as a gesture of an apology, but she refuses, point blank, to take it ensuring he is left stewing a little longer for his misjudgement of her situation.

Elizabeth breaks the thick air that surrounds us by beginning to speak, though less forceful than Diana, in an almost apologetic manner.

'I too wish for the safe return of our king to his seat in London, really I do father. I want also for my husband, William to be given the opportunity to explain his failings in Scotland, after being unable to prevent an alliance with Parliament.'

'I understand Elizabeth,' says my stepfather with enormous sympathy for her, having been in Scotland with Hamilton and witnessed his efforts.

Elizabeth doesn't pause for breath. She is caught in the moment, relaying her thoughts, wanting to be understood.

'Instead of allowing my husband, such a pardon, King Charles arrests my poor dear William and throws him in the dungeons of Windsor Castle. If it hadn't been for his faithful servant, helping him to escape, he would have been left to rot. I want to help this cause, but my loyalties are so confused and I must support my husband.'

Whilst Elizabeth maintains her dignity, she appears flustered by her outburst at reliving the situation as she relayed her thoughts and reasons. She sits back in her seat lowering her head, fighting back the tears and the hopelessness she feels. Poor angel. Thankfully, Diana, who is sitting closest to her, momentarily puts an arm around her, offering support.

I glance at Anne as she places her hands on the table, preparing herself to speak, appearing strong and composed. I wonder if Anne and me could work together on this? The two Ryder sisters, working hand in hand, showing what we can achieve. But that is not to be. Anne rejects her involvement on the grounds that her husband, Sir Thomas Bowyer, would fear very much for her safety after the torture he received when helping to set up the garrison in Chichester for the king. To which end, he lost his seat in the House of Commons. Anne explains that Sir Thomas and herself are fully committed to the Royalist cause, but she is needed at home to care for her family, keeping home for her husband.

As I listen to Anne, I picture her residing in Leighthorne, managing her home with extreme military precision. Imagining her surrounded by twelve children. Looking after twelve children. Who does that? Who has twelve children to look after unless you are a governess?

My stepfather then turns to me. 'Jane, do you have anything to add or to say?' What are your thoughts?' he says, somewhat disappointed with the responses he has so far received from his children; even though all legitimate reasons for declining his request.

'Come on Jane,' says Anne, 'where do your loyalties lie? After all, what has your so called husband given up for the cause? Has he been imprisoned, chastised, tortured? Or has he instead absconded from the ceaseless anguish we every day have to endure?'

'Yes, Jane,' agrees Diana, 'Anne does have a point, what has your husband sacrificed to help the cause?'

I blush on hearing the remarks they make of Brome. His feeble actions towards the cause is humiliating. Others have already fought and lost. Today, highlights where all our loyalties lie and shows how fast the dynamics of our family have changed. Where once we seemed as one whole, supporting each other against the world, we now, because of this wretched war are fractured from our core. One thing we can all agree on is, that Brome Whorwood is an embarrassment to us all and his country.

'Come on Jane,' says Diana impatiently, disgruntled. 'Please hurry-up with your decision, so we can all return to the rest of our day.'

'I shall do it,' I say.

'I shall help you stepfather in the Royalist cause.'

'Thank you Jane. Thank you', replies my stepfather, making his way to my side of the table, taking both my hands in his. 'I knew I could rely on my Jane.'

The others all stand, tucking their chairs neatly under the table, whilst I remain seated, a little excited at the prospect that my help could make a difference. Perhaps even fill the void that is ever present since my husband's leaving. Elizabeth places her hand on my shoulder as she leaves the room with my sisters, neither of them turn to look back as they close the door.

CHAPTER SEVENTEEN

Making Plans for a Gold Run
1644

Number 159, 161, 165. Here it is, 169 Bishopsgate Street. My stepfather is quite right, the house is unmissable with its splendid double-height frontage of a wooden ornate bay window, not unlike I have seen at Hampton Court Palace. Number 169 stands in all its glory exuding luxury and elegance like Phoenix raised from the ashes, juxtaposed against the simple facades of this East of London Street, on this humid mid-summer late evening.

Everywhere around me is quiet, but for the sound of cats screeching in the jitty adjacent to the house. I peer around to take a look. They fight over rubbish left in the alleyway which I observe for a while. Though this feline tussle is but a distraction, comfortably accommodating my resistance to approach the house and take up with the

Michelle Hockley

business in hand. I tear myself away to stand instead in front of the tired wooden front door to prepare myself to rap. My hand, looking awfully small, clenched, folded double, begins the agreed signal of four taps. The fourth is not stronger than the other three, but instead quivering, trembling, mirroring the beads of sweat that descend my forehead in the humid air. I wait quite still.

The door slowly opens with the operator pressed firmly behind. I see no one but a dimly lit hallway as I enter inside. The door closes shut without one word spoken. I take my lead up the narrow, wooden, creaking stairway until signalled to wait on the landing. I dare to look around from where I'm rooted, but move not one inch from where I've been instructed to stand. A large chandelier hangs low, desperate to shine, but denied such with heavy cobwebs that enshrines its beauty. Another door opens inwards, again without exposing the person standing tight behind the door against the wall. An arm shows itself, offering me entry. I take the smallest, quietest steps on the wooden floorboards towards the centre of the room, making each step count as if it be my last. A stout, balding man, sitting at a desk, turns his low wooden swivel chair to face me. We make eye contact. Each maintaining our gaze whilst the door closes leaving myself and Sir Paul Pindar, gentleman merchant, alone in this dusty, wainscot clad room where books and large ledgers are stowed against each wall.

'Madam Whorwood. Are you sure you know what you are doing?' says Sir Paul Pindar, with sinister, elongated, drawn out tones. A resonance that mirrors my concerns, that what I am about to embark is, dangerous, wrong and above all, illegal. If caught, I shall undoubtedly take up residence in the Tower of London to await trial, regardless of who my stepfather is. Regardless of my contacts at the royal court, which, in these circumstances, counts for nothing when faced with a charge from Parliament.

Stop it Jane, says the voice in my head as I hold composure in the middle of the room, confronted by one of the richest merchants in the land, about to loan his wealth to help the Royalist cause with me at the helm to pilot this scheme. I have a plan of course, but for now this has resided only inside my mind. In reality, it has yet to air itself. The main stay of my plan will be associated with the plague, which has once more made its appearance on the stage of our already war torn decaying London; terrorising our people of this once splendid capital. Having seen Sir Paul's house for the first time this night, I still have to think on my feet as he begins to interrogate my design.

'So. Jane Whorwood. You, who has come highly recommend by your stepfather, James Maxwell, what do you have to ensure your beloved King Charles gets his hands on urgent funds?' asks Pindar with both a look and sound of sarcasm, that says, this should be interesting, expecting me to retreat.

'Your wealth, Sir Paul, that you kindly offer, is housed in this building. Am I correct in that assumption, sir?' I enquire with confidence that has surprised even myself.

'Yes, that is quite true. Since the start of the war it is hidden in boxes and crates, in this room.' Having clarified that loose end, I continue to expose my plan.

'Sir, I shall be aided by sufficient manpower allied to the royal court along with gentleman merchants, who by the promise of payment, will carry out our first drop to Oxford.'

'May I enquire as to who these persons are, who will be carrying my wealth out of my house?'

'Yes sir. These persons are; Mr Maule, Mr Murray and John Ashburnham, who are Gentlemen of the Bedchamber. John Browne who, as you know, is John Ashburnham's servant. Mr Loes, merchant, Elizabeth Wheeler, royal laundress and myself.'

'You are certain these people all agree to be part of the plan?' he asks.

'Yes indeed. Each person is loyal to the Crown, wanting to help King Charles regain power in London, sir.'

'I am familiar with the people you list, except one. Who is this Mrs Wheeler, you speak of. Who is this Wheeler?'

'She is laundress to Our Majesty's royal household. I have known her for many years. You may know her by her maiden name, Cole, for she has only recently married Mr William Wheeler,' I explain.

'Does your stepfather know of her?'

'Yes, she is trustworthy about the royal court.'

'What next, then Madam Whorwood? What else do you have for me?' enquires Pindar.

I take a deep breath, wiling to be offered a chair, but I ignore my want and instead pray that my plan sounds as workable in this room, as it does in my head.

'Sir,' I begin, with a slightly timid sound, clearing my throat before I continue. 'Mr Murray and Mr Maule will wear the official uniform of a Plague Inspector; a long white gown, with a long beaked mask, supposedly filled with herbs to prevent contracting the plague. At nightfall, they will bring a flat cart to 169 Bishopsgate Street, carrying two empty wooden chests covered with tarpaulin, steering the cart directly through the side alley of your house'.

Having only seen the side alley this night, my mind tells me to use this as part of my strategy. So far, it sounds like the perfect scenario, even though I'm receiving no reaction from Pindar. Taking another deep breath I continue.

'...The wooden chests will be put down at the back window, on the ground floor, in your back garden.'

At least I'm certain there is a garden, recalling my mother's disappointment when my stepfather took supper here last year and spent until the early hours drinking wine in Sir Pindar's courtyard.

'...A pulley apparatus,' I continue, 'will be used to winch the gold down from this floor, to the ground floor several times or more, where it will be collected before being stowed in empty wooden chests. When the caskets reach the weight we require for the journey, they will be closed tightly, affixed with nails banged in with a muffled mallet. The tarpaulin will once again cover the entire cart that Mr Maul and Mr Murry will push out through the alley back on to the street; all the while with caution, heading towards the Thames.'

Sir Pindar adjusts himself more comfortably, crossing his thick legs, having all this time been squeezed into his swivel wooden chair.

'Mmm...What makes you so sure about this plan, Madam Whorwood?' asks Pindar, clearly contemplating in his mind what I've explained; which must be a good sign.

'I am confident of this plan sir. No one will freely approach us for fear of contamination, as we act as if we are carrying the dead from the highly contagious disease, the plague.'

'My you have been doing your homework, Madam Jane,' says Pindar in a somewhat condescending tone, as he uncrosses his legs, pushes back on his heels, taking a stretch, before leaning forward and placing his elbows on the arms of the chair. With the tips of his fingers together, not in prayer, but in a more relaxed pose, he requests me to proceed with the rest of the plan.

'Sir. Once we arrive at the river, having pushed the cart far from here, there will be two boats waiting for us. One of the crafts will be held by Mr Loes and the other, by John Browne. If, or when an Officer of Customs approaches the cart, Elizabeth Wheeler and myself, with our faces covered, will wail uncontrollably explaining in a slightly inaudible manner through our fictitious grief, that the unfortunates died from the plague out of parish, returning home to their final resting place, being their last dying wish. The gentlemen, still masked as Plague Inspectors, will confirm this by showing forged papers to the officers. If, at anytime, we are asked to open the casks, the gentlemen will remind the authorities of the dangers to their own health if the bodies are exposed to the air.'

Again I get nothing back from Pindar. This time, his blank repose doesn't faze me. Today I am light of tongue, feeling every beat of this scenario as if I were already standing by the river Thames. I charge ahead to bring life to the images I see in my mind's eye.

'Sir, if I may continue?' Pindar moves his head, which I take as permission to my request, for I am eager to hear the plan inside this room, given that it has spent many hours peculating inside my head.

'John Ashburnham will wait our arrival in Oxford, ensuring the coast is clear before we moor. When he sees our boats arriving, he will send up a flare to signal that we have clearance. We shall not proceed until we see the sign, but instead wait on the banks of the river some distance away. Once safe, we shall sail to the steps, where Ashburnham will help us disembark lifting the heavy casks from the boats onto waiting carts he has hidden in the bushes beside the water's edge.'

'Yes, yes, yes,' says Pindar circling his hand as if requesting me to wrap up my narrative, making me think I have given too much detail, boring his fast witted brain.

'Sir, in summary, your huge contribution from your good fortune, will arrive in Oxford, taken to the mint at New Hall College, where it will be melted down to produce funds to aid Queen Henrietta Maria to escape our shores, and for the Royalists to win this terrible war.'

'Madam Whorwood, thank you. I am impressed. It is

without doubt, you have been brought up in the Maxwell household having developed the cunning traits of your stepfather.'

Traits of my stepfather? Surely not. Though perhaps unavoidable with nature versus nurture. My mind throws up an image of my stepfather, many years ago, when I stood with my family in the parlour, and he singled me out as we listened to him telling us what it meant when Charles returned to London from Spain with his religion in tact. It was as if it would be me who understood his joy. But I shall not accept that I am made of his cunning, crafty traits. That is not who I am. I am doing only good for my country and my king. Surely if circumstances were different, I'd be at home with my tapestry frame, not here in combat against these merchant gentlemen, and these, so called traits, would never have seen the light of day.

'Please go ahead. Put this plan into practise Madam Whorwood. In the meantime, I shall arrange the engineering of the pulley system you describe.'

'Thank you sir.'

I watch as he swivels his chair towards his desk, turning his back on me, closing down the meeting with a clear indication that I am to vacate the room, being no longer required.

Standing once again on the landing, waiting to be

escorted out of the building, I plant myself beneath the dusty chandelier acknowledging that if I am to approach all the city merchants my stepfather has requested, then this encounter is but the first of many.

Pindar's discreet manservant soon appears to usher me downstairs, opening the front door without showing his face to me or to the world outside. I head off without hesitation down Bishopsgate Street before I've even found my bearings, not wanting to dither outside Pindar's home, wanting just to walk, to collect my thoughts. Passing the parish church on the corner, recalling its presence from last night, I advance with greater certainty; pounding the streets of London, taking the longest of strides, feeling elated by what I have experienced; exhilarated by what I have become.

CHAPTER EIGHTEEN

Hold on to the Crown Jewels
April 29 1646

I am either a natural, or born for espionage. The transportation of gold, from as far back as 1644, has been safely escorted to Oxford from London. The thrill of successfully deceiving our enemies is exhilarating. The royal court remains of modest fashion in Oxford, not yet returned to its power seat in London. However, Queen Henrietta Maria did reach France safely in her escape, July 1644, settling in the Summer Palace at St Germain, on the outskirts of Paris.

My stepfather continues as a favourite at the royal court, confirmed this year 1646, when bestowed the title, Earl of Dirleton. My beloved mother, now Countess, either enjoys residing at Dirleton Castle, East Lothian, or the recently acquired family home, on the vast Guildford Park estate, in Surrey. We still have our London home, along with the addition of a house, not far from Charing Cross, in Cannon Row, that my stepfather has recently rented. My mother continues to worry for my safety, wishing that my stepfather had not encouraged me to get involved in secret intelligence, but knows I am rarely dissuaded from my beliefs, letting me know she's there if I need her advice.

Brome returned from the Continent last year, 1645, and everyday is delighted to be with the children after being away for three long years. It's not yet apparent what he achieved by taking himself away, though he does harbour much distress from the continuing unrest in our nation, buoyed-up by an ever increasing alcohol consumption. When Brome returned to England he paid a one thousand pound fine to Parliament for the return of our confiscated home in Staffordshire. Although we own Sandwell Hall again, for the time being, we remain in Holton, leaving the Steward, Henry Ford, to manage the estate during our absence. For now, I am pleased not to return to Sandwell. I need to be close to the royal court which Holton House is perfectly situated, being four miles away from the centre of Oxford.

I strive hard to make Holton House as comfortable as we made Sandwell Hall, trying also to help Brome readjust to life in England, encouraging him to heed what has now become, excessive drinking. However, I feel I have my work cut out on both accounts, since I appear to be coming from a long way back. Moreover, domesticity is proving difficult with this double life I lead; that of housewife and undercover agent. My head is always cluttered with information which I must separate correctly depending on whom or what I am speaking. Everyday I'm aware that I could be caught out at any moment, which of course, only adds to the excitement, fuelling my new found desire.

Our servants here in Holton remain in good spirits. They have carried out my instructions to create a vegetable garden so we are self sufficient, reducing the need to rely on supplies from the village or venture into Oxford. I have added a herb garden, not only for cooking, but also for their medicinal properties to protect us from disease. I still carry the pomander filled with herbs for protection and encourage my little one, Diana, to do the same. Mary Hurles continues to work well with the children, covering-up for me whenever I'm away. I trust Mary, but I don't impart details of espionage, for she does have a rather loose tongue. Margery Bowyer and Joan Miller are still helpful as is Emmanuel who is always willing to drive me in the carriage if I request his services. The villagers, Lena Parker and Elizabeth Ball, came to visit the children, but since Brome's return, these guests frequent our home much less often. I believe I am keeping good house here in Holton and helping an ageing Lady Ursula.

I have not discussed with my husband my involvement in helping the royal court to transport funds, but my comings and goings have not gone unnoticed. Brome's displeasure of my clandestine habits are evident. He is currently forbidding me to make the journey to Oxford for the royal court. I have yet to decide if Brome is grounding me because of concern for my safety, or if he wishes to control the freedom to which I have become accustomed during his absence, these past three years.

Indeed, danger is everyday more threatening to us. The recently formed New Model Army, by Thomas Fairfax and Oliver Cromwell, positions itself in the environs of Oxford, where according to a recent report, ten thousand soldiers are preparing themselves to take this city from the king's stronghold. Tension is mounting. The war is reaching new heights of despair. Soldiers live in nearby fields held up in barns. Property is pillaged for arms and weaponry.

I am perhaps most secure when taking refuge alone with reading or focusing on my tapestry pursuits, which is where I find myself this evening; taking recourse in the drawing room with my needlepoint. As night closes in, I am making little headway, even after Derek Truman kindly lit all the candles in the three large candelabras to improve the lighting. I struggle on regardless, wanting to complete this lengthy sampler upon the frame, even though my eyes are somewhat heavy.

The rumblings of a carriage in the distance distracts me for a moment as I imagine in my mind's eye, it approaching the bridge to cross the moat. My ears, fully engaged with the outside makes it difficult to concentrate on the cross stitch. The carriage has halted. Not expecting quite such a determined rap at the main front door, I leap from my seat, causing my needle to come away from the thread, dropping to the floor. My whole body tightens as I remain poised to consider who has come to our door at this late hour. I prick up my ears, leaning in the direction of the door trying to hear the conversation between our footman and visitor. I can't hear anything clearly, not even able to establish the tone of language being used.

I return to look for my needle, which has by now rolled somewhere under the table. As I look for it, scrambling on the floorboards, there is a knock at the drawing room door, alarming me, making me jump again, banging my head on the underside of the table. My goodness how clumsy I am this evening. I hope my double life is not starting to affect my nerves, for I seem to be in a permanent state of high alert.

'Madam Whorwood...Madam...,' comes Mary's voice,

standing outside the drawing room.

'What can I do for you?' allowing her to enter, calling out as I continue to look for my needle.

'Are you alright Madam,' asks Mary as I curl up from beneath the table attempting to get to my feet, catching my foot on my dress, causing me to lose my balance slightly, before managing to hoist myself up by pulling on the chair, quite ungainly, to stand up right.

'Sorry about that Mary. I dropped my needle, but I've found it now, thank you,' I explain by holding the needle in the air to show her the evidence; somehow feeling the need to justify my rather anxious behaviour.

'Now what can I do for you Mary?'

'A letter Marm. The carriage won't leave without an answer I'm afraid,' she says standing with an outstretched arm, willing me to take it.

'It is late in the day for letters,' I reply as I release her from her responsibility of delivery. Leaning against the table, hoping to establish some firm ground to regain my composure, I start to open the letter, daring to bend slightly backwards to gain maximum light from a nearby candle, digesting the written request.

My first thought after reading, is to ask Mary to care for the children, but purposely omit to tell her where I have been summoned. She doesn't pry. I go quickly to the children, kissing them on the cheek, careful not to disturb them as they lay sleeping in their room. Without another word, I make my way downstairs to the front door where I find an awaiting carriage.

Standing in the vestibule, with the main door to the house closed tight behind me, I try to button my cloak but my fingers are fumbling too much with excitement to carry out such a simple task and instead, secure my cap. The adrenaline is pumping inside me as my heartbeat quickens. I take a moment to collect myself, trying to find a semblance of calm by taking the deepest inhale of breath, exhaling with the largest of grins about my face. Standing tall, I make my way to the waiting royal carriage.

'Good evening, Mr Murray.'

'Evening Madam Whorwood,' he replies, holding open the carriage door. 'I am expecting us to arrive at the royal court, in about one hour.'

'Thank you Mr Murray,' I reply as I make myself comfortable, sitting further back into the carriage seat, pressing my shoulder firmly against the window for support.

We move away from the house, crossing the moat. As we start to turn left onto the road within the estate, I see Brome holding a lantern, marching towards the house, waving one arm above his head, shouting for us to stop the carriage as he draws closer. I keep my head down, crouching towards the floor.

'Madam. Would you like me to stop? I see someone is trying to gain your attention,' calls out Mr Murray.

Shamefully, straight off, I think to myself, I've lived my life quite successfully for the past three years whilst you, Brome Whorwood, took leave of your senses on the Continent. Today, my dear, will be no different. I know I shouldn't punish Brome like this, but I am aware, that if he knows where I am going, he will disallow it. He has already made it quite clear since his return, that I am forbidden from taking flight from Holton when I please. In this instance though, I can justify my actions because I've been summoned by the king. Surely, to refuse My Majesty, would be a treasonable offence, would it not? I shall explain everything on my return; well, a fictitious version at least.

'Please do proceed Mr Murray and make good haste if you will,' assuring him that the flailing lantern, belongs to the gardener, and my husband will deal with any business of that sort; having no trouble in spinning yet another falsehood.

'As you prefer Madam. As you wish.'

An hour into our journey towards the royal court, tension is clearly building. Thousands of soldiers surround Oxford, ready to attack. As we drive closer to Oxford, the noise from the gathering crowds, in protest of our king, is deafening. It's difficult to drive past them as they bump against our carriage. I retreat from the window moving to the centre of the bench, covering my face with my cloak, praying for the unrest to be over, wondering when it will stop. Perhaps, this is what Brome wanted to warn me about? The soldiers bang their muskets on the side of the carriage making an horrendous din. They are so close. It is so congested. The carriage rocks from side to side when the horses lose their balance. Mr Murray ploughs on, keeping us upright as we strive forth.

Then all of a sudden, without warning, the crowds clear like the stern of a ship passing through unobjectionable waves. We must have passed the periphery where it is safe to cross to enter inside the centre of Oxford. A Royalist haven. Headquarters of the royal court. I lift my head from my hands to register the silence, whilst behind us in the distance, I see the army jeer in defiance.

Approaching the main driveway to Christ Church College is a relief. The difference in atmosphere is striking. I start to trust the serenity of new surroundings, though still not quite believing we have arrived safely to our destination. The anger from the opposition is fierce as they build a wall of men around our sovereign. Piece by piece, removing the backbone of our society in the most disgusting manner. Mr Murray helps me down from the carriage, both of us ashen, saying nothing, an experience that leaves us speechless.

I quickly run through the courtyard of the college, making my way past the scholars in the gardens relaxing from their day of studies. The students, who have chosen to remain at the university, despite the chaos of the country taking over their university, endeavour to continue with their studies. I am so relieved to see the outline figure of Edward Sackville, who continues as Lord Chamberlain here in Oxford, after Henrietta escaped to France leaving him without office. Something the court wanted to avoid, after the devastating loss of his wife, Mary Curzon, who sadly died last year in May, months after retiring from her position as governess to the royal children.

'Thank you for coming Jane. His Majesty has been asking for you. Apologies for the short notice at this late hour.'

I offer my hand, which Sackville takes to kiss politely, before leading me to the Privy Gallery, where I am requested to wait further instruction. Although I see familiar faces about the royal household, I can't help but notice something is distinctly different about all of them. Rather than going about their duties, they appear to be somewhat distracted, forming groups, passing notes to each other, saying no more than a nod of the head or a doff of their cap.

It's not long before I catch site of Mr Patrick Maule who makes his way towards me. Oh no, am I here for another gold run? Is that why I've been summoned? How much gold does this court and war need? Mr Maule smiles but says nothing as he hands me a tiny folded note. I take it discreetly, returning the smile. Not having time to read the letter before Edward Sackville returns, I squeeze the note in the palm of my hand pushing it up towards my cuff until it is safely secure in my sleeve.

'Please come this way Madam Whorwood,' says Sackville, more formal in sight of the courtiers.

I follow him through the court to outside the Presence Chamber, where the Knights Marshal permits me entry. A second Knights Marshal then escorts me through the King's Privy Chamber, knocking thrice, and I gain access to the king's inner sanctum.

The gentleman, seated in a semi circle flanked either side of our king, rise as I enter. Charles remains seated. I curtsey in front of My Majesty, before acknowledging each Gentlemen of the Bedchamber in turn, by slowly bowing my head as I move around the circle greeting John Ashburnham, Mr Patrick Maule, Mr Murray; whose colour has returned to his cheeks and Colonel William Legge, a recent recruit to our fold. Elizabeth Wheeler is on the far side, completing those persons who I trust as my comrades, after the tasks we have already carried out together. I take the vacant seat that awaits in the horseshoe that encircles Our Majesty.

John Ashburnham takes to the floor to inform us the purpose for this gathering.

'With the force of the New Model Army surrounding the city of Oxford, increasing their fold, our beloved king is in danger of being captured by the army, fearing for his life. As a consequence, His Majesty, who has taken everything into account after extended talks with his advisers, will offer himself to the Scottish Army, where he will find a sanctuary with the necessary support needed to return to his rightful seat in London.'

Without thinking, I immediately comment on what I have heard. I, in no way consider myself to be an adviser to the king, but I can see before me, my beloved Charles looking browbeaten, shrivelled and lost, as he clings to Ashburnham's every word.

'If the English Army are wanting our Majesty captured,' I ask, 'and Parliament are supporting them, are they going to allow a transfer of allegiance quite so easily as you describe sir?'

'This is a good question, Madam Whorewood,' replies Ashburnham. 'Parliament and the army will indeed view this move as most disloyal, but we are left with no

186

alternative but to leave Oxford. It is too dangerous here,' continues Ashburnham. 'We intend for Charles to make an escape from Oxford in the early hours of this morning, accompanied by myself and his clergy Dr Hudson, where we shall make our way to meet members of the Scottish Army at their headquarters in Southwell.'

This is serious. I can detect only danger at every juncture of this plan. However, I can also recognise there is no alternative after witnessing for myself, the hunger in the eyes of those soldiers surrounding Oxford. Charles would not stand a chance if they invaded, acting upon their desire to take the seat that Our Majesty is holding fast.

A knock at the chamber door and Babbington, Charles' barber enters. He is beckoned inside by Mr Maule as if expected. Elizabeth Wheeler hands a bundle of old clothes to James Daventry, dropping a mounteere cap from the pile as they move swiftly past me. I bend quickly to pick up the soft felt hat and go after her; grateful to help with the cap, because to be honest, I feel like a spare part. Everyone has a role to play, performing what is expected of them, whilst I, on the other hand, seem superfluous. I return to my seat where the semi-circle is now void of all persons.

'Jane.' I hear Charles call my name. 'Could you come in the chamber please to help with sorting my clothes.'

Finally, a reason for my being here. Though

completely absurd to request my advice on fashion. I make my way to a smaller room, adjacent to the Privy Chamber, where I find Charles undergoing a transformation with the royal barber, who is busy cutting his hair in a short, close cropped style, whilst William Legge, positions the felt hat to disguise My Majesty as an ordinary servant.

Instructing the servants to leave the room, Charles holds out his hands to me, which I take in mine.

'Jane, please don't look so worried. As you can see, disguised as a servant I can quite convincingly travel as Ashburnham's Gentleman, being quite content in the company of my dear clergy, Dr Hudson.'

'I have to admit sir, I am a little concerned for your decision to leave has come about quite suddenly. Your journey to meet the Scottish Army in Southwark is such a lengthy task.'

'I appreciate your concern.'

'May I ask sir?'

'Yes, Jane. Please go ahead.'

'Thank you. Are you going to the Scottish Army because you want to go home? Do you feel safer in Scotland, your place of birth?'

'That is interesting what you say, for I shall be safer in their care. However, the reason must be that the army are wanting my blood. You will have seen their hate when you passed them this evening.'

'Yes I did. Their rage has become so brutal with such force in such a short time.'

Still holding my hand, looking unlike Charles with his tightly cropped hair beneath that awful mounteere upon his head, he says, 'I want you to do something for me Jane.'

'Yes, of course sir, anything.'

He bends down to lift to his lap, a small wooden cabinet, closed with three seals; a crest of arms either side of a silver antique Roman figure.

'I want you take this chest Jane. Keep it safely hidden from everyone. I shall ask for its return when I believe the time is right.'

My eyes fixate on his thin fingers as they move across the cabinet and slowly lift the lid to reveal hidden treasure that lie beneath.

'Oh my word sir.'

The contents glitter and glisten against the candle light bouncing off the looking glass. I kneel down beside him to gain a closer look, wanting to touch the delicate pieces that lay within.

I look up to Charles, 'may I?' pointing to the contents.

'Yes. Please go ahead Jane, you should know what I am asking of you.'

'Thank you sir.'

Carefully lifting the first piece out of the cabinet, I hold the most exquisite diamond and sapphire encrusted Saint George, hanging from a Garter; an insignia for the Order of the Garter. The precious piece appears to be in need of repair, but this takes nothing from its beauty as it entwines my fingers delicately; twisting, turning, sparkling. Oh, how it sparkles. I choose another piece, where my eyes are set, then diamond earrings and rings. In this small cabinet there must be, four or five heavy handfuls of jewels.

'I shall look after them for you Charles. You can rely on me.'

He smiles, looking straight into my eyes. 'I know you will Jane,' he says, closing the lid, resting the wooden box momentarily on his lap, before handing me what remains of his wealth.

'In return for your loyalty Jane, when the cabinet is returned to me, I shall give you this ring,' pointing to the enormous emerald and diamond encrusted gold band worn on his smallest finger. I don't know how to reply to such a grand gesture, so I smile, remaining speechless, tucking the jewellery cabinet under my arm beneath my cloak.

Our silence is broken as the college clock strikes midnight, reminding us how late into the night we are progressing.

'You need to take your leave Jane. Mr Murray will

drive you to Holton. Please, return to your children and husband.'

I take Charles' hand and squeeze it reassuringly, aware of the dangers that lie ahead. Holding back the tears that are welling up inside me, I walk towards the chamber door, looking back one more time.

'Keep safe sir. Please keep safe.'

He raises his hand, nods his head beneath the felt, hat, smiling lovingly.

Outside, in the college grounds, the courtyard is deserted of students. Murray leads me to the waiting carriage where I take my seat, moving the box on to my lap, keeping it hidden under my cloak, completely out of sight. In the darkness, we make our way back towards Holton, having once more successfully ploughed our way through the waiting army. Clutching firmly the jewellery chest, taking this time to process details, I suddenly remember the letter stowed away in my sleeve and fumble around my dress until I find the small, hard parchment. I pat as a reminder to read when I am home.

Events of this evening have unnerved me. Measures being taken, by all divers, to satisfy their desired outcome in this conflict, are becoming ever more dangerous and ever more extreme. With the surge of secrets and unable to share their burden with those who love me, I feel isolated.

Michelle Hockley

Weighed down by duplicity, aware that I am sinking deeper and deeper into a labyrinth of deceit and doing nothing to set myself free from its clutches. I wonder, to what depths of deception am I prepared to plummet?

CHAPTER NINETEEN

Unexpected Guests
May 1646

O n waking later than usual after last night's meeting at the royal court, I lie in bed with thoughts drifting in and out; wafting, floating as I imagine the courtiers' shock on learning their king has absconded. Then, as if that thought is swiped sideways by a runaway carriage, the next thought comes charging towards me to replace it. Crown Jewels.

I sit bolt-up-right, then swoop down to look under the bed where I remember pushing the chest last night. As I recover myself, feeling stricken with the responsibility that proceeds me, I hear mumblings, then loud voices booming up from downstairs. Brome is shouting at the staff. Doors are banging, which I immediately interpret as his anger at my leaving last night, defying the restriction he previously placed upon me. I quickly go   to the children's room. Finding they are playing happily together, not wanting to disturb them, I close their chamber without saying a word and creep away.

Downstairs, Mary Hurles scurries through the corridor away from the kitchen where the servants are all huddled in confabulation. Brome and Lady Ursula are in the first drawing room where Brome leans against the hearth with his head in his hand, clasping a letter.

'Good morning Brome, Lady Ursula,' I say meekly, standing on the threshold, surveying the situation before I fully enter. 'Is something troubling you, my dear husband?'

'Yes. Something is troubling me considerably,' replies Brome curtly.

Lady Ursula seated in the salon chair, turns to me with an expression of shock, her eyes wide.

'I can explain,' I say, ready to conjure a yarn as to why I left the house last night.

'I doubt even you can explain this,' says Brome, throwing the letter in my direction, landing on the floor before me.

I don't comment on his rudeness. Quite honestly, I'm taken by surprise that my interpretation of the commotion is something quite different to what I'd anticipated. Instead, I quickly grasp that we have received a letter from Oliver

Cromwell. Without reading the letter in its entirety, conscious that Brome is wanting a response, it soon becomes apparent that Holton House is under sequestration. Whilst we are permitted to live in the house, it will become the headquarters for the Parliamentary Army during the siege of Oxford. Thomas Fairfax, along with his wife, Anne, who is sickened with a bout of Malaria, will reside here in five days time.

I stop reading to look at Brome, willing for him to take the lead. He returns to the hearth, covering his face in his hands. If Brome knew what I was hiding beneath our bed, he would need more than his hands to cover his face. A jewel case, from an escaped king, under the roof of the Parliamentary Army is unthinkable. Your timing Cromwell, is terrible.

Putting the jewels to one side for a moment I turn to Lady Ursula to ask how she feels about the situation. Brome replies abruptly before Ursula has a chance to speak.

'It is quite obvious Jane, my mother doesn't wish these Parliamentarians to come anywhere near us, let alone live in the same house.'

'May I take a seat beside you, Lady Ursula?' She nods, providing me the necessary permission where I hope to find a middle ground, because one thing is certain, we do not have the option to deny Cromwell's request without being severely punished.

'Lady Whorwood,' I begin, 'could we perhaps consider Anne Fairfax, who needs our help in her recovery?'

'What about the wedding?' shouts Brome sharply.

'What wedding?' I ask with utter confusion, wondering what on earth he is talking about.

'You've read the letter as I have. Cromwell is requesting that the wedding of his daughter Bridget to Henry Ireton, takes place here at Holton House on the 15 June.'

I choke a little. I hadn't read that far. I'm speechless. The civil war is making us all lose our senses. No one is thinking clearly anymore. How can such an idea be conceived. A Royalist home, entertaining a parliamentary family, during their Puritan matrimonial ceremony, whilst the army takes residence to boot, is ludicrous. The situation is quite preposterous. With no sway to consider our feelings, at Cromwell's request, we are expected to open our doors to something that our principles tell us is clearly unprecedented. We are but pawns under the Parliamentary regime. The Royalists, including our king, are only able to react to the moves directed by our opposition, leaving us without the mind to fight back; leaving us without a winning strategy. This cannot go on, we are losing our grasp. This is absurd. All we can do for now, is protect our own lives and ride out the high waves we find ourselves. Any morals we had prior to the war, are everyday being chipped away. Will we ever be whole again, or be able to look at ourselves in the same way as we once did? Shall we even recognise ourselves, knowing what we know?

'Off you go Jane. Clearly you are of no use here,' says Brome, dismissing me.

I'm pleased to leave, because I have my own problems to solve. I return to our bedchamber where I finally have the opportunity to read the letter given me last night by Patrick Maul, discovering my stepfather is requesting my services for yet another mission. I read, but the words are not penetrating my mind. Far too much is already swimming in my head to allow me to focus on one issue. 'Come on Jane, concentrate,' I whisper. 'Focus. What does it say?' It says, the current Ambassador of Constantinople has committed wrongful conduct with the Levant Company and a replacement will shortly to be found. Quite honestly, what has this got to do with me or the war? I continue to read. My stepfather's choice for a replacement Ambassador, is that of a Thomas Bendish, who was recently released from the Tower for helping the Royalist cause. Although he currently awaits full liberty, being restricted to maintain a twenty mile radius of London to encompass his home in Essex, according to my stepfather, he is a worthy candidate. Knowing my stepfather as I do, what he truly means is, this gentleman, if Ambassador, would be a useful source to his own business dealings in the Levant. I proceed to digest my instructions. I am requested to sing the praises of this Bendish to His Majesty, which won't be easy because I don't know a Bendish. Fortunately, I'm provided with his credentials to which I am encouraged to repeat. A price tag of three thousand pounds, I might have guessed money would be involved, is requested by the King's coffers in order to secure whoever takes the role. My mind quickens to devise a plan to acquire some of the funds needed, until I pull myself up short, agreeing with my conscience, that this will have to wait.

  I fold the parchment carefully but quickly, whilst all the time listening for footsteps on the stairs outside the bedchamber, looking for a place to hide the note. I don't want Brome, and certainly not Fairfax, to know that my stepfather may be eschewing the choice of Ambassador for Constantinople. It is a private letter and the contents will remain that way. I look about my person for somewhere to hide the note but choose instead, the large wooden linen chest under the window. I heave up the heavy pile of fresh laundry inside the trunk, placing the letter between the sheets. As I hold the lid up with one hand, I catch sight of myself in the mirror. What am I doing? I am supposed to be a mother and a wife. What is this war doing to us all? I pause a moment leaning the full weight of my head on my arm that holds the hefty lid, before closing it tight. Pulling myself off my knees to sit on top of the chest, I hold around my waist and rock forward and back to ease the knot that grips fast inside my gut. I contemplate the tension which is mounting in my shoulders as my body hunches heavy with the demands set upon me. Do I have the physical and mental strength to carry out these orders? My emotions are confused. On the one hand, the demands upon me weigh ridiculously heavy, yet at the same time, I am invigorated when these great men empower me with responsibility.

But the lies. Everyday I cast a web of concealment to avoid becoming muddled by the plans and secrets I hold inside me. Not wanting to disappoint those who trust me; believe in me; expecting me to do right by them. I'm starting to panic. Take a deep breath. Come on Jane. Breathe. Think logically and rationally. Take one step at a time. Carry out each task efficiently and carefully so as not to feel confounded by the number of issues already on the table. I release the clench from around my stomach and force my shoulders to release the tension they crunch and seize.

Today, I shall be mother and wife and tomorrow, deal with other issues in my care; for I have the Parliamentary Army arriving in five days time, and the wealth of the

Michelle Hockley

kingdom beneath my bed.

CHAPTER TWENTY

A Place to Hide

Early morning hours are disappearing as I lie alone in bed, staring at the ceiling, willing Brome to either come to bed and sleep, or pass out from his drunken state. Eyes stark. Body rigid. Still. I listen to the frequent, all too familiar sounds coming from the sitting room in our apartment, here in Holton House. The same routine, night after night, played out with either a stumble towards the decanter, already in a stupor, or the clatter or shatter of glass. But always a final thud before sleep from wherever he lands. I jolt on hearing the thud tonight, but it's a welcomed sound. I wait a few moments more to be certain he has passed out. Good. I hear no more. Now to hide these tormented jewels.

Releasing the covers from my tightened grip, conscious of every move I am making, leave the bed. A slit in the curtain gives me a slither of light from the moon.

Reaching under the bed I drag the smooth mahogany jewel case towards me until I can once again hold it in my grasp. As a precaution, in case Brome should return to the bed this night, I place a pillow beneath the covers as a substitute for my small frame.

The key in the main front door is heavy to turn but gives up the fight with a sharp snag. Sitting in the vestibule, pulling on my riding boots beneath my nightdress, I feel alone. Unlike Charles, who I now know is in Newcastle, in the hands of the Scottish Army, surrounded by his familiar servants including my stepfather. The faithful moon is my guide tonight, leading me away from the house towards St Bartholomew's church. The owls hoot as a reminder that I am not quite alone. At any stage someone could be watching me. I shiver at the thought. My breath is amplified as it resounds off the collar of my cloak. The heavy clomp of my riding boots echo as they hit the cobbled road. Everything sounds so loud. I take to my toes; not putting down my heels, moving faster, building momentum as if to begin a minuet with a lightness about my feet. Clinging all the time to the jewel case, keeping it close to my chest beneath the cloak.

Approaching the church door, I look back from where I've come. Something rustles in the shrubbery beside me between the grave stones, stopping me in my tracks. I've disturbed a fox, scavenging at night. I'm not sure which of us is more startled. The fox scampers away, but not before showing me its white, sharp teeth, as they shine in the star filled heavens. The church door is heavy. I push it strong to make my entrance. Thankfully, some of the light from the night sky finds its way through the stained glass window, creating a shaft down the short aisle. I stop to bow my head to acknowledge the altar, crossing myself; the Father, the Son and the Holy Spirit, before proceeding down the South transept to enter Brome Chapel.

I arrive first at the small tomb of my baby Elizabeth. A strong pang hits me knowing my little girl, who died at four years old, must witness in her resting place, my utter deceit. Her soul is in heaven, but her weak body still here on earth will surely sense what her mother has become. My mind turns to the two children sleeping, completely oblivious of the secrets their Mama is holding. I stroke Elizabeth's tomb as I kneel beside her, kissing my fingers to place my love silently upon the engraved name plate.

Getting to work, to unfold my plan, I turn towards Sir Thomas Whorwood's large raised tomb and feel for the heavy rope I placed behind, earlier in the day. Managing to catch the end of the coil I pull the length towards me. I need to hurry now. I can see first light. The birds are begging to wake. Standing on the dais, beside my father-in-law's tomb,

I'm able to reach the lid more easily. I pull with both arms to move the bevelled stone cover to provide me a small gap where I can tie the rope. It is much heavier than I imagined. My design hasn't taken into account the sheer weight. The plan has also failed to consider that God may disapprove of my disturbing those who've been laid to rest. I know my actions are illegal, but I shall plough forth regardless.

I am able to swing the rope over the lips of the tomb lid, gaining grip of the weight, I pull with all my might. It edges slowly towards me until I see a gap appearing at the head of Sir Thomas' tomb that will provide me enough room to squeeze the jewellery cabinet beneath the embalmed body. I gasp at the aromas I've released and hold my nose, cover my mouth, squint my eyes as they smart. I start to question my actions again. How could I ever have imagined moving a resting body in the good Lord's House? What was I thinking? I can't do this. I can't see what Sir Thomas has become. No. This plan won't work. I have opened the tomb, let out the stench, but there is no way on this earth I can look Sir Thomas in the face and lift his head to place the jewels beneath. I sit with my back against the tomb leaning on a stone finial on the edge of the dais, defeated. This is too much for me. I am finished. I'm ready to surrender to take my punishment.

In my mind I see again, the smile of Sir Thomas that

haunts me. Did he read deep into my soul and see the devious nature that lay beneath a facade of innocence? I can't do this. No. I shall close the tomb. I need to rethink my scheme.

I re-tie the rope to the other end of his vault and drag the lid towards me, closing it over Sir Thomas' head, making sure not to look inside, allowing him some dignity. As I pull to close, the lid moves more easily, so much so, that it over shoots the head to reveal a gap at his feet. That's it. I can do feet. 'I can't mess with your head Sir Thomas, but I can deal with your feet.' I jump down from the dais with renewed energy. Pick up the jewel case from the floor moving swiftly to the other end of the tomb. Without hesitation, for I am losing time, I aim to place the jewels beneath his feet. Taking one glimpse inside, I realise I see only his shroud. I can do this. The ease at which the lid moved when I pulled the other way, is a sign. I wipe the sweat from my brow and push the curls back with the crook of my arm. Come on Jane, get on with it. I lean my arm inside the tomb to fumble for the sheet. Clutching the cabinet in my other arm, I lower the jewels inside, covering with folds of fabric. Thank you Sir Thomas. You've owed me since the day I forewent my liberty to free you from imprisonment; from your sentence.

Taking a hold across the width of the lid, this time without the rope, I pull with all my power until it begins to slide towards me. I keep pulling until it finally slots back into place. With utter exhaustion and relief, my arms still outstretched across the shrine, I take a moment to rest my head. The cold stone against my flushed face is satisfying. I breathe lightly and calmly as the weight of responsibility floats away; overwhelmed by the comfort this brings.

Footsteps on the gravel outside, breaks the passive silence and my heartbeat quickens once more; really racing this time. I gather up the rope to hide beneath my cloak, contemplating my exit from the chapel. But no time. The door of St Bartholomew's swings open, banging against a pew. The almighty force thunders across the nave, echoing throughout the church. I hear heavy, slow, purposeful footsteps making their way across the transept nearing Brome Chapel. Quick thinking, I throw myself down over Elizabeth's tomb where I start to pray. 'So help me God.'

Conscious of every footstep drawing closer, my body quivers. I hear the scuff of a boot as the steps halt behind me. I keep praying. I don't move; still kneeling over Elizabeth.

'What in God's name are you doing here in the middle of the night?' asks Brome.

I stay hunched over, still tightly clutching the rope beneath my cloak, letting out a heavy sigh at the realisation that it's Brome and not Fairfax or one of his brutal men. I turn slowly towards my husband.

'Oh Brome. Thank you for coming to find me. I was lost this night when my thoughts turned to our baby Elizabeth,' I explain as tears of relief roll down my exhausted face, hardly recognising myself as the lies pour so easily from me.

Brome kneels down holding me in his arms. I can feel his hand discovering the rope held beneath my cloak.

'Jane. What is this my dear?' He lifts my cloak to take a closer look, as my arm tries to hide the criminal aid.

'Were you planning to hang yourself in God's house? Were you? You cannot be that upset. What about your beautiful children, what about me? I have never seen you like this, in such despair.'

I'm so taken aback. Not only that Brome could suggest I'd perform such an unforgivable act, but that he does in fact still care about me. I rarely encounter these sentiments since his return from exile because his companion is the bottle and they both continually shut me out. Our openness for each other since this war, erodes so fast.

'Brome, you have this all wrong. I found the rope on the pew. I was going to return it to the stables and then despair came over me again. I couldn't leave the church. I couldn't leave our Elizabeth.'

He looks directly into my eyes as he strokes my dainty neck, maybe contemplating our past. Warm and safe, wrapped in Brome's arms, I see an opportunity to unravel, upon the world, yet another lie; my quest to secure funds for my stepfather, to aid this person, Thomas Bendish, as Ambassador. I feel a slight tinge of guilt at my guile, but where needs must, must be ceased upon. Unprepared, so perhaps somewhat unconvincingly, I speak of my desire to spoil our children, pleading with him to supply me with funds so I can buy them treats during these times of austerity.

'They have your love which costs nothing. You can offer love in abundance if you were to spend more time in Holton, and less time at the royal court.'

'But Brome, life at court is part of who I am, dearest. It is all I've known, all my life. You understand that, don't you?'

'When we lived at Sandwell Hall, you didn't feel the need, quite so often, for the royal court. We were a family. Now we reside closer to the court, you seem drawn to the glamour it offers you.'

If only Brome knew that my time spent at court is far from glamorous. Transporting gold in the most despicable manner, watching the king dress to take flight from his realm and my journey to and from the court, fraught with danger. If Brome thinks time at court is spent watching a masque, then he is very much mistaken.

'If it will make you happy Jane, I shall find the money so you can shower our children with gifts as well as your love.'

We both come up off our knees to sit on the dais of my father-in-law's tomb and I drop the rope beside me. As Brome holds me, my conscience pricks for having used our children to enable my lies and disturbed his father from resting in peace. One day, when this war has been won, I hope we can tell our stories to each other. I can explain that I loved both him and our king and Brome can tell me what happened when he was in Holland for three years. He gently pulls me closer where I rest against his strong body. I can sense his smile of contentment, acknowledging the love I think he still has for me. Nestled against each other, with the dawn light shining, the quietness we feel floats to find its place. Maybe already this is a turning point for us, back to the days of Sandwell Hall, without the strains of our unparalleled lives.

Though the distant rumbles, promoting the sound of hooves on the road outside, confirms the arrival of the army delivering their inhabitants. Without a word, Brome takes my hand and together we walk out of the church to embrace still further changes upon our lives.

209

CHAPTER TWENTY ONE

Caught Inside a Web of Crime
1647

'Your carriage awaits you Marm,' informs Mary Allen, standing in the hallway of Holton House. I make myself comfortable for the journey ahead, taking a seat by the window as the carriage begins to pull away.

Mary Allen, who is known to us as Katherine, is a recent member to Lady Ursula Whorwood's household. She joined the staff last year when we needed additional help for the wedding of Bridget and Henry Ireton during the army's six week stay. Although pleasant enough and efficient in her work, she remains an outsider, choosing to keep herself aloof from the other servants. No one seems to know anything about her other than her father, prior to his death in 1642, was a baker in Oxford High Street and Ursula suggested she come to join the household, to ease the Allen family's financial burden.

I wish someone would help Our Majesty's burden and remove his strain. All he needs is an honest hand to guide him out of a situation that becomes ever more harrowing as the days and years roll on. The escape from Oxford proved futile. The Scots handed him over to Parliament in February 1647, who in turn, made Charles a prisoner at Holdenby House in Northamptonshire. According to my stepfather, Charles is awfully withdrawn these days after Parliament expelled his servants: John Ashburnham, William Legge and Mr Murray from the royal household, after being discovered trying to help Charles escape on a Dutch ship to France. This leaves my stepfather and Patrick Maul, as his original faithful Grooms of the Bedchamber, working alongside a newly established household installed by the Parliamentary Commission, consisting of a James Harrington, Thomas Herbert and Henry Firebrace. None of us know who to trust anymore. Henry Firebrace is himself a conundrum. Whilst secretary to Basil Fielding, the Earl of Denbigh, a devoted Parliamentarian, Firebrace managed to deceive both the Parliamentary Commissioners and his master by switching allegiance to align himself with the Royalist cause, acting as a double agent in support of the king.

Before Spring Came Summer

I too recently travelled to Northamptonshire, intending to offer my support to Charles but instead, to ensure my safety, was forced to reside twenty miles south of Holdenby in the village of Passenham, with Sir Robert Bannister and his wife, Lady Margaret. However, I have gotten myself another mission, which my stepfather secured after singing my praises to Lady Bannister.

My task is to submit payment, owed by Sir Robert Bannister, to the Committee for the Advance of Money; the body set up by Parliament, to collect twenty percent of each citizen's annual wealth to aid the war effort. The problem arises in that, the sum owed by Sir Robert is three thousand pounds but Lady Bannister believes the sum should be no more than one thousand pounds because duties of public faith, carried out by Sir Robert, have so far gone unrewarded. The task has become more difficult still, after my stepfather, perhaps having had one too many ports, suggested that his Jane could negotiate an even lower sum of say, six hundred pounds. It was quickly agreed, that if I can achieve the challenge set, the Bannisters will pay me forty pounds in expenses.

I, on the other hand, have a different idea, in part spurred on by the anger I am feeling after hearing that on the 15 June, Cornet George Joyce, kidnapped Our Majesty from Holdenby House, and is currently travelling him cross-

213

country to Hampton Court Palace, to reside as prisoner of the army. Our sovereign is being humiliated at every turn and everyday denied the opportunity to carry out his duties as our Lord God intended. I am more determined than ever to cease upon an opportunity that may help My Majesty out of this plight.

My carriage approaches the corner of Staining Lane, adjacent to Maiden Lane, in the East of London, pulling up at Haberdashers' Hall, where the Committee for the Advance of Money now occupy, and to whom I shall deliver the Bannister's request. I have chosen today for good reason, having word that the clerk, Martin Dallison, who is frighteningly fastidious in the work he carries out for Parliament, is absent. In his stead will be the Chairman, Lord Edward Howard of Escrick, who is rather more fitting for my purpose.

On arriving at the hall, I am directed to a seat in the long corridor, where the walls are clad with wainscot, making it terribly dark. A strong tobacco smell and dust lingers about the place, making for an atmosphere of austerity and masculinity as the clerks go about their business, dressed in long dark cloaks.

'You can go into the office now Madam,' instructs an approaching clerk.

At the far side of the room, near the window, sits a

scribe who keeps his head down busy making notes, as I enter. On the near wall, is a large wooden desk piled high with ledgers almost concealing Lord Howard as he sits surrounded in documents.

'Madam Whorwood. What can we do for you?' asks Howard.

'Lord Howard. I am sent by Sir Robert Bannister of Passenham, with monies owed from his estate.'

'Have you Madam,' he says with his head reverting back to his ledgers then across the room. 'Clerk McDonald, pass me the file for Sir Robert Bannister and the Bailiff's ledger for Northamptonshire,' he demands.

I continue to stand until Lord Howard points to the chair opposite his desk as he begins to digests the details of Bannister's outstanding payments. I am grateful for the seat, from where I shall conduct my business more easily, rather than standing over the desk. I wait for Howard to take the lead.

'I am seeing here Madam, that Sir Bannister owes three thousand pounds. Do you have that sum with you?'

I shuffle my chair closer to the desk leaning my arms on the table, bringing myself nearer to Lord Howard's ear, offering my plea out of earshot of the clerk by the window. I speak, but in a quiet, pronounced voice.

'Lord Howard, it is my understanding that public

215

faith has been carried out by Sir Robert without receiving payment, leaving a sum owed, much smaller than you are suggesting. He has helped tirelessly to collect Ship Money in his area bringing huge funds into the system. As you will agree, this is not an easy task with so many people opposed to taxation. Therefore, that which is owed, is much less than the three thousand pounds you request.'

'Do you have evidence of this public faith to which you speak?'

I take from my purse the neatly folded paper, listing these duties, and pass across the desk to Lord Howard. The office is quiet whilst he reads. I transfix my eyes to the crown of his head as I await his verdict.

'Very well,' he says, 'I agree. Considerable unpaid work has been carried out by Sir Robert. On this occasion, I shall reduce the sum owed to, one thousand pounds.'

'One thousand pounds,' I reply in alarm. 'What about the riots that Sir Bannister regularly breaks up and the manpower he provides to bring order to his manor during a garrison?'

'I am offering an excellent discount Madam and you would be advised to accept it before I change my mind on account of your boldness.'

'Lord Howard,' I start to clutch at straws, 'what about the monies already paid by the Bannisters?'

'Do you have Sir Robert's accounts to show the previous payments?' asks Howard.

I realise I am starting to lose a grip of the situation and need to up my game if I'm to win this round of negotiations. Inside my head I am more confident. Come on Jane. Think Jane.

'I don't have any previous accounts with me sir, but I have valuable information that I would be happy to impart if you were to ask the clerk to leave the room,' I whisper, speaking closer to Lord Howard, beneath his chin.

'I don't know what you mean, Madam.'

'Oh, I think you will. Let the clerk go sir.'

If nothing else, Howard is intrigued, obliging my request for privacy.

'Mr McDonald,' Howard commands, 'can you go to the basement, into the archives, to find details of payment for Passenham, 1642.'

'Yes, sir. Passenham, sir, 1642,' replies the clerk, eager to please his master, mumbling his instructions as he scurries out of the office, closing the door behind him.

'Is he likely to return very quickly with the documentation you have requested of him?' I enquire, wanting to assess how long I have on my own with Howard.

'No Madam. He will be gone for days. All the documents have been moved up to this floor and he won't dare return empty handed. Now, what's this information you have Madam?'

'Lord Howard. With the information I have, I was thinking you might waive the outstanding amount; wipe the slate clean so to speak. Would you agree on that?'

'No Madam, absolutely not. I am tasked with collecting these sums of money for Parliament which is what we are here to do. Whatever gives you the idea I could be bribed in this way?'

'I've heard you wipe the slate clean with your tradesmen.'

'That is an outrageous allegation, Madam,' Howard replies, pinning himself back into his seat.

'Is it? I would agree it's an outrageous way to do business, but not an outrageous allegation. I know that the tailor presents you with your outstanding account and you suggest calling it quits after showing him an extortionate, fictitious, amount he owes the committee. He believes you are doing him a favour but it's quite the reverse. Unbeknown to him, it is he who is doing you a favour. Are you ready to start negotiations now?'

I can hear myself sounding awfully scheming but I'm not ashamed, after all, I am only denying Parliament, for whom I do not care. I sit back from the desk, squeezing the little bag on my lap, wanting desperately not to give the six hundred pounds to this committee. I watch Howard process the information, aware that I am starting to get Howard where I want him.

'Madam, I shall settle this bill for five hundred pounds. How does that sound?'

'It sounds better, but it's not good enough Lord Howard.'

If I stick at five hundred pounds, I shall have made one hundred for the king, plus my expenses which is good, but I want more, so begin to pile on the pressure.

'I also know, Lord Howard...' As I begin to speak the office door opens so I stop. Damn, I have lost my chance. I don't turn around but assume it's McDonald.

'Not now Mr Crisp, can't you see I'm in a meeting?' shouts Howard.

I hear Crisp, whoever he is, retreat, shutting the door as quickly as lightening. All the time, keeping my eyes firmly fixed on Howard, I continue.

'...the silk merchant. What about him?'

Lord Howard stops me right there, without a chance to go on.

'Okay, Madam. I've heard enough thank you. It's frightening how like your father you are. My goodness you are.'

'No sir, I think you mean my stepfather. Yes, it has

been said before that I appear to be much like him.'

'I shall offer the amount to be paid of one hundred pounds. I can't go any lower.'

'The silk merchant, Lord Howard...' I remind him.

'Yes, yes, yes. You are a hard business woman, Madam. I can see that your husband, Brome Whorwood, has his hands full with you. Though what drives you Madam, is a mystery to me.'

'Thank you Lord Howard. That wasn't too difficult was it, sir? Please arrange for Sir Bannister's discharge papers to be certified today, I don't intend making this journey again. Oh, and your secret about the tailor and the silk merchant is safe with me, that won't go any further, I promise.'

'I can't sign the papers, Madam Whorwood, you know that, they must be signed by Mr Dallison. You will have to wait until he returns, bearing in mind, he is much less lenient than me and will ask many more questions,' says Howard, with a grin, stretching right across his face.

'Lord Howard, you're the chairman, that position must count for something,' determined not to have Dallison involved. 'Now, we wouldn't want him hearing about the tailor or the silk merchant, would we? So why don't you forget that rule and sign the papers, sir.'

Mr Howard looks beaten. Sighs. Squints his eyes,

tightens his lips hard, before calling for his clerk.

'Mr McDonald. Mr McDonald,' shouts Howard calling him back from the basement.

McDonald comes running into the room, out of breath with a worried look on his face, clumsily explaining, that he can't find any corresponding documentation in the archive.

'No boy. Come along. Please scribe the discharge papers for Madam, so she can leave our offices as quickly as possible. Madam Whorwood has paid in full. I shall sign the papers in the absence of Mr Dallison.'

'Yes sir. Right away sir,' replies McDonald.

I stand up slowly, feeling empowered, offering my hand to Lord Howard, but he doesn't take it. Instead he flaps his hand to indicate for me to move aside, away from his desk. He makes no eye contact, keeping his head down, returning to his mountain of paperwork, muttering under his breath, 'Maxwell, Maxwell, James damn Maxwell.'

As soon as the papers are signed and handed to me, I leave the office without saying a word, for I don't know what to say, nothing I was thinking seemed appropriate.

The footman approaches me at the main door of Haberdashers' Hall, to enquire if I need a carriage. With Charles now a prisoner, the fighting has ended in London making it easier to travel without the previous suspicion.

'May I ask where you wish to travel Madam?' asks the footman as he stands in the street, holding out his arm to an approaching Hackney carriage.

'Charing Cross. Anywhere in Charing Cross, thank you,' I lie, having no intention of giving any member of the Committee for the Advance of Money, the opportunity to follow me. I need to put them off the scent of my next appointment.

Once we roll away from Staining Lane to head west, I bang on the roof of the carriage. The driver stops and leans into the window.

'Is everything alright Marm?'

'Driver. I've changed my mind. Can you drive me to Ironmonger Lane please.'

'But Madam, that was walking distance from where I collected this fare.'

I ignore the driver's off hand comments, for he is quite right, but there is reason for my madness. I am instead, making my way to Alderman Thomas Adams, a woollen draper, who two years ago, was the Lord Mayor of the City of London, so a respected man. I have met him only briefly before, he is a staunch Royalist, known to my stepfather and the Bannister's. Lady Margaret has instructed Adams to reimburse me the six hundred pounds on receipt of the signed discharge documents for the Committee.

'Ironmonger Lane, Marm,' shouts the driver as he pulls up the horse to stop the carriage.

Ironmonger Lane is narrow, not wide enough for two way traffic being also busy with merchants as they cut through to Cheapside, a main thoroughfare to merchant's houses, markets and warehouses.

'Can you wait here, sir?' I ask, not wanting to hail my own carriage or hire one at the nearby stand.

'As long as you don't change your mind again.'

Pushing through the crowded narrow street I find the Alderman's house and bang heavily on the front door, hoping to be heard over the noise of the traders. The door soon opens. I move straight up to the first step to begin my business.

'Alderman, sir. I understand from Lady Margaret Bannister, she has written to inform you of my coming to your house and the nature of my business. I am Madam Whorwood.'

'Yes, I remember you Madam, please come inside.'

As he steps away from the door, I enter the house to stand in the dark hallway, as Adams continues his conversation.

'I have received word from Lady Bannister, though I wasn't expecting you so soon. I thought it would take time to oversee the public duties that Sir Robert carried out, before a decision could be made on the monies owed.'

I ignore what he has to say, because I don't enjoy being dishonest to the face of such a kind, gentleman. Instead, I hand him the documents so I can collect my money, leave this part of London and lay low for a while.

'Oh,' remarks Adams as he reads the document.

'Is something the matter, Alderman?'

'I see the discharge papers are signed by Lord Howard of Escrick. Did you not see Martin Dallison? I understand it's Dallison who signs the papers.'

'Dallison seems to be away from the office today, so the Chairman saw me. Is that alright, sir?'

'Yes. I don't see why not. If Dallison is absent, then I suppose Lord Howard is taking his place,' Adams says, completely unaware that I chose this day specifically, because I knew Dallison was absent.

'I am expecting reimbursement of payment today, sir,' trying to hurry him along with the funds.

'Oh yes Madam. I have a bill here for six hundred pounds. Is that correct or did you pay more than that?'

'No sir. Six hundred pounds is correct, as we agreed, thank you. I didn't pay more,' well, I didn't pay anything, but he must never know that.

Adams leaves the hall to fetch a promissory bill for the full amount, and I'm thankful that my task is complete.

'Madam would you like to take a small beer with me?'

'No thank you. I have an appointment which I am already late in attendance,' I say, falsely. Intending to sound polite, but wanting so badly to leave this part of town. I start to edge my way to open the front door.

'You take care then Madam. You are clearly a clever negotiator. One day you must tell me how you were able get those papers signed off in such a short time.'

From what Adams is saying, he doesn't believe for one moment that I received these papers by playing by the rules, which is slightly worrying. If he knew how much I did in fact pay or didn't pay, what would he say then? As I unlatch the front door, Adams continues to engage.

'I know you do so much to help the king,' he says, 'but you must be careful Madam Whorwood.'

'I am careful sir. You know yourself that it's important to help the Royalist cause now that the king is a prisoner of the army, making his way to Hampton Court Palace. It's even more important that we try to put an end to this horrid situation.'

'Yes, but at what cost? At what cost, I ask?' he says with a little panicked note in his voice. 'Tomorrow I take the stand at the House of Commons, reprimanded for the attack I made on Parliament last year. It is possible I shall be sentenced to High Treason and sent to the Tower.'

'Oh. I am sorry to hear that sir, but if we didn't help the king, how would we feel then?' I reply, as I take my leave, not wanting to hang around to console him.

Seated back in the carriage, I try to settle myself, but feel quite anxious after scamming the Alderman and being firmly entrenched in following a treacherous, dangerous path. I shall stay one night at Cannon Row, the newly acquired London residence of my parents, before returning to the country, where I intend to keep myself out of harms way for a while, which by all accounts, shouldn't be too difficult, being surrounded only by fields.

Driving through London, gazing out at the people going about their mundane business and daily routines, my concerns and fears start to subside. I clutch my little purse between my hands unable to hold back a smile as I ponder on having secured six hundred and forty pounds for my king.

CHAPTER TWENTY TWO

11 November 1647

Sitting close to Charles in the Barge House at Hampton Court Palace, looking out over the river before us, there is no need for conversation. Consumed in our own thoughts, or maybe the same thoughts, we seem at peace again on this crisp early morning with the mist lifting effortlessly from the banks beyond. A bevy of swans swim softly down stream without disturbing the moment. Come summer, during Swan Upping, it will be their turn to be disrupted although for their own protection, because we care. Who will protect us? Who has our best interests at heart? How can we ever feel safe when authority has been taken from our king, replaced by quasi leaders who fight amongst themselves for power; not for one moment considering our Lord God or the divine right of kings. What will our uncertain future bring? More fighting? More Tragedy? More heart ache?

Charles appears rested and certainly not defeated, as he resides under the watchful eye of the army, being afforded a degree of respect from his gaoler, the military leader, Colonel Whalley, whom I am familiar after his stay at Holton House. Charles is permitted visitors, some of which I think he looks forward to seeing, especially his children who are residing at nearby Syon House. Once again, familiar servants are about him, which must provide some relief to this plight we find ourselves. Can I dare to think that the end of our fight is in sight? That an agreement could be made to restore Charles to his seat of power? My contemplation is suddenly jolted back to life, when Charles starts to utter.

'Jane,' he says softly, maintaining his gaze upon the calm waters. 'I need you to do something for me.'

'Anything sir. You know that.'

'I am going to make an escape from here Jane. I must leave, it's becoming too dangerous for me to stay.'

'Are you quite sure of that sir?' somewhat taken aback.

'Indeed I am. I have it on good authority, that the Levellers, at their meeting last night in Putney, made their intentions clear, to make an attempt on my life.'

The Levellers, who are known agitators within the army, are most definitely stirring hatred for the king and with Charles being a prisoner of the army, it is understandable that he will feel unprotected, even though he trusts his gaoler, Colonel Whalley.

228

Before Spring Came Summer

My Majesty talks of danger, but I know he is not fearful of losing his own life. His concern will be in failing to protect kingship bestowed on him direct from God. It is this that he everyday defends, entrusted to him, by a divine power.

'Don't worry Jane,' says Charles, continuing to stare directly at the river as he relays his intentions. 'I have spoken with John Ashburnham and William Legge who both agree to help me to safety. John Berkeley, who Henrietta Maria has recommended as a trusted companion, has also agreed to help.'

'Where will you go? I ask.

'That is what I want you to find out for me Jane. I need you to visit the astrologer, William Lilly on The Strand, and request him to figure, via the astrological chart, which is the safest direction for me to flee? Bring the information back to me and I shall pass to Ashburnham, who will make the necessary arrangements.'

'Yes, Your Majesty.'

He takes from his pocket a small leather purse. I watch as he unties the cord and hands me twenty pieces of gold as payment for Lilly's reading, which I take, furling inside my gloved hand.

'Thank you sir. It will be an honour. I shall make my journey to London immediately.'

As I pass through the Privy Garden, leaving Charles in the Barge House, I see my stepfather standing in the doorway of the Privy Lodgings, in his role as Groom of the Bedchamber. His once strong stature now shows signs of the anguish that is everyday pressed upon us all. The troubles that have continued for far too long, are felt by everyone.

'Are you leaving so soon, my darling?' he enquires.

'I am stepfather, yes to London,' showing him the gold coins, confident he will know where I have been ordered to attend.

'Have you seen Mr Murray and Patrick Maule and Colonel Legge since you've been here Jane? I am sure they would love to see you.'

'No I haven't, but I am pleased they've been allowed to return to serve Charles, it makes it a little easier doesn't it?'

'Yes. His Majesty has quite a lot of freedom here. Princess Elizabeth and Prince Henry, both came to visit from Syon House at the beginning of the week and yesterday, your favourite person, Lady Fanshawe.'

I snigger when he says Fanshawe is my favourite person, for he knows too well, that I consider her slightly over dramatic.

'Have you heard about Alderman Adams?' he asks.

'Not for a while. How was his assessment at the House of Commons?'

'Committed to the Tower with a verdict of High Treason, for acting against Parliament.'

'Oh no, that is awful. He was worried when I saw him last, warning me to be careful.'

'I know you will be careful Jane. I shall bid you farewell.'

I hurry through the palace to make headway on my errand for my king, but regain a more dignified appearance when I see Colonel Whalley walking towards me.

'Madam Whorwood. To what do we owe this pleasure?' asks Whalley

'I came to visit my stepfather.'

'You are a long way from Holton, my dear. How is Lady Ursula and your husband?'

To be honest, I have no idea how they are, having given no thought to either of them. I seem to have only a fleeting acquaintance at Holton, before I'm off on another errand. However, since I am rarely honest these days, I reply with what I am sure he wants to hear.

'They are well, sir. Thank you for asking. I shall remember you to them.'

'The wedding at Holton was a marvellous day. Did you think so?'

The wedding was pleasant enough, but I don't have time for these pleasantries. If only he knew I was rushing off to help the king escape from his grasp. Poor Whalley, I quite like him.

'Yes, the wedding was glorious, however, I should be going now Colonel, if that is alright with you?'

'Yes, off you go Madam, I don't want to keep you from your family,' clearly assuming as all good wives and mothers, I would be returning to my domestic station.

'Thank you. Good day to you sir.'

For a member of the opposition he is pretty civil. I know Charles likes him. Apparently they have an understanding, a mutual respect for each other. As long as Charles agrees to keep his parole he is free to wander the palace and its grounds. Whalley even allows Charles his own chaplain and each evening, escorts him to the Palace Chapel.

When I arrive at William Lilly's house, it's early afternoon. The Strand is bustling with people and carriages but the house is desolate. All is quiet inside. I can't get an answer at the door. I peer through the closed shutters, trying for a gap in the wood, to see what lies inside; but nothing. I bang on the door again. Then rattle the shutters calling out, for I know I have to gain entrance to speak to him. I can't return without an answer.

'Mr Lilly. Mr Lilly,' I shout, relentlessly banging on the door. A neighbour pokes her head out of the small window.

'What with all the commotion Madam?' the neighbour enquires.

'I have an appointment with Mr Lilly, Marm, but he doesn't seem to be home, do you know when he might return?'

'I'm surprised you have an appointment Madam, he is not seeing clients on account of his two maids' recent passing with the plague. He has hauled himself up inside his house, writing his books, waiting for the air to freshen.'

The neighbour is quite correct, I don't have an appointment, but on hearing he is inside, provides me with the encouragement I need. With renewed hope I start all over, rapping the warn out wooden door until at last I hear movement beyond. The latch turns with an opening of the tiniest crack.

'Mr Lilly, thank goodness you are there. I need to see you urgently.'

'No. I cannot allow you to enter on account of a recent visitation from the plague.'

At that, I push the door with force to open wide. Lilly jumps back in surprise as I step inside.

'It is not the plague that worries me sir, it's the pox.'

I am of course worried about the plague but I have to risk life and limb for my sovereign. I am however slightly worried about the pox, not small pox, I am immune to that, but the great pox, a concern I've had after Brome's three years away on the Continent. Nevertheless, Lilly accepts my determination, closes the door, shutting out the busy street.

'I shall allow you entry as you are so determined, but if you are taken with the plague, don't come running to me for compensation, for you have been amply warned.'

I could hardly do that. I'd be dead. Lilly takes me upstairs to a small room, overlooking The Strand, where every wall space is covered with astrological charts. On his desk, is a large ledger where he is indeed writing a book.

'Now, Madam....?'

'Whorwood, sir. My name is Madam Whorwood.'

'Madam Whorwood. What can I do for you that is so important you are prepared to risk your life?'

'King Charles has sent me here sir.'

'King Charles, why didn't you say?' 'Sir, I am saying. I am saying now, sir.'

'Yes, indeed. Please take a seat,' he says pointing to an old chair on the far wall. He puts on his spectacles and looks at me with intrigue.

'Now, what can I do for His Majesty?

'The king is wanting to escape from Hampton Court

Palace, where he is currently a prisoner of the army. He wants to get himself away from the Levellers who are threatening to take his life with their aggressive cruel words about our king. Please sir, can you figure in which direction he should travel?'

Lilly carefully notes down the details using his Horary astrological system, asking particulars of time and place from whence this question was first posed to me. As soon as he has all the information needed, he turns back to his desk, taking to his work; making calculations and geometric drawings.

I sit in my chair looking around the walls at the charts, allowing Lilly the time he needs to make an assessment. I peer at the spines of the shelved books, which I soon realise I couldn't possibly understand, so return to my chair. I suspect, Lilly was expecting a more menial question from me, like so many others. The likes of; should I marry? When will I fall in love? I look down at the little gold ring encrusted with sapphires and diamonds that my mother gave me on my wedding day, on the hearsay of an astrologer, purporting good fortune. Good fortune indeed. I don't think so. It makes me smile and snort, forgetting where I am.

'Are you alright Madam?' asks Lilly, distracted by my titter as my thoughts turn to my marriage of little good fortune.

'Pardon me, sir. Sorry sir,' I reply apologetically before ensuring I remain mute.

'Would you be so kind as to light the candles, Madam? It is getting awfully dim as this winter afternoon begins to draw.'

I take the tapers from the pot on the table by the window, where outside, is indeed getting dusk. I start to light the candles. Some of them are sunken deep inside their brass holders, some are worn. It is evident that the poor maids are no longer with us, for they would have added fresh candles each day; it would have been one of their duties. Poor souls.

'Almost there Madam. Almost there,' says Lilly, with his head down over his charts.

I return to my seat to await the verdict; content to look around this small compact room that holds so much knowledge and expertise all in one small space. Lilly breaks the silence once more.

'I have it Madam.'

'Thank you. I am much appreciated,' I reply, drawing my chair closer to his desk, listening with close attention.

'I shall explain my findings to you Madam Whorwood.'

'Thank you sir.'

'His Majesty is advised, by the figure, to leave Hampton Court Palace in an easterly direction and continue until twenty miles outside London. The reading is advising a flight to Essex.'

'Essex,' I repeat.

I shall suggest the home of Thomas Bendish. With the Bendish family now in Constantinople, having achieved the role of Ambassador, the house will be unoccupied. Ashburnham and Berkeley can break into the property. Charles will be close to London, ready to return to his place of power.

'Thank you Mr Lilly.' I hand him the twenty pieces of gold, to which his eyes light up, looking pleased with himself, for such a fruitful afternoon.

'I shall show you out Madam.'

'Thank you Mr Lilly.'

'Please be sure to find some herbs to keep away the plague.'

'I am always prepared Mr Lilly,' I say, holding up the little pomander which I keep about my person, always filled with fresh herbs.

I am delighted to have an answer for Charles. Lilly never flinched on hearing that Charles was preparing an escape from the army. He is well known for his political sway towards the Parliamentarians, but equally known for his liking of the king, which is possibly why Charles feels safe to deal with this man. We do indeed live in complicated times.

Arriving back at Hampton Court Palace, the carriage takes the long drive through the iron gates to stand beneath the arch of Clock Court, where I alight, pleased to stretch my legs.

'Thank you sir.'

'Your welcome Marm.'

I take a quick glimpse at the astronomical clock on the tower above, reading nine o'clock, and make my way to the Great Hall. A soldier takes my details, recording that I'm here to see Mr James Maxwell, and then escorts me to the Watching Chamber where I wait for my stepfather.

So much time is spent waiting around today. Either sitting in the carriage or sitting with Mr Lilly. Now more standing around for my stepfather, which is more difficult, because I'm eager to let Charles know I have an answer for him and can even suggest a safe house.

'Jane. Jane,' calls out my stepfather as he starts to enter the Watching Chamber.

I quickly go to meet him, for his tone seems quite urgent and looking more aged than normal.

'Is everything alright? You seem troubled.' He comes closer to whisper in my ear.

238

'He has gone Jane. Our Majesty has absconded from the palace.'

'No. That can't be so. Nothing has been arranged. He doesn't know the best way to travel. Has someone taken him? Is he still alive?' I whisper back in a determined fashion.

I can't believe what I'm hearing. Who could have allowed this to happen? Our king is like a parcel, moving from one place to another.

I leave my stepfather to run through the palace, making my way to the Privy Lodgings, pushing anyone aside who stands in my way. I rush up the backstairs to the bedchamber, passing a page on the stairs who I don't recognise. He doesn't move out of the way to let me pass, causing me the need to squeeze along the passage. I change my mind, pulling myself up fast to address the Page.

'Who are you? Do I know you?' I ask without any manners whatsoever, annoyed at what has happened to Charles.

'My name is Firebrace, Marm. Henry Firebrace, page of the backstairs,' he replies with a smugness about him.

Enough said. He is the new servant, the double agent, who wriggled his way into the royal household, fooling Parliament, supposedly supporting the Royalist cause. Without saying anymore I continue to run up the

239

backstairs arriving at My Majesties Bedchamber door, where I see Colonel Whalley, Patrick Maule and Mr Murray, standing, looking shocked.

'What is going on Whalley?' I ask. 'You're supposed to be looking after the king. Has he been taken again, like he was from Holdenby House?'

Mr Murray peers over Whalley's shoulder, mouthing something I can't make out. Colonel Whalley then tries to explain.

'Everything was usual for a Thursday, Madam Whorwood. His Majesty was in his room to write letters until six o'clock. I was here to escort him to chapel but Mr Murray informed me that His Majesty is not to be disturbed, so I waited outside. When he did not emerge at eight o'clock, I took the back route into the chamber with Mr Smithsby, only to find he was not inside.'

This cannot be happening. Charles absconded without first hearing from William Lilly. It is surely not possible?

He only asked for advice this morning, no indication that I needed to return to the palace by a certain hour. Charles distinctly said, that once we hear from Lilly, Ashburnham and Berkeley will devise a plan.

'Paradise', I call out.

That's where he will be, Paradise Chamber. I quickly

start to retrace my steps until I stand outside the door of Paradise, recalling the last time I came to this room, remembering Charles alone, in his favourite chamber, sitting relaxed, consumed by splendour and fantastical items. The room is a sanctuary, an escape from the real world, so this is where he will be, I'm sure. If not, how will he fare in the dark cold night, taking a direction in an unprepared fashion? I take a deep breath. I don't knock. I burst open the door stopping in my tracks, enchanted once more by the beauty of this room. The same calm, glorious atmosphere, but no Charles. I rush to the window overlooking the park. It's black with night. No movement. Nothing. He has gone.

I close the door to Paradise making my way back to the bedchamber where Mr Maule and Mr Murray are still outside. Colonel Whalley opens the chamber door. I go inside.

Charles' cloak is spread out on the floor. His greyhound lying, panting on the rug. As I walk closer to the dog he looks up at me with frightened eyes.

'You know don't you boy. You know what is going on.'

I bend down to stroke him whilst continuing to look around the room. Outspread on Charles' writing desk are three documents. I leave the dog to take a closer look, calling Colonel Whalley.

Michelle Hockley

'Have you seen these letters, Colonel? One is addressed to you.' Whalley takes the letter to begin to read.

It seems odd that Whalley hasn't sent out the guards to re-capture Charles. Has he let Charles leave the palace voluntarily? Where is the manhunt for our sovereign? Has everyone given up on him? Has he become a nuisance to them; a thorn in their side? I am so confused. The Colonel begins to read aloud the letter sent to him by Charles.

'Dear Colonel Whalley. I assure you it was not the letter you showed me this morning that made me leave...' I interject abruptly.

'What letter did you show him this morning Whalley?'

He hands me that letter, still on the desk. It's from Cromwell, asking Whalley to put on extra guard after the Levellers' agitated meeting the previous night in Putney, threatening to do away with the king.

'Whalley, you have scared the king by showing him this letter. Could you not have put on extra guard as requested?'

He doesn't reply. I take the third letter.

'What is this letter, signed ER? Who is ER? Do you have a cipher key so we can at least know who is ER?'

'No Madam, no cipher,' Whalley replies.

I need to think. What does this all mean? Perhaps

242

Parliament have removed Charles from the army because he is being advised not to sign the Newcastle Propositions, which gives Parliament what they want.

I start to read the letter from ER, 'I cannot omit to acquaint you... at a meeting last night with eight or nine agitators who were in debate at Putney...it was resolved to take away your life..' I stop reading. I don't want to hear such cruelty. We don't even know who is ER.

Then it strikes me. It's possible that Charles has left for Ashburnham's house? He was expecting Ashburnham to make the arrangements for an escape when William Lilly had figured in which direction to leave. Living in nearby Thames Ditton, feeling safe with his servant, it is possible Charles has already taken his leave. Throwing the letters down I run out of the bedchamber towards the privy stairs across to the backstairs.

'Firebrace,' I shout.

'Yes Marm.'

'Can you get me a horse as soon as possible? Like now. Now. Now,' I scream.

'Yes, Marm.'

Firebrace runs to the stables to collect me a horse then beckons me to the door that leads to the park, which I find strange, as the tow path is a more direct route to the main road. Then it starts to dawn on me.

'You know how His Majesty left the palace, don't you Firebrace? You know that His Majesty has escaped. You turned a blind eye at the stairs.'

I mull over in my mind. Charles went out of Paradise, down the backstairs, past Firebrace, then to the door into the park.

'I understand,' I say to Firebrace. 'If that's what Charles wanted, I guess you did right by letting him go.'

But urgency returns to me. I still have to find Charles, because he is going the wrong way. He should be going east but by going through the park he is travelling west.

'Thank you Firebrace. Thank you.'

'God be with you Madam Whorwood,' he says, handing me a lit torch before returning to the palace, to take up his position once more as page of the backstairs.

As I prepare myself to mount the horse, my foot kicks against something hard. I ignore it, it will be rubble. Then my other foot kicks it. What is this? I crouch down beside the horse, lowering the torch to gain more light. It's a book. I wipe the mud on my dress, *A Broken Heart*. Immediately recognise the title as the religious tract, my stepfather worried he would never find for Charles. A work by John Shawe, based on psalm 51; poignant for these trying times, 'David would serve God with a broken heart.' I am even more confident this is the direction Charles took on leaving the palace, for I doubt he would intend to leave this religious guide behind. I slip the book inside my cloak for safe keeping and finally mount the horse. Keeping open the gate in the wall, I inch my way slowly, feeling my way until the ground levels out. Once the ground is flat, I start to canter, then gallop. Faster and faster, making my way towards Thames Ditton, to the home of Ashburnham, hoping all the while they will be there so I can tell them to change their direction and head east.

'Come on boy. Come on. Lord, please keep me safe on this night.'

CHAPTER TWENTY THREE

Time to Regroup
December 1647

I failed Charles on 11 November 1647. William Legge, John Ashburnham and Berkeley had already made haste travelling west, arriving on the Isle of Wight. Our Majesty is once again a prisoner at the hands of Parliament, held up in Carisbrooke Castle, without any of the privileges he was afforded by the army at Hampton Court Palace. In the eyes of the authorities, Our Majesty is but an hindrance, an irritation in their traitorous scheme and the outlook for us all is somewhat bleak.

My stepfather retired from service after Hampton Court, no longer wanting to travel across the country, chasing down his sovereign. Nevertheless, he has made an exception for me. Together, we have successfully completed our last operation; moving the jewels from Holton to

London.

'They will be safe here Jane,' confirms my stepfather as we hide the jewels beneath the floorboards of the family home in Cannon Row.

'Are you sure?' I ask, concerned we are four doors away from Derby House, where sits the Committee who advise Parliament.

'I am sure Jane. Trust me. Keep your enemies closer.'

I smile at the thought of these fated jewels, being always under the nose of the opposition. First they are hidden at what became the headquarters of the army. Now they are spitting distance from the Committee of Both Kingdoms. If they only knew. I concede to my stepfather's better judgement, not wishing to feel ungrateful for his assistance.

'Thank you stepfather. What a team we are.'

'No. Thank you Jane. I am proud of what you have achieved in trying to help Our Majesty.'

'Well, I had a good teacher,' I reply. Though, both aware that whatever we have done during this war, we have made few inroads towards success.

We both move our feet across the floorboards to ensure there is no sign of disturbance, before I take the rug to throw it back into place and move the chest firmly on top.

'We should be getting off now, Jane. I will be heading

for Guildford Park, where I intend to enjoy my retirement with your mother, whilst praying each day for this war to reach its conclusion so we can get back to something like normality.'

'Yes papa. Good idea.'

We say our goodbyes. I watch as he enters his carriage, heaving himself into the seat, heavy with the burdens from the life he has run.

My mind turns to the first time I saw him in 1619, when my mother was newly married. I smile as I picture how young and happy they both looked that day. His love for Anne and me; taking us into his care as if we were his own. Me, taking on his reckless qualities for justice and being the object in one of his many schemes. From the back of my carriage I wave, as we proceed in different directions, to continue our lives and this war.

Journeying back to Holton, I am relieved that the jewels are away from the Whorwoods who remain completely unaware that I used Sir Thomas' resting place to hide them.

When my driver turns into the road of the Holton estate, I see an unfamiliar carriage standing on the moat. I lean forward from my seat, with intrigue. I see Katherine Allen, the servant, at the door, talking to someone who I don't recognise. She sees the carriage, but doesn't see me.

As we drive closer, I hear raised voices between the two of them.

'Which Whorewood is it? Lady or Madam that you want?' she shouts. 'Is it the old lady or the one with the red hair and pockmarked face?'

I am horrified to hear such a disparaging description of me. How dare she describe me in that fashion. Such disrespect. As soon as she sees me walking towards the house from the carriage, she throws her arm up, pointing to me, before slamming the main front door of the house.

'Sir, may I enquire what is your business here?'

'I am Richard Cole, courier for the Committee for the Advance of Money, Marm.'

'What is your business with me?'

'I have come to request expenses for the work I've carried out, trying to retrieve money from Sir Robert Bannister owed to the Committee. I have travelled through treacherous conditions more than three times to the village of Passenham to collect the money, as a result am financially out of pocket.'

'What brings you to Holton? What does this have to do with me, may I ask?'

'Sir Robert and Lady Margaret suggested I come to you, informing me that you were given ample payment that will cover both our expenses.' I am flabbergasted. How dare

Sir Robert send this person to my home?

'I have no idea what you are talking about Mr Cole. I can only assume you have the wrong name and address. I suggest you return to Sir Robert and explain that. Now, good day to you, I have my children to attend.'

'No. You were given forty pounds for expenses,' he continues. 'I need only fourteen. Do you hear,' he says, catching up with me, pulling at my arm as I try to walk to the main door of the house.

'Away with you,' I say, shrugging off his tight grip. 'Off you go. You are on private land. You are trespassing. Good day to you.' He comes no closer, but continues to shout after me.

'This is not the last you've heard of me Madam Whorwood. Not the last, I can assure you.'

I watch him go to his carriage, leaving me feeling somewhat shaken. I never expected him to be the fall-out of the escapade I had with Lord Howard. Where did he suddenly spring from? That has rather thrown me. If only he knew how much I did manage to make from that episode. Well, he can run for his fourteen pounds. I have six hundred and forty pounds secured safely within the King's coffers and have no intention of retrieving any of this for the likes of him. My head is banging with rage. Possibly from the thought of having to conjure yet another excuse to my family if they ask about this shenanigan. Hopefully this is the last we hear of that nonsense.

When I eventually enter the house, I see Katherine Allen coming out of drawing room.

'Everything alright Madam?' she says with a smirk on her face.

'Yes thank you Katherine. Everything is fine,' doing all I can to hold my tongue, for I would like to berate her for her description of me. I'd also like to know why this servant remains within our household after almost two years since Bridget and Ireton's wedding, when she was apparently employed for that sole purpose. Maybe if I spent more time at Holton I might know the answer to that.

'Madam. Mr Whorwood is wanting to see you. He is in the drawing room.'

'Thank you Katherine.'

I drop down my bag, handing her my cloak, which she takes half heartedly. As I go towards the drawing room I can feel her eyes watching me, even though I don't turn around. I knock on the door.

'Come in,' shouts Brome.

'Hello Brome, my dear. How are the children?' I say with a huge smile, hoping to appease him after my being away again.

'Ah, my wife, good of you to join us. How are the

children you ask? If you were here to tend to them, in your supposed role as mother and wife, you wouldn't have to ask,' he says sarcastically.

'What has brought this on? You knew I was needed to help my stepfather as he starts his retirement. You saw him here, he explained I needed to go to London.'

He holds a document raised in his hand.

'It is this, that's brought this on Jane.'

I try to second guess its contents, wondering if it's a summons from that horrible Mr Cole, having already presented an invoice to my husband for the money he is requesting.

'I can explain Brome. It has nothing to do with me.'

'I think you will find it has everything to do with you my dear,' he says in a loud, bold, deep determined voice. 'Jane, do you know what is in my hand here?'

'No Brome, how could I? Stop playing games.'

'In my had, Jane, I have a receipt for money; a bond of security for three hundred pounds.'

'What has that to do with me?'

'It comes direct from the King's coffers to acknowledge monies sent to help secure a Thomas Bendish, in a role as Ambassador in Constantinople.'

I gulp at hearing this, taking me completely off guard. I did indeed send the promissory note, he gave me for the children, to my stepfather as monies to help secure Thomas Bendish in the role of Ambassador. I had expected Brome's name would be removed when the bill was cashed, not add his name to the ledger and record him as a donor.

'You look confused Jane,' says Brome.

Dam right I'm confused. I feel like I'm standing on a sheet of ice right now. I can find no grip or friction at this point in time.

'According to the dates,' Brome explains, as if I didn't already know, he continues, 'this is the three hundred pounds I gave you to spoil the children.'

Indeed it was. In truth, when I received this huge sum, I couldn't quite believe it. At the time, I thought maybe Brome felt he'd neglected the children, wanting to make amends for the time he'd been away. What he thought I wanted to buy the children with such a vast sum of money, still remains a mystery to me.

'Instead of treating the children as you requested, Jane, you sent this to a Thomas Bendish, who I assume to be your lover.'

'My lover. How dare you suggest such a disgusting accusation. I am your wife and yours alone,' I say; delighted to hear something leave my lips that is truthful.

'Oh come on Jane, you were desperate for money to help your secret rendezvous. You used your children as an excuse to help this man, who you are clearly overly familiar, intimate even. You are rarely at Holton. So where are you? In the arms of this gentleman?'

'I would never take a lover. I don't need to take a lover, I have you Brome, my lovely Brome,' I say holding out my arms as a sign of embrace, hoping to soften his anger. He ignores my gesture. 'Brome, if this was my lover, I wouldn't help him to go to Constantinople, now would I?'

'Get out of here Jane. I don't want to see you again today.'

'Brome you are being ridiculous. I don't know a Bendish. I am sure there is a plausible explanation. Clearly a misunderstanding. I did send the money to the king. He needed money Brome. You were right all those years ago, the court is running out of money.'

'Get out. How dare you insult my intelligence in this way. You know what I feel about lies and deceit. You assured me you would never let me down yet look at you. Standing before me is a blatant liar. You are never here. I never know where you are. Your children never see you or know when their mother is coming back to them. This is the final straw to stoop so low as to use their money to help your lover. You disgust me. Get out.'

Brome raises his voice like I have never heard before, which makes me take my leave of the drawing room. I am

255

not afraid, but I don't want to upset the whole house. If Ursula hears all this screaming she will only side with Brome making things worse for me.

I'm not so clever as I thought. My stepfather would never have made such mistakes. Oh, this is so embarrassing, I wasn't expecting that. My excuse was appalling. I said I didn't know this Bendish. He knows the money he gave me for the children was sent to the king for Bendish, which could only have come from me. Then I back tracked, saying I did send the money to the court for the king. He can clearly see I am lying, any fool can see that. This is serious. I have gone too far. I am fast failing Charles. Now I am failing my husband and my children too. Brome despises liars. Where can I run? What should I do next?

I feel at a loss, unable to justify what I have done. To use Brome and my children in this way is appalling. The war doesn't allow for honesty. Nothing is honest anymore. I haven't been honest for years. I am fast becoming tangled in the web I've spun.

In the hallway, Katherine stands outside the drawing room door, conveniently polishing the wainscot nearby. She is everywhere that woman. I don't acknowledge her as she slips past me, entering the drawing room before I close the door.

As my little girl comes running towards me, I

couldn't have wished for a better sight.

'Hello Diana, how are you?' I say, lifting her up to spin her around as she giggles.

'I have made a picture of our horses, Mama.'

'My they are splendid looking creatures. You are a clever girl. Have you been good for your father, Diana?'

'I have, but Brome junior is refusing to learn his French language properly. Papa has been most annoyed with him.'

'Oh, that's not like Brome junior is it?'

'It is Mama. He hates his school work more than anything in the whole world.'

I am surprised to learn this, not having received a report from his master. What a bad mother I am. My mother would never have been so neglectful with us. I must take stock, spend more time with my children and win back the trust of my husband. What an awful day. I shall be glad when this one is over.

CHAPTER TWENTY FOUR

King Charles Still Needs My Help
May 1648

For the past six months, since it was discovered I'd used the money to secure an ambassadorial role for a Thomas Bendish, relations between Brome and myself have remained raw. He never returned to our marital bed, punishing me for something that is false. I suspect he is hurting too as he attempts to wrestle with this situation. I promised, all those years ago, that he could rely on me. I still believe that to be the case; except war has come between us. It has damaged me; it has damaged all of us and we move further and further away from anything remotely close to rational thought. It is very easy to be swept up in the moment, believing you are doing right by your country, when in reality, you cannot hope to satisfy everyone. By striving to bring order to our lives, forcing a struggle against the tide of life, we have created chaos.

Our king remains a prisoner on the Isle of Wight, held up in Carisbrooke Castle with Henry Firebrace and Thomas Herbert, two faithful servants and firm allies to the Royalist cause. I am regularly informed of their progress through coded letters, but quite honestly, we are further away from Charles returning to his seat of power, than we were in 1642 when civil war first broke. After six long years we have nothing to show for our efforts other than time-worn by this unforgiving conflict. Charles continues with his highest devotion to God and his subjects. He fights with relentless determination to bring about a solution of peace that will satisfy his kingship. My Majesty is far from passively accepting his lot. Already he has made several foiled escapes from his gaoler, Colonel Robert Hammond, who persistently maintains a tight grip on confinement, receiving tip-offs from the Parliamentary Committee of Two Kingdoms, who are more adroit at intercepting our schemes.

On this fine spring morning, I have positioned myself at the far corner of the grounds at Holton House, away from prying eyes, longing to read a letter received yesterday morning from Henry Firebrace. Recently, since embarrassing myself with Brome over the Bendish debacle, and Robert Cole arriving at the house, I have maintained a low profile with the Royalist cause, allowing for the heat of that day to simmer down. However, I am confident, that this inactivity will only sustain itself until I am sent direction to take action. If the truth be known, whenever I receive a letter, I pray for that day to arrive sooner, rather than later.

Pulling the letter and cipher key from my pocket, I buckle down to an arduous read, but almost immediately realise, today, my prayers have been answered. Hardly able to conceal the joy that is bubbling inside me for once again, my services are required. Thank you my Lord. Without doubt, the past six months have given me the opportunity to reflect on my behaviour, but I would be deceiving you and myself if I didn't admit that I'd missed the thrill of the danger. This is good news. To know I am still a worthy link in the chain to win back power for my king, being given the opportunity to put behind me the failure I felt when I arrived too late at Hampton Court, is such a relief. I put the letter in my pocket as I run back to the house, calling in on the stables to request Emmanuel take me to Oxford, where I can hire a carriage to London, to carry out my orders, and attend another meeting with the astrologer, William Lilly.

Arriving in The Strand, it's a relief to gain access to Lilly's house, without the previous confusion, even though I've arrived, again, unannounced.

'Madam Whorwood. I didn't expect to see you again. Though it's good to see you didn't die from the plague,' says

William Lilly with a wry smile as he opens the door to me.

'Thank you sir,' I say, walking confidently into the hallway, taking the narrow stairs, being familiar with my surroundings.

Lilly continues to chatter as we enter the small office. Both of us take a seat with him at his desk and me quite close by, where he begins the consultation to discuss the purpose of my visit.

'So, Madam, what brings you here when obviously you don't take the slightest notice of the information I give you?'

'What do you mean sir?'

'Well you defy me on the plague notice, then on the direction to take the king. By all accounts, His Majesty appears to have gone south-west, rather than east as I advised, and look where we are now. His Majesty is a prisoner, once more. I am happy to take your money, but you'd do well to act upon the reading I give you.'

'Sir. I can explain. When I arrived back at Hampton Court, the king had already left the charge of the army. I was one hour too late to provide the king with your valuable information.'

'Very well. So, what can we do for you today?'

'His Majesty would like to make another escape. This time from his cell in Carisbrooke Castle, and requests your advice on how best to achieve this. He has made several attempts already, but without success. On the last attempt he became stuck between the bars of his window. His body became so wedged he was forced to recoil and call off the escape.'

'His Majesty wishes to make yet another escape, you say? Oh my Lord.'

'Mr Lilly. It is not for us to question His Majesty's wishes?'

'It might be preferable if we did. But no, probably not.'

'Well then Mr Lilly, can you help me please?'

'I can only advise that you go to see my good friend Mr Farmer, a locksmith, in Bow Lane. He will supply the tools needed to ensure success. Here is the address. This note will explain the tools and equipment that I recommend you need.'

'Thank you Mr Lilly, I shall do as you say.'

'Yes, but will you do as I say? Lilly repeats. I smile, rolling my eyes, as I take the instructions from him.

'Take care Madam Whorwood.'

'I shall Mr Lilly,' I say as I enter the waiting carriage to take me to Bow Lane.

As we drive past Ironmonger Lane, I peer down the narrow street, knowing that poor Alderman Adams has since been sentenced to High Treason, residing in the Tower of London. How easily things can change. So much uncertainty.

Arriving at the ironmonger shop, with an inscribed banner outside, G. Farmer establishment, I hand the proprietor the note from Lilly. Without saying a word, he sets about his work, giving the impression of being rather suspicious of me. When he's finished, he places on the counter, a bottle of aqua fortis and a file. The plan is for Charles to soften the iron bars by dousing them in acid and then file them away from their support. He will return each bar back to its original position and remove when he is ready to make his escape; providing a more efficient exit from his cell. When I've inspected the items, Mr Farmer wraps the equipment carefully, but firmly, in brown paper tied with string.

'Thank you Mr Farmer,' I say, handing him the coins, being the only words spoken between us.

On my return across London, heading west towards Westminster, I can't believe my eyes.

'Driver stop,' I shout urgently, banging on the roof. 'Stop please.'

We pull up fast. I disembark at the top of Cannon Row, still holding the packages in my arms. It's Diana, my sister.

'Wait for me please sir.'

'Yes, Marm.'

'Diana. Diana,' I shout, picking up my pace to catch her, as she heads towards Derby House in a purposeful manner.

'Jane. What a surprise. How are you?'

'Diana, I haven't seen you for simply ages.'

'No. We have all been rather busy with one thing and another. Are you still hell-bent on helping the king?'

'Oh yes, he is always extremely grateful for my help, though we haven't made much progress. He's still a prisoner. Poor dear.'

'You know, no good will ever come of your interfering. His Majesty would be wise to let Parliament take power so they can do right by the nation and our good people.'

'Why do you say that Diana?'

'It's obvious, my dear. Parliament has the king over a barrel. He's spent, at least the last six years being pushed from pillar to post. He keeps escaping and getting caught. Simply, nowhere left for him to turn.'

'We have to keep trying though. We can't give up on our sovereign.'

'Well I did, a long time ago.'

Knowing there is never a good reason to argue with

Diana, I allow her space to point score and air her views.

'King Charles was brought to Hatfield House on the way to Hampton Court Palace. Did you know that?'

'No I didn't Diana. I hope you made him welcome.'

'The army took over. We let them get on with it whilst my husband and me did our best to carry on with life as normal.'

'How is Charles Cecil? Well, I trust.'

'He is well thank you. Feeling more in control of this whole mess, now he sits on the Parliamentary Committee of Both Kingdoms,' she says with relish, as she swivels around to point at Derby House at the end of the road, where they are currently in session.

'They have a great deal to resolve. It takes time,' I say, determined not to show my utter contempt for this committee or start an argument with her.

'They do indeed have a great deal to resolve because Our Majesty is unable to admit to his wrongdoings and constantly refuses to agree to a more acceptable form of government.'

I scrunch the paper around the parcels in my arms, doing all I can to suppress my rage as she gives her unwarranted opinion in such an arrogant, forthright manner. How dare she says those things?

'What have you got tucked in your arms, Jane? Not

something for the king is it? He is not planning another escape is he?'

'No, Diana. Whatever gives you that idea?'

'I'm messing with you Jane. I hope the war hasn't taken away your sense of humour.'

'No. No, not at all.'

'What have you got there Jane? The packages certainly do look ominous,' she says, coming closer to pull at the string. I let out a nervous laugh.

'These are toys I've had made for Brome junior and Diana. I collected them today.'

With my children being thirteen and nine years old, having long since stopped playing with toys, this is a terrible excuse and I start to feel my blood run cold. Thankfully, she ceases to tug at the string and smiles.

'Be careful Jane. It can only end in tears,' she says, turning in the direction of Derby House to meet her husband.

As I watch her walk away, I make myself feel better by remembering the crown jewels are hidden beneath the floorboards of a Maxwell dwelling, just a few doors away from the Committee. If she knew that, it would definitely end in her tears.

'Good day, Diana.'

'Au revoir Jane,' she says, tossing her purse in the air,

dangling from its drawstring.

'Take good care of those children and stop worrying about the king,' she adds.

I walk towards the carriage at the top of Cannon Row, slightly bemused by our opposing views and just how close I came to putting Charles in danger.

CHAPTER TWENTY FIVE

Honesty Comes With Some Relief

Descending the carriage at Gosport, the last stop before employing the services of a fisherman to take me across to the Isle of Wight, I struggle to find enough space to stand without being pushed about by the determined crowd. I move towards the waters edge where people gather to meet the early morning catch. As I do so, I think I hear my name, but since there is so much noise, that is hardly possible.

'Jane. Jane. Stop Jane.' I hear it again. I look around but don't see anyone I recognise.

'Best price ladies. Can't get fresher than this,' calls out the fishermen as they set up their stalls beside the mooring.

People continue to nudge and bump me as they walk past. I push my way forwards regardless, determined to arrange a crossing and hire a ride before they are all full.

'Ouch. Do you mind,' I say, starting the motion to swing my bag, the best I can in this tight space, fully intending to clobber the person who seems to have taken charge of my shoulder.

'Jane. It's me,' says Anne.

My sister ducks away from the object towards her, but it's too late to stop the momentum.

'Anne. What are you doing here?'

'Ouch. You have some weight behind that swing, young lady,' she replies rubbing her back.

'I am so sorry Anne. I didn't know it was you. What are you doing here?'

'I've been travelling through the night.'

'My, the fish must be fresh to make that much effort. Can't you find somewhere closer to Mundham?'

'Don't be ridiculous Jane, I'm not here for fish.'

'Oh, sorry.'

'I came to find you.'

'How did you know I was here?'

'Diana seem to think you were heading here.'

'Diana? I saw her yesterday.'

'I know, she told me. Parliament have already raised the alarm to the army, that Charles is attempting to make another escape.'

'What's that got to do with me?'

270

'Diana has her suspicions that you're involved.'

'That's absurd. All I want is to see Charles. To see if I can speak with him.'

'Don't Jane. Please don't,' she says, encouraging me to walk away from the water.

'I can't change my plans, people are expecting me. No Anne. I have to go,' I say, moving away, not wanting to miss a crossing.

'Jane, you must not go. Diana has it on good authority, that letters are being intercepted. They are rather suspicious of a Fire..br..a..ce. I think that was the name she used.'

'What does Diana know?'

'Listen Jane. They know of an escape being planned and Diana has got it into her head, that you are involved.'

Struck by what I'm hearing. Information coming left, right and centre. Wind blows up from the sea and in my mind I'm pleading for it to carry me in the direction I should be going. Anne doesn't have the remotest idea of the level of deceit I am drowning, or the errors I've already made, as pieces of the jigsaw start to emerge with my name on them. I wonder how we ever managed to smuggle all that gold across London to Oxford from the merchants' houses, without getting caught? Everything now, is one problem after another.

'Jane. Jane. Are you listening to me?'

'Anne. No. Please don't suggest I let down those who are relying on me.'

'Come on Jane, you can trust me. It really is for the best. I cannot watch whilst you destroy yourself.'

'I can trust you Anne, but I'm not sure I can trust Diana. Do you remember when we were quite young...'

'Not now Jane. We haven't got time to go down memory lane, this is serious. Why don't you go back to Holton and forget all about this? I'm sure Brome worries about you running errands across the country as you are.'

'Anne, I can't do that.'

'Jane, this is what we are going to do. I have taken it upon myself to find Elizabeth Wheeler, who I discover is in service for Charles on the Isle of Wight.'

'Yes, I know that. I could have told you that. Elizabeth is expecting me.'

'Jane. I've made arrangements to meet her when she arrives to collect the local catch, which apparently is a normal routine for her. She will be accompanied by a Mr Thomas Herbert, who has been installed by parliament as Groom of the Bedchamber...'

'Yes, I know Mr Herbert. You are not telling me anything I don't already know. What have you arranged with Elizabeth Wheeler?' frustrated that my plans are being interfered with.

'Pass me the items you've brought for the king, Jane.'

'What items?'

'Come on Jane. Whatever you have to help Charles escape.'

'No. I shall not put Elizabeth Wheeler in danger.'

'You have to Jane. This really is the end of the road.'

Not knowing which way to turn, feeling bulwarked, I reluctantly concede, taking the parcels from my bag, which she places beneath her cloak.

'I have also wrapped inside, the religious tract, *A Broken Heart*.'

'Jane, I'm sorry it is ending in this way.'

'I found the book on entering the park at Hampton Court Palace. I know Charles will appreciate having it to read. It reinforces his belief to continue his fight in the way he knows.'

'I'm not sure we want him to fight in quite the same way as he is currently, but I shall give the book to Wheeler, all the same.'

'I hope I've made the right decision Anne.'

'You have. Otherwise, you will be walking straight into captivity, which would be foolish. Come on then, let's get your coach.'

'Anne there is one more thing I'd like to talk to you

about if you have time.'

'We don't have time. We have to meet Elizabeth and this...Herbert person...Thomas Herbert. I have no intention of coming here and missing them.'

As Anne starts to point me in the direction of the carriage stand, I see Elizabeth Wheeler approaching.

'Anne. Look there's Elizabeth. Behind you.'

'Wait here then, we don't need you to get involved.'

I take myself off to crouch behind the wall, leaving enough of a vantage point to see Anne make her way towards Elizabeth, to see with my own eyes that she makes the drop. She opens Wheeler's basket to place the brown packages inside. It's satisfying to know that at least the equipment is on its way to Charles. I continue to watch as Anne takes control to protect her older sister. Little is said between the two conspirators, before Anne starts to return and head back in my direction.

'All done Jane. Now come on. Let's get out of here,' she says, taking my arm, promoting me to move faster.

Neither of us dare look back, sensing impending danger and neither of us stop at the waiting carriages, which pleases me, because I'm not ready to go home just yet. Instead, I keep time with Anne's energetic pace, that seems to be born out of a nervous energy, and continue to walk away from the sea, further into Gosport. She pulls up fast outside an inn, where we both catch our breath.

'Jane, my dear, I shall treat you to refreshments. I've developed quite an appetite.'

Surprised by Anne's impulsiveness, I am more than willing to accept her offer, if only to spend more time with my sister.

The inn is busy with traders and travellers. We push our way to a seat in the corner of the small, dingy, smoke filled room to take a table by the window, affording us some light, with a glimpse of the sea and blue sky.

'Ladies. What can I get you two beauties?' asks the landlord, quick to descend on new customers.

'Ale please mister. Two ales,' says Anne.

'What can I get you to eat? I have a lovely fish pie, fresh today.'

'Yes. Two fish pies please,' says Anne.

'Is it always this busy here in Gosport, mister?' I enquire.

'It's always this busy when the fish comes in of a morning, but nowadays with the king prisoner at the Castle, in the Isle of Wight, it's busy all through the day. Are you here to see the king Marm?'

'To see the king?' I chuckle, 'whatever makes you think that? I don't think the king would be interested in the likes of me,' I say, trying to relax my vowels.

'They say, tens of thousands of soldiers reside on the island. You could be a soldier's sweetheart.'

'No. Not me.'

'That's good, cause the soldiers and locals don't get on you know. Not on the island, anyhow. Fights break out at night, and there is such a to-do. Mind you, having the king as a local resident has done so much good for business. Long may it reign.'

He chuckles a huge belly laugh as he moves away, clearing the nearby tables before making his way back to the bar with our order. I consider his drop in trade, as soon as Elizabeth Wheeler helps the king to escape.

'Anne, I can't begin to tell you how good it feels to be here with you. It seems so long since I've been able to talk to anyone. I always have a million things on my mind. Sometimes it becomes too much.'

An old lady approaches our table, holding out her hand; wearing a distorted smile of one long front tooth. As she shuffles towards us I question in my mind if she's a spy. Has she followed us from our encounter with Elizabeth and Thomas Herbert, or am I paranoid?

'Ladies. Fortune? Would you like your fortune told pretty ladies?'

'No thank you,' I say. As she continues to come closer to our table, I can't decide if in fact she is a man dressed as an old lady or an old lady. Either way, she moves along with little trouble. 'Now Jane. What is it you want to talk to me about?'

'Ladies. Ladies. Two ales and two lovely fresh fish pies,' shouts the landlord.

'Thank you sir,' I say as the delicious smell rises up to my tired head, making me feel quite satisfied.

'Sir,' repeats the landlord. 'Now I like that. I could get used to that ladies,' he continues as he goes about his business with the appearance of taking everything in his stride. Good for him. I wish I could be like that. Once he is out of earshot, I begin to let Anne in on my concerns.

'Anne, one week ago, I received a personal letter from Charles via Henry Firebrace. Having deciphered it, I'm wondering if it was meant for me, or what to make of the content.'

'Do you have the letter and cipher key with you, Jane?'

'Yes. I don't dare let it out of my sight.'

I take it out of the pocket in my dress to hand it to her, hoping I am doing the right thing by sharing a letter from Charles. Not wanting to be dishonourable to him or our friendship.

Anne starts to check everything against the cipher key as she reads. To give her time to concentrate, I tuck into the fish pie, looking around the inn, avoiding eye contact with anyone, choosing to fix my gaze on the blue sky and a glimpse of the sea beyond. It is so good to be sitting here with Anne. What a strong woman she is. I hope Elizabeth Wheeler stays safe. I would hate for her to think ill of me for not delivering the items as I said I would. I am sure Anne is right, it seems the safest option.

Anne nudges my elbow as she continues to decipher. I look at her, thinking she has finished, she raises her eyebrows before continuing to read. I think she is getting to grips with the text. By the look she is giving me, even enjoying this saga a little too much.

Our silence is broken again by the landlord.

'Ladies are we all finished here then?' he shouts over the noise of the other customers.

'Not quite mister. The pie is good. We want to savour the flavour, if you don't mind.'

'No, I don't mind. You enjoy yourselves.'

'Could you get us two more ales please,' I ask, thinking we need more refreshments and the landlord either wants his table back, or make another sale.

'Two more ales coming up for the lovely ladies in the reading room.'

He may well describe us as being in the reading room, as he puts it, but if he knew what we were reading, he wouldn't believe it. If the trash journals got hold of it, they would have a field day. A pamphlet would certainly be published for a daring read. Anne nudges me again.

'Okay, I've read it. I am not sure this is meant for you Jane. Tell me, is Charles expecting Henrietta Maria to come back from France?' she says in a whisper, though no one would hear us, it's too noisy.

'No, I haven't heard anything about her coming back to England. I know Prince Charles is expected with a fleet of ships on his way to Norfolk, but no mention of Henrietta coming with him. Why?'

'In this letter, Charles is wanting to spend time alone with you, arranging how you can enter the castle, have a meal with a Captain Mildmay before he interrupts that meal to take you away, promising to make love to you, using the most vulgar language I have ever heard. This is not how Charles speaks to you. Or is it, you naughty girl?' she says looking down at me as we sit shoulder to shoulder.

'No. Never. This is what I've been thinking. We are friends Anne. Only ever friends.'

'You are good friends, I know that, but this is more than a step over the mark of friendship isn't it.'

'Yes. Which is why I haven't responded. I didn't know what to think. He is so dedicated to Henrietta Maria and his children, he would never commit adultery to defy a union of God or encourage me to do so in my union. I don't think he would see me in that way. Surely not after all these years of being friends.'

'More importantly,' says Anne, 'this letter is addressed to sweet 391. According to the other cipher keys you are either 715 or N. I am quite confident that Charles is expecting, or asking Henrietta to meet him, quite possibly when Prince Charles returns to England with the fleet you mentioned. Don't you think?'

'It was my first thought, that it's someone else's letter. I love Charles deeply. I would do anything for him, but in this letter he has taken leave of his senses.'

'Well, let's not forget, he has been a prisoner for a while now. You are perhaps the closest woman he knows, but I can't see him saying this to you. I would say, this is for Henrietta Maria. He is expecting or hoping, maybe even encouraging her to make the journey incognito, with Prince Charles. Let's look together at the ciphers. Here you are 'N' according to these other keys. So, if Charles is 390, Henrietta is most probably 391 because every other key runs in order of importance. Sorry Jane, you are important, but not as important as Henrietta. It makes far more sense for a sequential order for Charles and Henrietta rather than a sequential order for you and Charles.'

'I know Our Majesty is writing many, many letters

each day,' I explain to Anne. 'He has been known to sends Thomas Herbert to deliver several times a day. Sometimes even in the middle of the night if he's requesting hand delivered letters across the country.'

'Again, more evidence for confusion. He has written the letters, folded them up into so many pieces then got mixed up when he comes to address them. Feasible, isn't it?'

'Yes, quite possible.'

'I am sorry to say also Jane, that it wouldn't surprise me if letters were not going back to Charles sealed with your seal, using your identity to fool the interceptors. Deception is at every level since this war began.'

'Yes, I am aware of the deceit, I am pretty much in the thick of that. What you say of the letter, I think is quite right, it was not meant for me was it.'

'No. I think we can be pretty sure of that.'

'Don't you think the King of England could take a fancy to Jane Ryder?' I ask, preening myself in jovial, playful manner.

'I am sure he could, but we both know he would never act on it. He would never encourage you to deceive God by disobeying the marriage vows you promised in front of God. His loyalty to God is too great. Also, his loyalties to his wife and children are too strong. You know that. You've known him long enough.'

'Thank you Anne. You are right. I can see this so clearly now. Thank you so much.'

'Jane, you look relieved,' says Anne, smiling as we sit bunched up, engrossed in our conversation.

'I am relieved. I don't ever want Charles to address me in such a manner. Our love for each other is so pure, I want it to stay that way. I want him to have eyes only for his wife. She has worked so hard for Charles throughout the war, by collecting troops and selling jewels.'

'Forget about the letter. Don't respond. Put it all behind you.'

'Two more ales for you ladies,' announces the landlord, as I fold up the letter beneath the table.

'Jane. Did you order these? Or do we have a secret admirer somewhere in the establishment?' I laugh as I take a sip from the pewter mug.

Anne starts to organise us again, which, may I add, she is doing extremely well.

'Let's pay for our refreshments,' she begins, 'then take these drinks outside to watch the people for a moment, before we get you on a coach back to Holton and me to return to some sort of normality, far away from your eccentric existence. I think I've had enough excitement to last me a lifetime.'

What a good sister she has been to me today. I am

grateful, but I am also completely exhausted. For once in my life I think I could happily swap the chaos in which I am living for the twelve children she has in her care. Now that is a first for me.

CHAPTER TWENTY SIX

Darkness Descends Upon Us
January 1649

N ot once did I have the opportunity to discuss the infamous letter with Charles, and all access to him is now barred. Parliament removed their prisoner from the Isle of Wight at the end of 1648. The newly formed Rump Parliament, containing members who despise Our Majesty, wanting rid of him, have taken it upon themselves to summons him to Westminster Palace where he is currently being tried for supposed wrong doings during the civil war.

Every morning throughout the trial I walk to Westminster Palace from the house in Cannon Row to be nearby Charles. He is heavily guarded, residing at the late Sir Robert Cotton's house in Old Palace Yard, making it almost impossible to gain even a glimpse as he enters and leaves the Hall each day. I wait on the street until I hear the Court Clerk announce the start of proceedings, praying for our king, wondering how it came to this. Then, in the early evening, I do the same; stand alongside the crowds hoping to see him being escorted from these legal proceedings.

During the day I read transcripts of the trial as they are reported in the news-sheets where I learn that Charles is refusing to co-operate with this mock Parliament, as he describes it, adamant they have no authority to place him on trial, believing only God can question him. He repeatedly espouses that to acknowledge this Parliament as official, would put the liberty of his people's future, at risk, destroying the country's long established legal system. Reading between the lines, it's clear that Charles is leaving his fate to God, adhering to his belief in the divine right of kings. Whilst this is of course, admirable, I am in despair, willing Charles to speak out to tell of his innocence.

Yesterday was a dark day, when upon the printed page, I read Our Majesty was accused of being a tyrant, a traitor to his people, and a public enemy of the Commonwealth of England. This is slander. It has never been his intention to hurt his people, only to defend their rights and those of God. It's as if we are playing out the court masque of 1638, *Britannia Triumphans*; the horrid land, the distortion of life. Though these scenes are not written by a famous playwright. This is real life. There will be no golden palace or flying dolphin. All we have is a harsh reality of this treacherous time. Our Majesty must defend himself against this damming sentence; against the liars who have brought him to trial. Lady Anne Fairfax, whom we cared for at Holton House during her bout of malaria, is strong now. Even though she is the wife of a general in Cromwell's Army, she shouts from the spectators' gallery that this sentence, brought against Charles, is not a reflection on how people feel. I should be there too. I should be shouting from the gallery to defend Charles, except, I am not afforded admittance to Westminster Hall.

I am a little later than usual this evening. As I leave the house I hurry along the River Thames taking a short cut from the other end of Cannon Row, knowing the crowds will be less dense along this route. It is cold. The winter January air is biting through my body. I don't mind. I must make a visit, it has become my routine over the last five days. My time is filled with nothing other than the brief visits, like bookends encasing an empty day. As I draw closer to Westminster, I hear jeering and booing. Something isn't right. I scurry faster and faster lifting my dress as I run more quickly into the crowds. The people are gathering momentum, moving in the opposite direction. I run to follow them as the waves turn towards Whitehall. Soldiers line the streets. Shopkeepers stand huddled, crying in their doorways. What has changed? Why the emotion?

Arriving at Whitehall, I see Charles step out from an enclosed sedan chair dressed in a black cloak and a tall wide brimmed black hat, looking much older than his forty nine years. Shoulders leaning forward, dragging his gait, supported by Thomas Herbert, taking the arm of his last remaining and faithful servant. Have they let him free? Is he free? My Majesty is returning to his palace, which must mean he's been successful in convincing the court of his innocence. Oh Charles, does this mean you have finally spoken out to tell the truth. You have at last, explained to the court that they have it wrong, that you are not a criminal. You have stood up to this vile sentence and explained the truth.

The crowds are still jeering. What is going on? Groups of people gather around a man on a soap box, on the other side of the road, opposite the Banqueting House. I run to join them. I get closer to hear what he's saying.

'The king found guilty of High Treason and sentenced to death. The king will go to the gallows.'

What am I hearing? No. This can't be right. Why? I am rooted to the spot; frozen in time. I look around to speak to someone. Anyone. All I see are blank faces. Unfamiliar faces. Bodies gaining momentum, moving forward as they listen to the rant of the crier. I find my legs again and run across the road to the Banqueting House. I attempt a route into Whitehall Palace, squeezing down the alley at the side entrance, trying not to be noticed or recognised. I have to see Charles. I need to see him. Suddenly I am pulled back, halted by two guards.

'Not here me lady. On your way now.'

'Let me in. Let me see King Charles. I need to get inside.'

'Yes that's what everyone is saying me lady. A quick shifty at the prisoner. Get out of here.'

'No, not just a quick look. Let me in.'

A third guard comes up behind me, lifting me off my feet, throwing me out onto the street where I land on the hard, cold ground, with a bang. I slowly pull my heavy, tired, defeated body, to my feet, staring back at the guard with revolt. I look for someone I can plead with, for I can't force my way past those guards, not anymore. Where is Colonel Whalley, or Fairfax or even Cromwell? No one can help me now. Times are instantly different. Gone is court etiquette. No special treatment. No formal invitation. The crowds start to disperse for they now have their news. They've learnt the king's fate.

I start to walk back to Cannon Row. So cold. So harsh. After all those years of fighting, of fleeing. Living a fractured existence, of hiding. 'Hiding.' That makes me instantly remember the jewels. Charles will make contact with me to reclaim the jewels. I try to recount his words spoken when in 1646 at Oxford he made the escape, when there was a chance to be free, '...please look after the jewels until I am ready for them.' I have to believe My Majesty will contact me to arrange to take back the jewels. This thought gives me a future again. I quicken my step, as I start to think how to release the jewel case from beneath the wooden floorboards. Maybe when he comes for the jewels we can both choose a disguise in which to flee far from here. Can we keep running? Could Charles keep running? Either way, I feel energised from a glimmer of hope that I shall see Charles again and decide what to do. Perhaps put him on a boat to France to be with Henrietta, taking Princess Elizabeth and Prince Henry too. Yes, that's what I shall suggest, for it cannot end like this, not now.

* * *

Each day, all day, I listen for unfamiliar sounds or movement outside the house expecting Charles to call to request the return of his jewels. Tonight, the third night, I sit again, holding the jewel case on my shaking knees, watching the flame of the candle flicker silently. On hearing footsteps outside I brace myself. At the sound of a knock at the door, I jump. This is it. Deep breath.

'Jane. My darling, Jane.'

'Mama, oh Mama.' I throw my arms around her as we walk inside to the drawing room.

'I had to be with you Jane, the news of Charles is too awful for you to be alone. I have been travelling all day from Guildford. I thought you would be here. I hoped you would be here.'

'How could it come to this Mama? Charles is to be taken from us in the most dreadful manner. All he ever wanted was to liberate our people, to save his nation from the tyranny of Parliament and preserve his religion.'

'It has been a terrible time for everyone. To end like this is shameful,' says my mother in her beautiful calm way.

'I tried to help. I honestly did. I have taken it upon myself to help in anyway I can, but it was all in vain.'

'You did indeed. These are horrid times. No words can describe what is happening to us all, even your stepfather has been arrested.'

'What? Why? No. Why? What has he done?' taking hold of her hands, as I listen to her news about my stepfather.

'Years ago Jane, he imported huge amounts of pepper. The business deal has, I'm afraid caught up with him. He is to pay huge sums for the money lost by so many city business men.'

'We are not as clever as we think. I too seem caught at every turn like my stepfather, who I thought was invincible.'

'Maybe you are not always as careful as you should be, my darling.'

'Is Elizabeth alright now Mama? I haven't seen her since she lost her little boy, James.'

'She is getting stronger, that is apparent, but has travelled to the Hague with William who is terrified of being captured for his association with the civil war.'

'I heard that his dear brother James is held prisoner for his involvement with the Scottish Army. His life hangs by a thread.'

'We do indeed live in anxious times Jane.'

My mother changes the subject.

'Please may I ask what is that little box you are keeping by your side?'

'You won't believe it, but these are the crown jewels. This is the last of Charles' possessions, which he put in my care when he escaped from Oxford. I have looked after these for three years. Everyday, since the sentence was read, I wait for Charles to come and collect them, as he said he would.'

'You two are so close. He trusts you to the bitter end.'

We both sit back in our seats, our minds start to remember the good days.

'Do you remember,' I start, 'how I used to love to see Charles from your bedchamber, shouting his name through the window in the most ungainly fashion?'

'I do Jane. Oh for those days to return to us. We had our tragedies to contend, but somehow the future was brighter. Of course, being young we had more hope for the future. Now everything seems so raw and disjointed. Nothing is secure. Far from it.'

As we continue to indulge ourselves in the excesses of our past, we are interrupted by a heavy thud at the door, an urgent awakening. We both sit up straight, startled.

'This is it Mama. Charles has come for me,' I say with a wide smile. Without a moments hesitation, I make my way to open the front door onto a dear friend, wondering what disguise I might see him wearing.

'Good evening Madam Whorwood,' says Thomas Herbert.

'Oh. Mr Herbert. Good evening to you.'

'Madam, I have been instructed to bring this small package to you on return of goods you have held for the king.'

Herbert hands me a small velvet box. My heart sinks as I open it slowly to reveal a small emerald and diamond

Michelle Hockley

ring from his own finger. A gift promised by Charles, on the safe return of the jewel case. I know now, that this is the end of our relationship, the swansong of our journey.

'I have what you are requesting, Mr Herbert.'

'Thank you Madam. I am sorry.'

Handing him the box, there is no conversation. All I can do is bid him a safe night. Closing the door to this final encounter, means life on earth with Charles is truly behind me. The fight is lost and we are undone.

* * *

I have stayed in London during Charles' execution, but I couldn't witness the loathsome event. Prior to the day, purely out of curiosity, I saw the scaffold placed in front of the Banqueting House in Whitehall, with black drapes slung around the railings to hide the worst from the crowds. Yesterday, 30 January 1649, brought an infusion of hatred and delight from the people of our nation. Some thankful by the outcome where Parliament can proceed to take the reins. Some in despair of what Parliament sanctioned upon our heritage. Though in that fusion, nonetheless, when the axe fell, a sudden gasp, from all the people, filled the air that gives us life. At that moment, change poured down upon us by the so called authorities who took away our sovereign.

Before Spring Came Summer

The most precious possession, life, that any of us will ever own, and the Rump Parliament believed they were justified to take away Our Majesty and his last breath. It disgusts me to the core of my very being, that their actions were carried out to satisfy their own ends. Without our Monarchy, London is empty, unreal, soulless and I am more than ready to take my leave to the country. I intend to pick up the broken pieces of my life in Holton, and put them back together again. Maybe we can return to Sandwell Hall, to our pretty garden, where the landscape is wide and green.

As I pack my belongings this afternoon, ready to depart from London, I try to make sense of the last few days; to understand the devastation caused by less than sixty commissioners, who thrust their beliefs upon our nation without any regard for the people. The decision made by so few to affect so many. To live in a nation without a sovereign is an unnatural feeling. We are all left in a state of mourning. Not only those people who were close to Charles, but the whole world is grieving. Whether our king was liked or disliked, ridiculed or praised, he was our king, given to us by God, descending from a line of royal persons, chosen by God to serve the people. A huge wide gaping hole, where once was our sovereign, is left open as we drift into the unknown, entering something Parliament are calling a Republic, setting us adrift into previously untravelled waters, and expecting us to float.

I move sedately to my carriage with my heart saddened by defeat. In despair, but at the same time, quiet in my thoughts.

'Where to Marm?' shouts the driver from his seat, muffled in a large collar coat, keeping the freezing, bitter air at bay.

'Holton village, Oxford, please sir.'

I sit as usual, leant against the cold window to begin my journey out of London, leaving the future to right itself in the best way known only to themselves; leaving our destiny in the hands of the minority. I calm myself by appreciating the crisp, clear, blue sky. The air is cold. The ice on the road is precarious. Yet, as I peer out of the window, the sky gives me hope as it watches down on me.

The driver turns unexpectedly off the main road to Oxford. I wonder where we are going, though worry little, as we are travelling west and the road remains somewhat familiar to me. Catching sight of Windsor Castle brings forth images of those wonderful Garter Ceremonies organised so precisely by my then energetic stepfather. Recalling the day we said our goodbyes to baby James. It is so sad at the realisation, that all the wonderful ceremonies will now cease. No more pomp and ceremony for which the English court became the envy of all the world. It is so difficult to digest all the changes we shall encounter after one sharp blow of the axe. I shiver at the thought. The carriage stops.

'Driver why have we stopped? Why here at Windsor? Driver. Driver,' I shout.

'Madam. I'm sorry to alarm you,' he says as the carriage door opens.

'Mr Maule. Mr Patrick Maule. I didn't realise it was you. Why are you driving me?'

'Mr Murray requested I drive you Madam. I hope you don't mind.'

'No, but why am I here?'

'To stop awhile. For awhile,' he says still holding the carriage door open.

'You are playing tricks on me Mr Maule. This is not acceptable.'

'Please Madam. It's fine. Please follow me.'

As I leave the carriage the blue sky seems to disappear, dulling over, replaced by a sky full of white thick clouds and a soft wind starts to pick-up. I stand at the edge of the castle grounds, adjacent to St George's Chapel, looking back at Mr Maule. He signals me to move closer to the door of the Chapel, though I don't know why he has put me in this situation. Obediently, I edge forward, little by little. As I proceed, in the far distance, is: Mr Murray; Henry Firebrace;

Michelle Hockley

Mr Ashburnham; Mr Berkeley; Elizabeth Wheeler and Thomas Herbert; walking either side of a coffin, covered in a black pall without a hint of insignia.

'Charles', I whisper to myself as I stand tight up against the wall, watching their sombre parade. I don't move closer. The wind swirling about me increasing its pace. I pull my cloak tighter around me. Moments before they enter the church, snow flakes begin to fall, the wind subsides. All at once, the atmosphere changes to one of complete calm and serenity. The loving group who stood by Charles right to the end, move inside the chapel. I look down at my cloak, completely covered in snow. My eyes are drawn to the sky where I see, a chink of blue breaking through the thick clouds with a hint of sunlight. He's arrived in heaven. It is God who will take care of him now. Thank you God. Warm tears fill my eyes and start to fall. I am not inconsolable.

'Thank you Mr Maul. I appreciate your kindness.'

'Your welcome Madam Whorwood. All that you did for the king, that is the least the royal household could do for you.'

I smile. Everything has now been observed. That path has been travelled. My work here, is complete.

'Please drive on, Mr Maule.'

CHAPTER TWENTY SEVEN

Consequences Show Themselves
1650

'**G**ood morning Mrs Bower. Something smells good?' I say with a slight lilt in my voice as I enter the kitchen at Holton House, clutching a large bunch of fresh herbs from our burgeoning herb garden.

'Morning Madam Whorwood. You seem a little more yourself today.'

'It must be your cooking. All this country air,' I reply, whilst becoming distracted as I watch Brome junior walking past the kitchen window, carrying a musket over his shoulder.

'How is your mother keeping, Madam?'

'My stepfather's death is still raw, but I'm hoping her stoicism will help the immense loss,' I reply, bringing to mind the funeral a few months ago, dwelling on the fact that life as it once was, is chipping away at itself, leaving us more vulnerable each time it takes away our loved ones.

Mrs Bower offers me the pestle and mortar. I start to pummel the herbs, preparing an ointment for Mr Ball's aching joints, which his wife Jane, is collecting today.

'Don't leave on my account Mrs Bower,' as I see her making her way to exit the kitchen.

'It's not you Marm. I need to find Katherine Allen,' she replies with a furrowed forehead. 'She is supposed to be running an errand for me, but I've not seen her for a while.'

'Very well.'

'Now, where is that girl?' mutters Mrs Bower.

'Help. Help,' screams Mary Hurles from one of the bedrooms, causing me to drop what I'm doing and rush upstairs to her aid.

'What is it Mary?'

Without a reply, I stand at the open door of Brome Junior's chamber.

'Oh no,' I say, horrified, halted in my tracks.

'Who did this Mary?' I ask.

I see before me, inside Brome junior's bedchamber, his desk, chair and bed frame lying on their side. His bookshelves pulled down flat, and the trunks, open wide. I trip over the books scattered on the floor as I run to the open window. Saving myself by catching the sill, I peer out, expecting the worse, and see all his clothes strewn on the ground below.

'What has happened Mary? Please speak to me.'

'It's Brome junior. We are having such a lot of trouble with his behaviour, Marm.'

'This is not normal. Where is his father?'

'He left early with Katherine Allen. I think they've gone into Headington again Marm.'

'What do you mean, again?'

'I don't know what I mean,' she says, trying to tidy the room, avoiding eye contact.

'Come on Mary, this is not like you.'

'I've tried to keep the children happy but Brome junior is so headstrong. I can't keep him under control. His father and Lady Ursula always look the other way.'

'How long has this been going on?'

'It's been steadily getting worse since last year Marm, but he's never done anything quite as dramatic as this.'

'Not to worry now, Mary,' I say, holding her trembling hands in mine.

'Go to ask Mrs Bower to make you a mint tea and when you see Mr Truman, request he repairs the room. I shall go to find my son.'

Outside, the estate is quiet. I walk around the back of the house towards the stables hearing gunshots. Oh Lord.

Brome junior, what have you done? The shots continue, one after the other. As I get closer to the stables, three horses charge past me; one knocking me off balance as I hit against the barn wall. No, this can't be happening. Not my boy.

I rush inside the barn coming face to face with two more horses who both buck in unison, intent on liberating themselves from this nightmare. With seconds to spare, I throw myself out of their determined path. Their hooves drum on the ground beneath, freeing up my entrance to continue inside.

'Brome junior,' I shout. 'My darling.' Willing for there to be the faintest hint of life. A whimper or an angry roar. Anything.

As I move further inside, I see all the stables, except one, are empty. Doors flung wide. Silence has fallen, but for the padding of the lonesome horse inside its stall. I shut the door closed to continue down the barn.

'Brome, it's your Mama. Please Brome, are you here?'

Finally, sunk down, against the far wall, with gun still held under his arm, I see my boy. His shoulders quiver.

'Oh thank God, you are still alive.'

I calmly remove the weapon from his grip and sit down beside him.

'Oh my son. My poor, poor son,' holding him tightly in my arms, rocking him; feeling his heart beating.

His red, flushed face turns towards me. 'I'm sorry Mama.'

'Me too, Brome Junior. I too am so sorry.'

All I want to do is hold my boy. But there is no time to waste. The horses are scared for their lives and out of control, heading for the precious white herd on the edge of the estate.

'Now this is what we are going to do, Brome. Are you listening, my darling?' I hold his cheeks in my hands to be sure I have his attention.

'Oh Mama, I need you to help me.'

'I shall my darling. First, we must help the horses before they hurt someone in their panic or scare the deer?'

'Yes. I am sorry,' he replies.

'Come on then. Come on,' I say, pulling him to his feet, gently, but purposefully.

I jump on the last remaining horse and signal for Brome to jump on behind me.

'Quick, Brome.'

Having no time to tack up, I manage to balance the horse for us both; grabbing the mane as we gallop out.

'I see one,' shouts Brome junior. Over there, by the boundary wall.'

I pull the horse up, and Brome junior jumps off. He quickly manages to tame the escapee, enough to mount the stricken beast, before riding back to the stable. I grab another, keeping it by my side as I trot back, collect Brome junior, and ride out again together. Gradually, by either riding or walking the horses we bring them all, safely inside.

'Phew. Well done, my dear,' acknowledging his achievements.

Then my stomach somersaults, gathering all my senses, realising how damaged my fifteen year old son is. I guide him out of the barn into the sunlight suggesting we take a moment before returning to the house, sitting a while against the oak tree.

'How could they kill our king Mama?' blurts out Brome junior as he starts to lower himself to the ground. 'No one, but God, has the right to take away our king?' he says, hitting the ground with his clenched fist. 'They have killed a man, our king, sent to us by God.'

I put my arm around him, leaning against his broken body. But I'm speechless. I simply have no answer for my boy, because I too don't understand how to justify those evil signatures scribed upon that death warrant of a king who was chosen for us by God.

I am somewhat taken aback by Brome junior's distress of losing his king. If his upset was caused by the loss of his grandfather, I would not have been surprised, but for the demise of our king, is a surprise. Keeping our children off the battle field, was our way of protecting the young, but they have been on the front line the whole while; living in such turbulent times, creating enormous insecurities in their lives. I, being so wrapped up in the loss of a dear friend in Charles, hadn't thought how this might affect my children. Brome junior spent time at the royal court in his younger days, but somehow you think this loss, being predominately bound up in politics and religion, will effect only the adults, which of course is an oversight on my part. He is grieving for his king in a way I could never have imagined. The majority of his life has been blighted by war. The world in which both my children will grow is completely unknown to any of us. So how can we advise them on what to expect? We can't assure our children that everything will be fine because a nation directed without a sovereign, is something none of us have ever experienced.

'Mama. Why did you leave us so often?'

'I went to help King Charles, darling, but you were always on my mind, I never forgot about you. You do know that, don't you?'

'If you were helping Charles, why is he now dead?'

'Sometimes Brome, things are out of our control. We do not always achieve the outcome hoped for, but that must never stop you from trying.'

'Is this how it was for you and His Majesty?'

305

'Yes, darling. Parliament won in the end which meant the king could not be saved.'

'Does King Charles blame you Mama?' he enquires, as he draws himself closer to me.

'No, Brome. He knew I did what I could to help, even though in the end it was in vain.'

'I thought he'd be safe in the castle on the Isle of Wight, did you?'

'Yes. John Ashburnham and Berkeley thought so too, when they took him there from Hampton Court Palace. But they should have taken him in the opposite direction. It all happened so quickly, they couldn't be stopped from making that mistake.'

'Did you help Our Majesty when he was on the Isle of Wight? Did you go there?'

'I did yes, though it became more dangerous as intelligence became more sophisticated. One time, your Aunt Anne went to great lengths to stop me from travelling to the castle, to protect my safety.'

'How did you get there?'

'I hired a boat from the fishermen to make the crossing.'

'You were brave, Mama.'

'Come along now. Let us not dwell on the past. Let's get you inside.'

Standing up, pulling him to his feet, I link into his arm, to make our way back to the house.

'Mama. I think you quite enjoyed that ride didn't you?'

'Well, it was certainly energetic. Quite exciting for the first ride out, but by the fifth, it was not so good.'

As we approach the house, I see Jane Ball.

'The ointment. I haven't even started the prescription. Come on junior, we must run.'

'Hello Mrs Ball. Sorry. I was finishing the ointment. Please come inside. It won't take long,'

When I arrive in the kitchen I see two bottles already filled, labelled and placed on the table. I smile at Mrs Bower as I take them off the workstation.

'Thank you Mrs Bower.'

'You're welcome Marm. I could see you had your hands full. I too know a thing or two about recipes of this nature.'

'It would seem you do. Thank you,' I smile.

'Mrs Ball. Here we go,' putting the bottles inside her basket, wishing her husband a speedy recovery.

Mr Truman the footman, comes down the stairs, looking a little worse for wear.

'All done Marm.'

'Thank you Mr Truman,' I reply, hoping that we may

be getting on top of today.

A carriage draws up outside, and from the kitchen I hear doors closing, one by one; upstairs and downstairs. I make my way to the hallway. Mrs Bower closes the kitchen door. Mary Hurles appears to collect Brome junior before recoiling upstairs. Lady Ursula moves through the corridor towards the sitting room where she takes a long hard stare at me, as if to say something, but instead, closes the door behind her. Everyone has disappeared leaving me quite alone.

I hear giggles coming from outside. I recognise my husbands voice. The main door springs opens, spewing my husband and Katherine inside. Entwined in each others arms they manage to save themselves from falling to the floor, which for some unknown reason, their lack of control, appears to have caused them both, much hilarity. The two reprobates stand in front of me and their irresponsible guffawing comes to an abrupt end. Without releasing their hold of each other, they look directly at me.

'Brome, what is going on? Where have you been?'

Katherine steps forward creating the stance of a wench, with one hand on her hip, as my husband stumbles for balance at her release of him. Her breath, hot with spirits, she starts to belittle my authority, mocking what I have said.

'Brome, what is going on? Where have you been?' she repeats with an artificial voice.

'Thank you Miss Allen, that will be all, you can leave us now please.'

'Thank you Miss...' she starts.

I quickly interject. 'That is enough Miss Allen. Now Brome, what is going on?'

'What do you care Jane?' says Brome.

'Don't you have something to do for your stepfather? Oh sorry, I forgot, he's dead,' I gasp in shock which Katherine, refusing to leave, finds comical.

'How dare you Brome. How dare you. You disgust me, you drunken oaf.'

'You disgust...' starts Katherine about to repeat what I have said, thinking she is quite the charmer.

'Yes, yes, alright Katherine, that is quite enough, we get the picture. Maybe you need to go to your room to sober up, young lady.'

Katherine looks at Brome, who suggests it a good idea. 'Go on Katherine, you heard the lady. Though no lady is she, for she is a whore.'

'You are drunk Brome. I cannot communicate with you in this state, we shall speak when you are sober.'

Katherine stops half way up the stairs to shout to me in the hallway.

'In whose chamber shall I go to get sobered up me lady? Brome's or mine?'

Brome pushes past me to enter the sitting room.

'Not in here Brome,' calls out Lady Ursula.

'Sorry, mother,' he whimpers as he tries to close the door before losing his grip on the handle, slipping down the wooden clad wall, until he lands on the floor and begins to weep.

'Pull yourself together Brome,' I say as I go to help him back to his feet, bending down, grabbing one hand.

'Leave me Jane, you don't care about me. You have never cared about me.'

'That is not true Brome. You know I care for you. You know I don't like it when you drink heavily like this.'

'It's because you don't love me, that I drink Jane.'

'Now we know that is not true don't we. You know I love you, very much.'

I don't know why I do it, but every time he is despicable to me, I always try to make it better for him. The cruellest of actions are being played out before me, yet here I am, crouched beside my drunken husband, willing him to get to his feet; for everything to be alright. Why do I do that? Why not leave the useless specimen to find his own way back to normality?

'Come on now Brome. Do you want to go into the

drawing room, or upstairs to your room?' wherever that may be these days.

'To our chamber Jane. Our marital bed,' he says, which surprises me because, since the day he assumed I had a love affair with that Bendish person, he has never been in my bed, almost four years ago.

'Alright Brome, I shall take you to our bedchamber, though you'll need to help me to your feet. You are too heavy for me to do this on my own.'

'You'd do it for the king though,wouldn't you,' he shouts, which I ignore, realising how troubled my family is.

'Mama, what has happened to my father?' asks Diana as she comes bounding into the hallway from upstairs.

'Your papa has fallen over again Diana, but he will be fine once he is rested. Can you take one arm please? I shall take the other. Thank you, there's a good girl.'

We both manage to get Brome up stairs. Brome junior is nowhere in sight. His bedchamber door is tightly closed. I should imagine he is delighted at his father's state, being too preoccupied to learn what has been going on with the horses in his devilment today.

I put my husband in our bed to rest after removing his coat and boots.

'Come on Diana. Let us see if Joan has some fresh milk for you. Mrs Bower might have your favourite biscuits.'

'Can we take some to father and to Brome junior, please Mama?'

'Yes, of course we can my dear,' holding out my hand for her to take, praying she is made of stronger stuff than her father and brother.

CHAPTER TWENTY EIGHT

Not So Clever Now Are We?
June 1651

We desperately need respite from the sadness we so often endure. I sit in the drawing room at Holton House, writing a letter to keep in touch with my sister Anne whose husband, Sir Thomas Bowyer, sadly passed away four months ago, February 1651. I too struggle with my own domestic situation as Brome continues to ignore his wedding vows, openly spending time with Katherine, betraying me to the core, expecting me to turn a blind eye to the situation. Whether I am able to keep up this pretence is a different matter.

I finish my letter writing for the day, ready to open letters delivered this morning, though expecting nothing but the mundane without letters from dear Charles or Firebrace. The first letter on my pile today is excellent news. Brome junior has secured a place at St Mary Hall, Oxford University; beginning in October, Michaelmas term. I do hope this opportunity will provide him with relief from the problems at home and the past.

This second letter looks rather official; signed on delivery by the postmaster. As I register what I am reading, my heart misses a beat, blood drains from my face until I'm left cold with fear. It is a summons, for me to appear in court at the trial, already in progress, for the fraudulent dealings of Lord Howard Escrick. I don't disagree with his corrupt actions, but what has this to do with me? Perhaps I'm called to give evidence of his dishonest workings with the tailor and silk merchant. If so, that will be awkward, because I promised Lord Howard, I'd never divulge that information.

I read on, '...called to the stand through evidence supplied by a Mr Robert Cole.' I stop reading. Who is Mr Cole for heavens sake? Then pieces start to come to me. He was the courier who called, unannounced, to Holton. I struggle to recall details of this episode as so much water has travelled under the bridge since then; about four years ago. I remember him coming to the house. Think Jane. I remember him asking for fourteen pounds. Which seems to open the flood gates, because memories rush to my mind. I remember at the time I was adamant not to give him one penny of the money that I'd worked hard to obtain, wanting to give it all to the king. I take a moment to think, resting the letter on my lap. Surely I'm giving evidence associated with Lord Howard. Yes, that is it. I continue reading under my breath for this helps me to concentrate.

'Madam Whorwood. You are requested to take the stand at the House of Commons on this day, 21 June1651, after evidence raised by the plaintiff, the Committee for the Advance of Money, where you shall be read your sentence in association with case number 603.' Oh no. A sentence? What do I do? How is this possible? I sit quietly, trying to think about my dealings in this matter. Surely I can talk my way out of why I didn't give Mr Cole his fourteen pounds, but what does this have to do with Lord Howard? I can't make sense of this until I know exactly of what I am being accused. I look down at the note, my hands are shaking, the summoning is today. Do I go to them or do them come for me?

A knock at the door makes me jump in my seat. This must be a coincidence. I become flustered and quickly fold the letter and hide in the sewing box beneath the ribbons. I listen for Mr Truman to open the door. Another loud knock. No one goes to open. Where are our staff? Everyone has vanished today. I leave the dining room to walk towards the door, muttering that we employ servants yet I have to open the door myself. Where is everyone? Getting closer to the main door I'm hoping for it to be anyone but...

'Madam Whorwood? Madam Jane Whorwood?'

A stern looking man stands before me. A black carriage with tiny windows is paused on the bridge over the moat. Two more officials wait either side. I try to take it all in. Is this happening? I stare at the scene beyond.

'Yes sir.' I say, to the unfamiliar person in front of me from whom I take the papers he offers me.

'We have a warrant for your arrest Madam. If you come quietly, it will be better for everyone.'

'Arrest? You don't have the right person. I'm sorry, but you've had a wasted journey.'

'We can talk about that at the House of Commons Madam. My orders are to arrest you.'

'I should at least tell someone.'

'Yes, do Marm. Let your husband know. He can come with you if he chooses, we can take one for the Spectators' Gallery.' Oh Lord, there are going to be spectators.

I rush into the house intending to speak to the first person I see, which fortunately, is Mary.

'I have to go to London, Mary.'

'What again Madam? Are you sure? I thought, with the king gone and all that, things would quieten down for you,' she says standing confused. So much that Mary doesn't know about me, yet I've held her in my trust for almost seventeen years.

'I won't be long. Can you let Mr Whorwood know I have been called to give evidence at the House of Commons?'

'Yes. How long will you be?'

'Sorry Mary, I am not sure.' Knowing full well that I've been arrested, so it could be a number of years, but I don't mention that.

'Madam, please. We need to be getting along. I have my orders,' says the commissioner for the Commons.

'Yes, yes. Give a woman a moment please,' I bark, unable to contain the anguish I am feeling.

I reluctantly proceed to the carriage with the commissioner who grabs my arm to hurry me along. I leave Mary on the steps, but I don't look back at her. Closer to the carriage, I see John Stampe coming towards the house.

'Hello Madam.' He doffs his cap politely.

'Hello Mr Stampe. Lovely to see you,' trying to sound as normal as possible whilst being hauled by the commissioner, hoping to avoid a conversation.

'Is everything alright?' asks Stampe. 'These trappings look awfully serious.'

He recognises what is happening here, nothing gets past John Stampe.

'Yes, thank you. Everything is fine. I am going to speak for a friend of mine,' I reply, trying to loosen the grip on my arm as they shove me into the black carriage.

'That's good of you,' he shouts.

I see him wave as I look through the tiny window, knowing he hasn't believed a word of what I have said.

When I arrive at Westminster, it's not long before I am ushered to take the stand. From what I've grasped, this trial has been in session for some months now.

The Court Clerk begins, 'Madam Whorwood, you have been brought to court to hear your sentence for the involvement you had with the late Sir Robert Bannister's discharge papers for monies owed to the Committee. Can we call the first witness please? Mr Dallison?'

Monies owed? What is this? Is it the fourteen pounds, to this Cole? Oh no. Not Dallison, he is the clerk I took great pains to avoid for his scrupulous attention to detail. What has he got to do with Mr Cole's fourteen pounds? I listen carefully to what he has to say, as two officers stand beside me.

'I wasn't present on the day Madam Whorwood came to the Haberdasher's Hall, My Lord. Instead, she met with Lord Howard, who, may I add, has collected thousands of pounds for the Committee and the good of the land.'

We know how he got his hands on that don't we? I

318

say to myself. Knowing how he deceived so many tradesmen for his own self gain.

'She,' continues Dallison, pointing right at me. 'She forced Lord Howard to sign the papers in my absence. Mr Cole, courier, came to me a week later, upset by being out of pocket for the efforts he had made to collect Sir Robert's dues. Mr Cole informed me that Madam Whorwood refused him any money for expenses from that which Sir Robert Bannister had bestowed upon her. Though I should add that Mr Cole has since received the sum from Alderman Adams, in his role as executor to Sir Robert Bannister's estate.'

The problem is solved then. If Mr Cole received his fourteen pounds, why am I here? Did I force Howard to sign? Yes, I suppose I did. Though I had my reasons. We were in the midsts of a civil war, for crying out loud.

'Thank you Dallison. Is that all?' asks the Judge.

'For now, My Lord.'

Alderman Adams, now released from the Tower, takes the stand next, explaining that he saw the discharge papers that I gave him, reimbursing me with six hundred pounds as requested by Lady Margaret Bannister. Again, to me, all this seems straight forward. I know my plan was solid. I am quite confident that I didn't leave any loose ends in this one. The authorities can't blame me for not giving Mr

319

Cole his fourteen pounds, for it was not my responsibility to pay his expenses. Cole has nothing to do with me.

As the trial continues, I realise that I am but a cog in the wheel of Lord Howard's trial, where during an extensive investigation of his financial misconduct, the Commons have unearthed the small matter involving, Howard, myself, Bannister and Cole. I listen to further evidence being brought to the stand including Lord Howard's version of the day I went to Haberdashers' Hall, where he reports to the court, that I put him under a good deal of pressure.

'Mr Dallison,' enquires the Judge, 'do you wish to report any further findings after what you have heard?'

'Yes My Lord. I have the corresponding ledger here, as further evidence,' says Martin Dallison, holding up the exhibit for the court room to see.

'You will see My Lord, there is no record of payment for six hundred pounds on the day Madam Whorwood received

the discharge papers signed by Lord Howard; further evidence that Madam forced the papers to be signed without payment.'

Stupid Lord Howard. Why didn't he at least write in the ledger that the money had been received, regardless of whether the accounts tallied?

'Mr Adams,' says the Lord presiding officer. 'It is not

the first time you have been sentenced, having already spent time in the Tower. Do you have anything more to add?'

Mr Adams rises. 'I did question Madam Whorwood when she came to my house, as to why the discharge papers were signed by the Chairman of the Committee. She informed me that Mr Dallison was absent from the office and Lord Howard was covering that role.'

'Adams,' starts the judge. 'You know the discharge papers can only be signed by Mr Dallison, so why did you believe these papers acceptable?'

'We were in difficult times My Lord. I didn't question any further I'm afraid. I see now, that I should have. If I had been under any suspicion that these papers were inferior, I would not have handed Madam Whorwood the six hundred pounds, My Lord.'

'Thank you Mr Adams. We have heard all we need to hear. I shall prepare my verdict.'

I quickly interject. 'Can I speak, your Lord?'

'No Madam Whorwood. You are not here to speak. We have all the evidence we need. You are here to listen. I am here to prepare a verdict.'

I look across at Alderman Adams, but he drops his head. Then I turn to Lord Howard, who looks quite concerned, for this is not the only case in his long drawn out investigation.

'Order. Order. Members of the court. Order please,' demands the Court Clerk as the Judge starts to give his summary.

'The papers were without doubt produced under duress from Madam Whorwood. No money was paid to the Committee for outstanding monies owed. Lord Howard, has expressed that he felt uncomfortable signing the papers in Mr Dallison's absence, but Madam insisted they be signed that day. Lord Howard appears to have fallen into the trap set by Madam Whorwood and I am sure the reason for him feeling under such pressure, will surface during the course of our investigation into Lord Howard's fraudulent conduct. In the meantime, continuing with case 603, it is clear that the Bannisters paid Madam Whorwood's expenses in good faith and reimbursed her for the papers they received. Mr Cole has added further evidence of Madam Whorwood's deceit, but has since been compensated for his out of pocket expenses by Alderman Adams. Therefore, it leaves the matter of the discharge papers, not being signed by Mr Dallison, as regulation demands and the amount of £600, a payment due to the committee and still wanting. I am therefore, left with no alternative, but to deem the documents under court ruling, null and void.'

'Please all rise for the Lord to give his sentence to Madam Whorwood,' calls the Court Clerk.

Oh no. I should be allowed to say something in my defence.

'Please let me speak My Lord,' I yell across the room, until I'm yanked back by the two officers standing beside me.

'Quiet in Court,' says the clerk.

'No. I should be allowed to have my say. It was not like that.'

'Madam. Do you want me to double your sentence? Or do you want to be quiet?' demands the Judge.

'But sir...' I start.

'I commit Madam Jane Whorwood to prison until the sum of six hundred pounds is paid to the court for her involvement in receiving discharge papers through deceit and wrong doing, acquiring six hundred pounds fraudulently from Parliament and the Bannisters' estate.'

I start to pant as my heart quickens. I am not a criminal. I did none of this for my own gain. The room spins. I feel myself drop to the floor and momentarily black out. I feel someone grab my shoulder.

The clerk shouts, 'Take her down.'

I try to struggle, but it's no good.

'I did it for the king,' I shout as they pull me out of the court room. 'Our King. Not for me. Not like Lord Howard, feathering his own nest. You have to let me go. Let me go. Get off me.'

I make a final tug with the little energy I have, but my arms and body are held so tightly I can't break free. A cell door bangs open wide, and their grip eases as I'm pushed inside amongst criminals.

'You can't do this. I'm not a criminal. You have to let me speak. Someone will pay the fine, I am sure.'

Though of course in reality I am not sure about that, because no one knows where I am. No one until today, even knew I was involved in this scam. If my stepfather was alive, he would understand.

* * *

Six days have passed and no sign of anyone paying the fine. I can do nothing except bide my time as do my fellow criminals who sit around the wet walls, languishing in sores of puss. The food is disgusting and so far, I've refused to eat this muck. Each time the warden enters this holding pen with a plate of gruel, I ask the same question, getting the same answer.

'Someone needs to tell my husband where I am.'

'We keep telling you, Whorwood. We've contacted that drunk of a husband and he's asked us to let you rot and we are not asking him anymore.'

'No. He wouldn't say that. Ask him again. I can't

stay here.' I spit at the door for I am helpless, showing my disdain for the authorities.

Where is everyone on the outside? Why are they not helping me? Perhaps Brome hasn't told my family? Wouldn't the authorities tell my family? They must know my mother is the Countess Dirleton. Nothing like this seems to matter anymore; no more privileges now the king has gone. Oh Charles, if you knew what sacrifices I made for you.

My daydreaming goes on. Day in and day out. Nothing else to fill my time. I keep track of the days by scratching a mark on the ground beside me each time we are brought a meal.

'Come on then,' shouts the warden, 'let me have your attention,' he says, as the cell door is thrown open with more force than usual.

I lift my head from my knees expecting to see either a plate of gruel or another reprobate joining our family of criminals. I stay seated. I am not moving to make room for anyone. No one enters the cell, other than the prison warden who comes inside, without substance or crook.

'Prisoner, 132789.' A pause. I've no idea what the warden is requesting.

'Do we have prisoner 132789?' he repeats.

'Why don't you tell us who is prisoner 132...or

whatever the number is? Then that way, we shall know to whom you wish to address, won't we?' I demand, for I have no idea what number I am. I didn't even know I had a number. Goodness.

'132789,' repeats the warden, continuing to get no response.

Maybe it's me? Maybe everyone else in here knows their tag. Though looking at them, it's hard to imagine they know their own name, let alone a number consisting of at least six digits. I wonder how long they've been in here, held up in this pen. Does no one care enough to collect at least one of them?

'Is it me?' I shout.

'It's a Madam Whorwood.'

'Yes, that's me.' Why didn't he say that in the first place? Perhaps it's to allow us anonymity. Either way, 132789, is me.

'This way prisoner. This way. Quickly now.'

'Where are you taking me?'

I eventually manage to get to my feet without the help from anyone but I can barely move, let alone quickly. On leaving the cell I'm pushed up a corridor towards a desk at the far end.

'Sign here Madam.'

'Why? What is happening?'

'You are free to go. A fine of six hundred pound has been paid.'

'Free?'

'Yes. Now on your way. We don't wish to see your pockmarked face in here any time soon. Do you hear me?'

'Charming, I'm sure.'

I turn to the prison warden, 'see my husband does love me. He came good in the end. I knew he would, he must have been busy with estate management, busy time, summer,' I say smugly. Proud of my Brome, even though it took him so long.

'No, Madam. Not that drunken oaf. No Marm. It was the good, Countess Dirleton. She came good for you. Now off you go.'

I leave the basement, being escorted up the stairs. In the distance I see my darling mother waiting for me. Even though I feel weak and drained, I try to run to her.

'Mama I am so sorry. Thank you for helping me.'

'You are the double of your stepfather Jane, its like he was still alive.'

'Sorry. I thought I was doing right. At the time, it felt right, when I thought I could help Charles, Mama.'

'Let's get you home shall we? Would you be okay to stay in London for a night before going back to Holton? You ought to get cleaned up before you see your husband and your children.'

'Thank you. Yes, that would be good.'

Feeling safe again, thankful not to face Brome in this emotional and physical state, I settle into the short coach journey back to our Charing Cross home. I let out a sigh as we drive past the royal mews, recognising that Rayleigh has long since left us, taking with him the secrets we learnt together, especially that of my marriage. Tears come forth at the realisation, that if my mother had not paid the six hundred pounds, then my husband would have left me in the prison for ever. He must despise me more than I could ever imagine.

CHAPTER TWENTY NINE

Spring 1657

I try to call out again, 'let me out Brome, please let me out,' but it's all in vain. Within this forgotten, neglected room, high in the narrow turrets of this loathsome Holton House, where Brome locks me away for days at a time, I know I can't be heard. Lank hair falls about my face. The clothes I wear are heavy about my weakened frame. I try to gain control of my trembling body by curling tight upon the thin, worn blanket, laying on the damaged floor. The hunger pangs are all too familiar. The cold air would leave me numb but for the constant beat of my nerves jumping inside a malnourished body, that clasps to what remains of the most precious gift; life. A crack in the roof affords me some light, though heavy eyelids fight to view the changing sky as it rotates from blue to dusk, until dense darkness yields this blackened space.

My gaoler, Brome Whorwood, offers me less and less reprieve from the cruelty he has imposed on me for five long years; since the day I arrived home from prison in June 1651. It is that summer day, when I thought I was free, that plays over and over inside my aching skull. I fought back that day. I tried to make him understand.

'Where are you taking me Brome?' I shouted. 'Why are you pushing me up these narrow stairs? Let me go I tell you.'

I struggled with him and I struggled fiercely.

'You are a criminal,' he said. 'Criminals will be imprisoned,' he shouted, twisting and pulling every strand of hair, holding me tight beneath my chin, yanking and snagging my head. I remember him opening the door to the smallest rooms in one of the tallest turrets at the top of the house and pushing me inside, slamming the door shut, turning the lock.

'Brome my darling I can explain. Brome, please let me out,' I shouted. 'Please let me see my children. Brome. Brome,' I begged him as I banged hard on the door.

'I don't want to hear your explanations anymore,' he said. 'You are a whore and a low life thief.'

'I can explain Brome. I did it for the king. They imprisoned me for what I did to help the king.'

'Oh yes, you'd do anything for that stubborn, incompetent, ineffectual idiot, who had no intention of listening to reason. Instead, wasting everyone's time and money chasing him around the country after his pointless escapes.'

330

'Brome that is unfair. Our Majesty wanted the best for his people and his country.'

'You left a family who loved you, Jane. A family who needed you. And for what? I shall tell you what, to be a whore and a criminal. You disgust me Jane Whorwood. How dare you bring such shame upon our family? How dare you?'

His voice eventually cracked with emotion that day. You see, I think he did love me then, but he hurt so much because he thought I'd betrayed him. I listened as his body slid down the wall outside of this little room, sensing he was sitting scrunched up with his head in his hands letting the warm tears drip through his pain. I knelt close to the wall, as if by my touching the cold hard stone of the room, he would feel the warmth of my heart against his. I begged for council. But instead he shut me out, like the door he had just locked.

'I don't want to hear anymore lies or the fantasies that live inside your head, or the promises you cannot keep,' he said.

'What promises Brome? The promise to love you? I do love you Brome.'

'You promised to be my wife and a mother to my children.'

'I kept those promises,' I argued in my defence. Then

rage boiled inside me to retort his injustice upon me. 'It is you who shunned the vows we made before our Lord, whoremongers and adulterers God will judge. It was you who left me for another. It was you who left the family when we needed you; taking yourself into exile for three long years whilst we waited here to fight your battles, to help our country.'

I knew I had said too much. Too much truth for him to bear. Then for a moment, as I heard the lock unlatch I felt hope return. He will open the door and take me in his arms once more. No. Instead, his heavy boots turned from me that day, to descend the cold stone steps from the turret, to enter the arms of a servant, where my path was set. I knew then, I had lost him.

When lady Ursula died in late 1653 I had every intention to start afresh, taking my position as Lady of the Manor. That was not to be. Brome had a different idea. At every turn I was thwarted by the rampart that is Katherine Allen, her behaviour fully supported by my husband, leaving me superfluous in our marriage. I am but a thorn in his side. A living obstacle to their true happiness. The severe harshness I receive from their reprehensible acts towards me, make themselves felt. Whilst the cuts, bruises and broken limbs do eventually ameliorate with an ointment or a splint, it's the emotional heinous that remains matted and tangled in this doomed backwater, this atrocious pile consumed by its sullied moat that surrounds it, refusing to mend. If stone walls could be built by Satan, then this house surely has all the markings of the devil's work, tainted further by the insidious Katherine Allen with her relentless maleficent schemes upon my husband.

During this past week the situation has gotten much worse. I do believe this time, my husband has every intention to release me when I am dust that he can sweep beneath the cracks of time. Once I am deceased, the law will allow Brome to marry another. Whilst I am alive, stalemate will remain. I want her gone from the house so I have the opportunity to restore my marriage, without this third party tantalising our happiness. Though tonight I find myself all but defeated; struggling to cling to one last breath. My head is lighter than ever before; floating far away from me. I can be assured that I fought to the end even though I have lost every piece of dignity I ever owned. Everything is slipping away. I feel limp. I can't curl tight anymore, it's too painful. I feel myself fading fast. 'My Lord, am I to come to you this night? Please tell me what I am to do?'

An owl hoots in the stillness. White deer scream their cry. I urge them to jump to clear the wall that keeps them bound as I should have done, when I had the chance. Another noise I hear, one coming closer to the house far below the turrets. I try to lift my head. Carriage wheels crunch over the gravel. Is it arriving or leaving? I don't know. I lose the battle against my eye lids again. I have to rest. I am weak and thirsty the sores on my dry mouth smart. I fade again. Am I leaving this world now? Is this what it's like to release oneself from this contaminated existence? Footsteps tap on the stone steps outside my room. They come closer. I hear my name. It's Mary Hurles she must have been away these past days.

'Madam,' she shouts as she tries the door. 'Oh no you're locked inside again. I am so sorry.'

I don't reply, I don't have the strength.

'Stand back Marm. I shall try to push the door open.' I don't move. I can't move. I hear more footsteps on the steps. A scream outside the door. Twists and turns upon the shallow landing.

'Ouch. Get off me Katherine. Who do you think you are?' says Mary.

'Trying to help the interloper are we?' says Katherine, gloating at what I've become, as she has done so many times before.

'That is my Madam you are chastising. I am sick and tired of your behaviour. Your disrespect for her is of unacceptable proportions. Because you sleep with the master of the house, doesn't give you the right to speak to another human being in this way or behave the way you do. Madam Whorwood is ten times braver than you. She is more resilient than you will ever know. You won't get what you want. You will never marry that disgusting man. He will spit you out as look at you for Madam will never leave this world so you can take her place. Give me the key to this room. Do something good for once.'

I hear Katherine's evil voice. 'What? You want me to let her out to cause trouble between my love for Brome? I don't think so. He doesn't want her pockmarked skin anywhere near him, he wants youth to love, not that ageing wench. She's been locked in there these past five days without food or water so she should by now have rotted and gone to Hell as my dear Brome intends.'

'Five days. Oh my Lord. We must open this door fast,' shrieks Mary.

'Get off my hair,' shouts Katherine. 'I shall call my Brome if you carry-on.'

'I shall carry-on. So get him up here and fast, preferable with a key. We have a woman in there who has done more for her country than you would even care to know, yet, she is being starved before our eyes.'

All I can do is listen to the scuffle on the other side of the door as the fight continues, until I hear a well aimed slap, which from the scream is a blow delivered by Mary.

Then silence. Oh know, Mary has knocked her out. As much I want Katherine gone, I don't want Mary in the dock for murder.

'You dog. You will pay for that,' threatens Katherine.

'That is only the start, you ugly harlot. If you don't get the key and let my Madam out of this room there will be plenty more where that slap came from. When you've done that, please do the next right thing and pack your bag, for you are not wanted here.'

I hear Brome's heavy footing. The roar of his angry tones bellows inside the turret.

'What is going on here? The pair of you are like cat's in the alley.' 'Katherine my darling, you are hurt, let me kiss that better for you, come here my love.'

'For goodness sake, Mr Whorwood,' says Mary, 'open the door. You don't want to be accused of murder like your father do you?' I hear her run down the steps away from the fallout of her rhetoric. Where has she gone? I hope she's not leaving.

I hear the latch turn to open. I pull myself along the floor to take my chance. I feel for the handle in the dark but I have no strength and fall backwards. I try again. This time getting to my feet. My instinct is to leave the house, but where shall I go? As I open the door, clinging to the wall, my eyes are out of focus. I see only the outline of Katherine and Brome embracing; parting briefly as I stumble through their hold. I teeter on the edge of the first narrow stair letting myself fall forward hoping to engage some sort of momentum in my limbs. One flight after another I manage to remain upright, being drawn by the candlelight downstairs. Without a thimble full of energy left, driven only by fear that Brome will catch me, I keep moving. I see the last flight, still not knowing where I am going. In the hallway, Mary stands with my cloak, hat and gloves.

'Madam, quickly,' she whispers.

'Where are we going Mary?'

'You have to get out of here. I shall stay and talk with Diana.'

Mary slings the cloak around my shoulders. As she puts on my hat, she comes close to my ear.

'Walk in the direction of Elizabeth Ball and William Elliot's cottage. Mr Stampe will meet you along the way to help. I know you can do it Madam. You have to do it.'

'Mr Stampe? Why is he involved in this commotion?'

'I've seen him. He was concerned about the noise. Now go Jane. Quickly. Go before Brome gets bored of consoling Katherine and comes to look for you.'

I take my gloves from Mary as she hands me a lantern, encouraging me out of the door. Slowly, tripping over my steps, barely able to hold the lantern in my hand, I stumble in what I believe to be the right direction, but I can't do it. I can't. I don't have the strength of mind or body. I don't even know if I want to be saved. I shall give up now. God is calling me tonight, I know he is. The torture I endure everyday from my husband has gone too far. My body is heavy. No control over my legs. I fall against the shrubbery landing at the base of the oak tree, still within the estate, dropping the lantern on the ground. I am sorry Diana and Brome Junior – I cannot go on but I shall always love you. I feel a reassuring grasp around me as I'm lifted gently into the air, this is it, I am leaving this world.

'I got you now Madam,' says Mr John Stamp. 'You are safe now Marm.'

Mr Stampe starts to shout out for someone. We must be nearing the cottage for I hear Elizabeth Ball, then feel the soft divan and warmth of the fire against my skin.

'Oh my good Lord,' cries Elizabeth. 'What has happened to Madam?'

'From what Mary Hurles tells me,' replies John Stampe, 'she's been treated badly again up at the house. She's been denied food and water for five days. I think she is close to the end. Can you make her comfortable in her last hours?'

'Brome Whorwood?' 'Yes, it is. He's taken to one of his turns again I think,' says Mr Stampe.

'Taken a turn? That is generous of you Mr Stampe. You are too forgiving. He's the double of his father. Sir Thomas was the same, which is why Lady Ursula never spoke to anyone, too scared of the consequences. Oh but she should have supported this poor soul, and helped her. Not looked on whilst her son took his father's mantle, leaving this poor girl to fight her own battles.'

They think I'm asleep or unconscious, but as I drift, I can hear everything they are saying, but too weak to respond. It's not long before William Elliot comes into the room. Mr Stampe bids farewell as Elizabeth takes William to the parlour. I drift into a deep sleep but woken by the comforting aroma of home cooking. Taking every spoonful of thick broth, I'm fed like a baby. The quivers in my body gradually subside. I know Mary will settle Diana, for she is good at explaining and consoling. Well, she's had plenty of practise over the years. Brome junior need never know anything of this, as he continues his tour of Europe. I pray for a good night's sleep without being disturbed by Brome, demanding me to return to the house where I fear, next time, I shall not survive.

* * *

My concern, that Brome would demand my return to the house is so far, unfounded. I have resided at Ms Ball's cottage for two weeks and in that time, no attempt has been made by him to even look in on me, let alone try to make amends or apologise for his harsh behaviour towards me. The villagers visit, though sometimes in large groups, which is tiring. Last week I saw Margaret, our servant from London. She arrived on behalf of my mother who is too sick to travel. She visited again yesterday, with the final arrangements for me to leave Holton, with the help of my mother's financial support until an alternative solution can be found. I have toyed relentlessly with this decision, for to save my own life, I forego all access to my children, leaving them without the presence of a mother in their lives; abandoning my little ones. Who, although are not so little anymore, still need their mother - they will always need their mother, as I do mine. Perhaps in time, we shall meet and be together when I can explain. I know she is in good hands for her father adores her with all his heart. Mary Hurles promises she will stay to keep an eye on her so she doesn't suffer too much from my abandonment. The alternative is too bleak. If I remove Diana, I shall be sent to gaol for stealing Brome's property, which in turn, will deny her of any financial support and she will be left to fend for herself. Whilst it seems so very awful to leave her behind, the alternative actions are beyond selfish. My mother and I are in agreement, that I must come away from Holton and accept that the marriage has failed. To stay in the house with Brome and Katherine has obviously become untenable, so I must be strong, and walk away.

* * *

Alone in the carriage, early evening, I arrive at my safe passage, taking refuge in the parish of St Andrew's, Holborn, in the City of London; a secure haven arranged by my mother.

'Here we are Madam. This is the address Countess Dirleton gave me. Is this right?' asks the driver as he peers into the carriage.

I look up at the rows of houses before me. The despair I sense, tells me this is wrong, but for now, this is right.

'Thank you sir. Yes.'

'You go on in. I shall bring your luggage.'

I find the key but fumble to locate the lock on this unfamiliar door. A little nervous I think. I feel uncomfortable. The smallest task seems difficult. I hear footsteps behind the closed door. I drop the key to the ground. 'Damn. Why does nothing go right?' The door opens.

'Language Jane Ryder. Language.' I look up quickly,

recognising the voice.

'Sarah. I didn't know you were here.' I hug her so fast, almost losing my balance, as the driver interjects after carrying all my baggage to the door.

'Will that be all Marm? All your luggage is here.'

'Thank you,' offering him a coin for his excellent service.

'Leave those, Miss Jane. William will bring them in for you,' says Sarah.

'William is here too?' My mind flashes back to times when Sarah and William would greet us at the home in Kingston-upon-Thames when we visited the country. We would hardly wait to greet them, because we were so eager to see our rooms.

'William and I are now wed, Miss Jane, so we have to move in a sort of duet ensemble.' I smile, recalling how Sarah always manages to take life in her stride. Always making the best of whatever is laid in front of her.

'How will you fare in the City of London, Sarah, after the sleepy village of Kingston Upon Thames?'

'Oh we shall cope somehow and if we don't, we shall have to call on Margaret, your London servant, for help,' she replies, having an answer to bolster her claim.

Sarah shows me around the house which is neat and tidy, with a small yard outback that I can just make out, as dusk starts to draw-in. Small, but perfect for my stay with a charming, friendly atmosphere. Sarah always makes sure of that, which is, for now, all that matters. The fresh flowers placed in each room add a little brightness too. She is as thoughtful now, as she was all those years ago, long before the unrest of the civil war. Even when I contracted small pox she was encouraging. What a long time ago that now seems.

'Hello Madam,' says William.

'Congratulation William, on your marriage to Sarah.'

'Thank you Marm. It is good to see you after so long,' William replies, in his usual quiet, considered manner; quite the opposite to Sarah, who is most often excited, organised and forthright. Sarah starts to coordinate her ship.

'Miss, if you go into the sitting room I shall bring you your supper. You must be starving my dear.'

'Sarah, please don't worry about formalities today, I shall stay with you as you prepare in the parlour. I don't want to be away from your side yet.'

'Alright as you please. This way then.'

'You realise,' Sarah says, I had to fight off Margaret to get this position, she so wanted to be here with you, but she is with your mother, who I understand, is not so well.'

'No. She sometimes is a little weary, getting older you see.'

343

I follow her around the parlour from one work station to another, before taking a seat at the large wooden table adorned with a sumptuous bowl of fruit.

'Now let's see what we can find young Jane to eat to fatten her up,' mutters Sarah, bringing out from the pantry an array of already prepared pies, cheeses, and ham.'

'That should do it Sarah, thank you.'

'Not quite, young Jane,' as she goes to fetch the newly baked manchette, which she remembers is my favourite.

'For my first meal here, Sarah, can I invite you and William to join me please. We have so much catching up to do.'

'You will get me sent to Tyburn Hill, if anyone finds out,' replies Sarah.

'After what I've been through these past few years, I shall hang, if anyone will.'

Sarah is flattered by my invite, looking at me in slight disbelief, then sets down the plate of food and goes quickly to fetch William before I change my mind.

* * *

As night falls heavy, I'm reluctant to enter my bedchamber, but I can avoid it no longer. It's inside this room where I am sure to meet solitude, where my mind will toss and turn, keeping me from sleep. As I enter, already my stomach turns with the reality of my failings as a wife and mother. I watch the street below as I close the drapes. Carriages going past on their final fare. People walking to close their day. I recognise how tired and run down I am, but I must find strength to fight back for the sake of my children. I owe that much to them. This is a good place to give me thinking time. This is what I need. I blow out the candles. The soft clean linen is kind to my tired, aching body, but I don't let go. Instead, I clench the covers as my mind winds up like a spinning top. I am not relaxed. How could I be? I am not afraid. I am angry.

Thoughts start to gather speed, taking on a life of their own, as I churn over and over in my mind, fretting about this and that. I can't sleep. I sit bolt up right. Pounding the pillow to refresh the feathers before placing it back beneath my head. Irritated. Frustrated. Why are women expected to forego their independence to these useless men? If, in 1634 I'd taken charge of my own life, I wonder where I would be now? What dreams could I have fulfilled? Instead, I was whisked into a despicable family to save a brutal tyrant from a sentence of murder, buckled to a half-witted husband, who in the end when he so elected, left me washed up and done in, replacing me with another.

'Ten of the clock. Red sky. Shepherds' delight,'

Michelle Hockley

The Night Watchman's shout, recovers my rational thinking. The chain of constant, rapid thoughts is broken. I surrender the charging battalion inside my mind and welcome the silence of sleep.

CHAPTER THIRTY

19 September 1657

'What is she doing here?' screams Brome, seeing me standing at the back of St Bartholomew's church in Holton. 'Get her out of here. It's her fault. Get her out of here,' he continues.

I flinch, pressing my back closer into the wall as four ushers make their way towards me at my husband's command, halted by the voice of reason from solicitor, Mr Davies.

'Enough Mr Whorwood. At least allow your wife to grieve for her son. Can't you see her heart is broken from this tragedy.'

Brome doesn't retaliate verbally, instead he throws his arms in the air and stomps away.

Mr Davies leads me to a seat some distance from my daughter, who I see standing close to her father's side. A semblance of calm is being restored against a backdrop of gentle, soft tones from the choir. The purity of voice becomes more voluminous, filling the small chapel with their sound as my son's encased body is carried slowly and purposefully towards the altar, lowered upon the trestle. Through my tears I see Diana look in my direction. I manage to raise a smile, but in a moment, without expression, she has turned away her gaze, leaving me as cold as the stone beneath my feet. I want to tell her everything will be alright. But nothing is right. The death of her dear brother without her mother by her side will be too much for her to bear. She will never forgive me. How can she ever understand such betrayal from her mother?

I'm weaker than ever having lost my son in his twenty second year, who I believed one day, would blossom into a fine young man. Though Brome junior never did settle at anything. He showed uncontrollable behaviour on the European tour, which I tried to convince myself was high spirits. He was disrespectful to both his tutor and travelling companion. He refused to learn any of the foreign languages he encountered; constantly in strong debate or disagreement, remaining headstrong and frustrated. On returning to England, finding his mother had abandoned the family home, he took it upon himself to travel to the Isle of Wight, taking an unseaworthy vessel, where he met his maker, tossed out to the high seas in ferocious waves. Was it my fault as my husband believes? Did he embark on such a deathly voyage to find answers of his mother's wartime ventures? I think of the time he set free the horses across the estate, where his frustration blinded his common sense, where he was wild and unseasoned. I expected one day he would tame himself, but that was sadly not to be.

The pallbearers walk slowly from the altar, taking my child to enter Brome Chapel where he will find peace at the side of his sister Elizabeth, grandfather and grandmother Whorwood. The choir resounds once more, attempting to lift our spirits, to take away the pain we feel. The college of Arms will not carry out any formal protocol or pomp and ceremony. No ensigns of gallantry awarded to embellish the black pall. No honours. What did the world offer my son other than conflict? His final struggle on this earth, in the waters of the Solent, was to save himself in that leaking boat, to which he did not have the strength to overcome. Was he drunk that day, like his father? Was he running away from something? Did he instigate the crossing or his friend, George Croke, who was older than him, who he'd met at Oxford? So many unanswered questions that will forever remain inside that tomb.

As Brome turns to follow our son's body into the chapel I lower my head so as not to make eye contact. His feet stop at my side. I feel his alcoholic breath brush my face as he bends down to my ear to speak in an overly pronounced whisper.

'You can leave now Jane. You have seen all you need to see here.'

I pull back from his face that smothers my space to look towards him. I see he is full of worry and wretchedness. I want to reach out to him. We have history. It's our son who is lying cold in the chest he follows. We were happy once. We adored our little family. I need my husband to reach out to me. I am no longer strong but torn apart at every juncture.

As Brome leaves the church with shoulders hunched, I follow after him; quickening my pace to catch up with him as he walks away.

'Brome my love. Please don't shut me out today,' I say, stroking his back that is turned on me. 'We are both hurting more than ever. We need to be here for each other. Is that too much to ask of you?'

He turns around slowly to look down on me. He is not angry any more. He is expressionless. His eyes black, vacant, boring into my soul.

I gently touch his arm again. 'Please Brome. Let us be kind to each other today.'

I'm relieved as his face softens. I follow his gaze. But he isn't responding to me, it's something beyond me, over my shoulder towards the church door. He smiles at someone in the distance. His face lights up again. I follow his eyes to turn towards the lightness of his regard. It's Katherine Allen. She strides forth to receive Brome's loving smile, snuggling by his side, supporting her protruding stomach. I gasp aloud. I can't help myself. I'm aghast. I am hurt. My eyes transfixed on her hands as they circle the bump she incubates, highlighting their baby within. Without moving my head, still transfixed on her stomach, I lift my eyes up to Brome, saying nothing, with an expression of waiting for an explanation. He looks absently at me once more, putting his arm around Katherine's shoulder to hold her closer. His reassurance confirms that he is there for her, when today, he should be here for me.

'Come on Katherine my sweet. Are you feeling unwell?' he says.

'No, my dear, we are both feeling fine,' she replies, continuing to gently caress her tummy, drawing Brome even closer as I stand rooted to the ground, feeling hollow inside.

'Where is young Diana? He asks. 'Where is my poor, suffering child?'

Immediately, hoping to enrol myself in membership to the happy fold, I join in, 'Diana is coming,' but no one acknowledges me. My addition is not welcomed. I am but an outcast as Brome encourages Diana to join them.

'Diana, my darling Come along precious one. Let us take you back to the house for something to eat,' he says.

Diana does as her father suggests, without a second glance to her Mama. She was once my little angel, now she takes the arm of her father and his mistress to walk away from the church nestled between her guardians. I wave as they take the slight incline towards the house, but no one turns to wave back. Not even for one last glimpse. Instead, I watch as my family disintegrates before me, wondering where is the justice? I, who was forced to leave my home and my daughter, whilst this drunkard, cheating husband, walks back to Holton House with my daughter, his mistress and their love child. An unborn child conceived out of wedlock, inside infidelity, is forced into my face on the day we entomb our son; our first born. How dare he? How dare he take away my chance of a home and family, leaving me helpless and an outsider. I drop my waving hand as I lose site of them and look on to an empty scene.

'Madam. Madam. Madam,' calls Mary Hurles. I rush to greet her friendly face.

'Mary. When will all these tragedies end?'

'Oh Marm. I wish I knew. It's too much isn't it.'

'My little boy, that we both cared so much for, gone. He grew up to be quite damaged. What did we do wrong?'

'I blame it on the war Marm. To have the king taken

from us was a huge shock for everyone. It was too much change. No one in parliament considered how we might feel to live without a king as they decided our fate. I think Brome junior was too sensitive Marm. He couldn't move on from the shock; leaving him defeated, letting the demons take over his mind.'

'Do you really think so Mary?' barely able to unravel any of this mess in my mind.

'I think so Marm. Though he did pick up some bad habits with drinking too much, I fear.'

'Oh I don't know anymore Mary. All I know is, we did what we thought was best at the time.'

'Madam. I must tell you. I'm leaving Holton House. Diana is happy with her father. I can't work in Mr Whorwood's household whilst Katherine Allen takes your place, believing she is the Lady of the Manor. I'm so sorry, I tried for as long as I could.'

'Where will you go?

'I have a position in London, at Mill Bank House in Westminster, Marm.'

'That is good news. Well done on your new position. If you need references, you must let me know. I shall write you the best report.'

'Thank you. I shall let you get off before that black cloud bursts to soak us both,' she says pointing to the blackened sky, pulling her cloak closer beneath her chin.

I move quickly towards the carriage feeling the first few drops of rain. Mary closes the carriage door fast, running back to the house at the first clap of thunder. Rain trickles down the window, distorting my view of St Bartholomew's church to gain one last glimpse of my boy. The wheels turn to make our advance. My sobbing is silenced by the rumbling sky.

'Good bye my boy. Sleep tight.'

CHAPTER THIRTY ONE

Time to React
March 1659

Mary Hurles runs across the street towards my home in Holborn. I wait for her to rap the front door to welcome her inside.

'Marm. Are you alright? What's so urgent you had to see me today?' she says, as I lead her into the sitting room before uttering a single word.

'Thank you for coming Mary. I had to see you. I have a plan.'

'Oh no Marm. Where are you going this time?' she replies, rolling her eyes and lifting her eyebrows.

'I am taking Brome Whorwood to court. I've submitted a petition to Chancery, raising a Bill of Complaint. The Lord Commissioners have agreed to take up my plea.'

'Marm. That's a big step you are taking. Are you sure? Do you think you can win? What if you lose?'

'I've nothing more to lose Mary. I've lost my darling daughter, my home and my dignity. Brome Whorwood must be held accountable for his actions. He cannot be allowed to get away with this.'

'Oh, Marm, you are shaking,' she replies, taking hold of my hand.

'Is there anything I can do for you?'

'Yes, there is Mary.'

'Go on Marm, what can I do.'

'Can I ask you to bear witness, relaying everything to the court of Chancery? Tell them how cruel Brome treated me and the servants?'

Her eyes widen as her mouth opens. I've never seen her look so scared.

'Marm. You want me to speak to lawyers and judges?'

'Yes. Tell them everything.'

'What you mean everything?'

'Yes. How Brome held me prisoner in my own home. How he left me for dead. How he treated the servants who tried to help me.'

'What you mean like, when he pushed Joan Miller down the stairs after she tried to bring you food in the turret?'

'Yes. That sort of incident. All those incidents.'

'Like when he fought with Margery Bower.'

'Yes. She didn't deserve that treatment. All she did was confront him about Katherine's behaviour in the house. He challenged her when she spoke out, throwing her against the wall. Tell them that. Tell them how...'

'No Marm,' she interjects.

'Mary. Please. If not for me, then do it for Diana. My beautiful daughter who everyday is turned against me by that evil man. She has a right to know that her mother didn't abandon her for no good reason.'

'Oh Marm. No Marm. It wouldn't be for the likes of me to speak out. I'm so sorry.'

'Mary, you wouldn't have to see Mr Whorwood. He won't hear what you have to say. The lawyers will send their clerks to your place of work to take your statement. Could you do that Mary?'

Aware that I've shocked her with my request, I take her hand to ease her discomfort, disappointed in myself for even considering her involvement in such a painful task.

'You are a good girl, Mary. I accept your decision and your honesty. Now, let's forget about all this horridness. I've prepared supper for us. Would you have time to eat with me?'

'Alright Marm, that game pie does look inviting.'

She slips off her light coat folding it over her chair as she pulls it out slowly, appearing slightly more relaxed with the possibility of changing the subject.

'Have some claret. You will like this I think.'

'Thank you Marm, I don't mind if I do,' she says as the colour starts to creep back into her cheeks.

'Look at me Mary, things are not so bad. I might not have my beautiful daughter with me but you have to agree I am getting stronger. One day I shall have my independence from Brome Whorwood, I am certain of that.'

'I don't doubt your determination for one moment, you are stronger than anyone I know, but can you ever be free from him? After all, isn't your bond, as long as you both shall live?' says Mary, holding the pose of a priest, standing before a happy couple.

'You are quite right Mary. We were united in front of God, but unfortunately for Brome, in the eyes of the law this union can not survive adultery. For this too, he must pay.'

'But Marm, you would have to prove it. How can you do that?'

'Effortlessly,' I reply with a smugness about me as I replenish our glasses.

'What do you mean, effortlessly?' Mary replies, taking the glass in her hand.

'What more proof do I need than Katherine Allen

358

giving birth to my husband's child? To be honest, I can't believe I've waited this long to bring him to court. They fell right into my hands when she gave Brome, a son.'

'But Marm, don't you see? Mr Whorwood and Katherine Allen will deny there ever was a child,' replies Mary, somewhat surprised at my suggestion.

'How can they deny it? She was heavy with child at dear Brome junior's funeral and we both know she gave birth to a baby boy.'

'Oh, Marm. You don't know do you?

'Know what Mary?'

'Brome and Katherine fostered the child out to a Thomas and Audrey Juggins in the village of Forest Hill, near Oxford. The child doesn't even reside at Holton House. It will be so easy for the two lovers to deny the child is theirs or that Mr Whorwood even fathered another.'

I can't quite believe what I'm hearing. I'm flabbergasted. The one certain truth to make Brome pay for his crimes against me, has come to nothing. Thoughts start to rush forth. Maybe I'm clutching at straws but regardless, I proceed anyway.

'What about the physical harm he did to me? What about proving how monstrous he is? The villagers; what about them? They have plenty of evidence to support my case. For the most part they saw with their own eyes the bruises and cuts laid upon us at that lunatic asylum that is, Holton House.'

'Marm, what are you thinking?'

'What do you mean? What am I thinking?'

'Even if the likes of Mr Almond did speak to lawyers, those big-wigs in Westminster won't listen to the likes of us. No one listens to us. Our opinions don't concern the likes of them. Why should they? We don't have any rights, not like Brome Whorwood. If those villagers and servants said anything against him, they would instantly lose their employment to be chucked out onto the streets to fend for themselves.'

'Oh Mary, what was I thinking.'

'Marm, you must remember how shocked you were when I bad mouthed Sir Thomas Whorwood. How scared I was that you'd report me to Lady Whorwood that I'd lose my position at the house.'

'Yes, Mary, but I wouldn't have told on you, you know that.'

'Marm, we have no rights. We are brought on this earth to serve. Keep our mouths tightly closed and take whatever cruelty or dishonesty is sent our way. We survive because we know how to keep our mouth tightly closed. It's different for Mr Whorwood, it's even a little different for you too Madam.'

'You are quite right Mary. Whatever was I thinking. Please forgive me. You will forgive me won't you?' I say, feeling somewhat appalled that she had to speak so specifically to make me understand. Though there must be a way around this, there is always more than one way to skin a cat. True to form, I hear myself pushing to find a way.

I ask about Elizabeth Ball and William Elliot, who were not in service for Brome Whorwood, wondering if they could give evidence of the night I arrived at their cottage, hours away from my own death.

'Mr Whorwood evicted them from their tenancy soon after they helped you Marm,' replies Mary. 'They are already casualties of this plight,' she tells me.

'But they saved my life,' I say, quickly realising that Brome had wanted me dead, so he was free to marry his mistress. Those who bulwarked his plans were punished. He despises me even more than I ever can imagine. I look down at my lap, where my hands are wringing with anxiety and frustration.

'I'm sorry Marm. Perhaps I should leave?'

'No. It's me who should apologise. Now please, eat something more, there is plenty here. The game pie is wonderful.'

'Will you still go ahead with the hearing, Marm?'

'Yes. I shall name and shame that man even if I'm not

taken seriously. I shall at least be content that his antics have been aired to the highest in the land,' I reply trying to reassure us both that I still have strength to fight this man.

Though in truth, I am but a lamb cornered before slaughter. I don't have the slightest hope of proving anything to the Lord Commissioners. Brome Whorwood has covered his tracks at every turn. He will do exactly the same to the keeper of the Great Seal; avoiding any come back from his infernal actions.

'Now, no more of this depressing conversation, Mary. Instead, tell me all about your new position. Is your employer as kind as I am to work for?'

'Well,' she starts, taking a deep breath as a smirk begins to emerge across her face, which pleases me. 'My employer's life is not as exciting as yours Marm, but at least I know where she is most of the time, which makes my work slightly less difficult.'

We both raise a glass to her astute observation as laughter begins to return. It's uplifting to hear Mary's renewed hopes and dreams as she ventures forth into a new phase of her life; something that for me, I now realise, is impossible.

CHAPTER THIRTY TWO

Judgement Day
June 1659

The small court room, here in Westminster Palace, is cheerless. I wait alone to hear the Lord Chancellor's final decision on the evidence he and his clerks have collected over the previous three months. Court officials make me nervous since my involvement in Lord Howard of Escrick's case, even though the Lord Commissioners and their clerks have been patient, allowing me to log my evidence without interruption.

Adding to my anxiety is the outcome of a visit, yesterday, to the astrologer, William Lilly. I took it upon myself to request a prediction of how I might fare today. Lilly was kind enough with the usual humour and banter. He felt the need to remind me of my stubbornness the day I insisted on entering his house after being visited by the plague. His forecast however, whilst no surprise, is not pleasant, confirming that my husband will fight bitterly until he proves his innocence. He also predicted that Brome's bitterness is stimulated by the fury boiling inside his body that is consumed by gout and calcified stones. On first hearing this diagnosis, I felt sorry for Brome, but quickly suspended all sympathy, knowing his gout hadn't stopped him from taking a lover to his bed. At this moment, sitting here in the court room, I don't know who I pity more.

'Please rise,' says the clerk, alerting me to the immanent arrival of the Lord Chancellor, Keeper of the Great Seal, reminding me that proceedings are now in progress.'

This is it. I feel weak as I rise. I can't stop my knees from knocking. I appear to have lost complete control of my nerves. Nevertheless, I am determined to hold my ground. The room is so stuffy, but protocol reminds me I cannot remove my coat.

'Madam plaintiff,' says the Lord Chancellor. 'You have called upon this court to request a hearing against the brutality you suffered at the hands of your husband, a Mr Brome Whorwood of Holton House, Oxford, and the accusation of committing an act of adultery.' Is that correct Madam?'

'Right Honourable, Lord Chancellor, that is correct,' I

reply with an inaudible squeak.

'Speak up Madam, my clerks must hear your answers to record your response.'

'Pardon, your Lord. Yes, my Lord, that is correct.'

Come on Jane, I say to myself, pull yourself together. But I can't stop the verbal tennis match taking place inside my head. I'm pathetic. Now is not the time to start feeling sorry for yourself. Woe is me. Not now Jane. What's the worse that can happen? I am humiliated yet again? That's what could happen. Probably what is about to happen. Remember Pindar? You stood up to him. How you fought off Richard Cole when he came to the house? I didn't win him over though did I? It was because of the way I dealt with him that I ended up in a rotten cell with Brome finally disowning me. It was more than that though wasn't it. Whilst I believed the web of deceit I'd spun was for the good, it left others, such as Brome Whorwood hurt, feeling betrayed. Oh, what about the fact he left us? Were we supposed to ignore that? What about fighting for our country, for our sovereign. Surely that counted for something? Enough now Jane. Not now. Your conscience has heard quite enough.

'Are you alright Madam?' enquires the Lord Chancellor, lifting his head from his documents.

'Yes, sir. Though I am little warm, sir.'

Michelle Hockley

'This won't take long. Perhaps you can take a seat.'

'Oh yes, thank you, Right Honourable.'

That's better. That's steadied me a little. The room is silent, but for the tick-tock of the clock on the wall, but beyond the room, there is such a commotion going on. Perhaps they too are waiting for a hearing, uneasy like me. Goodness, they are noisy, don't they know that etiquette is expected when in such a building? Though of course there is less of that since Charles left us, leaving us to fend for such a code. The country seems to be in an even worse state since Cromwell died last year. His son, Richard Cromwell, the supposed successor, has already been removed by the army. Oh, everything is in such a mess. No one knows whether we are coming or going. We need a leader. We should have a sovereign leader to guide us out of the controversy between army and parliament.

'Madam,' begins the Chancellor, 'perhaps you would be more comfortable to wait in the corridor? Though what you will find on the other side of that door, with all that chatter going on, is beyond me.'

'I think I might do that sir,' I reply, hoping for some fresher air.

As I turn the handle, there is such a force from the handle on the other side that it opens, taking me by surprise.

'Are we late for the hearing, Marm.'

'Mr Stampe. What are you doing here?'

I prompt him to move away from the open door back into the corridor, where I see, seated in a line; Margery Bower, Joan Miller, Mary Hurles, Elizabeth Ball, William Elliot, Mr Truman, Emmanuel, Jane and George Ball, Elizabeth Towersey, Mr Almond, to name but a few. The site is overwhelming. I don't know whether to cry or smile I'm that emotional.

Joan Miller, who is so small in stature, pulls ranks, breaking away from the line to greet me.

'We've come today to hear the outcome Marm. We've all given our evidence you see, like you wanted. Those official people called on us. They wrote down what we told them, what we knew,' she says, swinging her arms as she retells what she explained to the commissioners, that Katherine, brought her to the ground, when she took orders from me instead of Miss Allen who Mr Whorwood had promoted to Lady of the Manor.

'I told them also,' she continues with her eyes wide, 'how when I tried to free myself from harm by running out the house, heading for the moat, Mr Whorwood caught up with me, and beat me with his riding whip.'

'So, you all gave evidence for me?' I ask.

Margery Bower stands up to walk purposefully towards me.

'Those good men from the court, Marm, they listened ever so carefully to me when I told them how Mr Whorwood cornered me in the scullery when I confronted him about the poor treatment he gave you. Telling him that he shouldn't take a servant to his marital bed. They wrote down what Mr Whorwood said to me, that it was good for Madam to be locked in the turret, to teach her the good ways of a wife.'

Emmanuel sits alongside her, always so quiet. I thank him for coming, for I wasn't sure he liked me, being always so close in service to Lady Ursula.

'I told them too, Marm,' he says. 'I told them of the journeys I made to take Mr Whorwood and his mistress Katherine, to rendezvous outside Holton village.'

'Thank you Emmanuel. I hope this doesn't get you into any trouble with Mr Whorwood.'

'Oh no, the clerks seemed pleased we spoke out. Mary Hurles warned us that we shouldn't, but when they arrived at the house, we decided we would. In the end Mary did too. She'd always want to help you,' he replies so eloquently.

When I see Elizabeth Ball and Mr Elliot, I feel quite ashamed. It's because of me, they lost their home. I apologise for what happened.

'No matter Marm. Mr Elliot and me are settled again. It's done us good to shift some of our old stuff that was cluttering up our home. I told the clerks as well. How Mr Stampe held you in his arms when you were close to death, with your lips all sore for want of nourishment. It broke my heart that day Miss, truly it did.'

Mr Stampe then pulls at my arm. 'Come and meet Mr and Mrs Juggins. They fostered Mr Whorwood and Miss Allen's baby boy.'

Not having even met the Juggins before, only recently aware of their existence, I feel so humbled in their company, that they've taken the time to come here to support my case.

'I explained Marm,' says Mrs Juggins. 'I thought it only right to do so, seeing as you are in such a pickle with that man from the big house who has caused you so much pain. Especially as you helped to save our beloved king as you did. You were brave then and we are brave for you now. I told those men from London when they came to hear my story, how Miss Katherine brings clothes for the child she bore out of wedlock, plays with young Thomas like a mother should, but hides her shame by leaving him behind in my care.'

'Thomas,' I repeat. That's an interesting choice of name. I hope the child is more charming than his grandfather.

'I know Katherine did wrong Marm,' Mrs Juggins

continues, 'but I look after her boy as if he were my own.'

'I am sure you do Mrs Juggins, you are a good and faithful citizen. Thank you for what you have done for me, in telling what you know.'

Jane Ball taps me on the shoulder, 'I shall never forgive Brome Whorwood Marm, for forbidding me entry to Holton House, to collect the ointment you made so carefully from the herbs you grew in your kitchen garden.'

'I am sorry Mrs Ball, it has all been so awful.'

'George, tell Madam how the ointment helped your arthritis,' she says, encouraging George to speak.'

'Without the ointment,' Mrs Ball starts again, 'he is in such pain. Look at him,' she points to her husband, 'he's so crumpled up, aching all over.'

'I am truly sorry Mrs Ball, I appreciate you coming here today.'

'Mr Ball insisted. I thought it might be too much for him, but he wanted to come, we all did to support you in whatever the outcome is today.' She starts to cry. I too tear up after hearing what Brome has put us all through.

The door of the court room opens. I become awfully aware that the noise has far from abated since I entered the corridor and afraid our behaviour might annoy the Lord Chancellor, perhaps taint his decision.

'Can you return to the court room, Madam

Whorwood,' requests the clerk.

Once I arrive inside the room, I apologise to the Right Honourable for the noise, explaining they are associates of mine from Holton House, taking full responsibility for any disturbance they may have caused.

'Madam. You don't need to apologise,' replies the chancellor. 'It is to their honesty and their courage, you owe a great deal. Now please, take a seat.'

'Thank you your Right Honourable,' ready to hear my fate.

'I have considered each of the seventeen witness statements as recorded by the officers. I have afforded Mr Whorwood the opportunity to retaliate when questioned, to which he has declined, firm in his belief that he has committed no crime, convinced it unnecessary to defend himself. The evidence we have received against him is most damning. A husband who believes it proper behaviour to treat a wife in this way, is wholly unacceptable, for which, Mr Whorwood should be ashamed. He is either sick in mind or ailing in body to treat another in such an appalling way and maintaining a belief that he has done nothing indecorous.'

I start to feel tears forming in my eyes. Not because I am sad this time, but because someone in authority is understanding what myself and the servants have had to endure.

'Based on these findings, along with proof of adultery committed whilst in a marriage union,' he continues, 'we are ordering Mr Whorwood to pay the plaintiff, Madam Whorwood, the sum of three hundred pounds per annum in separation, as alimony, which I can legally oblige. In the eyes of the church, you will remain husband and wife. Neither party is at liberty to re-marry whilst one of you remains alive. Under common law, your sole living child remains the property of your husband to which we are satisfied she is in no danger from her father. However, based on the evidence we have received otherwise, Mr Whorwood has committed a damming offence to which I pass the great seal.'

Relief comes over me only momentarily. For the outcome remains bitter sweet with the law leaving my daughter without a mother, even though my arms are always open for her. The relief is blighted too that whilst I have been recognised as a deserving case, those witnesses, as Mary Hurles pointed out, will be out of a position the moment Brome discovers they have spoken out against him. Perhaps there was never going to be any real winners in this situation. I start to collect myself, ready to receive the papers to take my leave.

'Madam, not in such a hurry,' says the Lord

Chancellor. 'I am placing an addendum to this hearing to the official documentation which is of the utmost necessity.'

'Pardon me sir.' I start to listen with intent.

'Mr Whorwood will be prohibited, for the next five years, from terminating any witness from their employment or removing any tenants from their property. Should he wish to do so, he will be obliged to address the court of Chancery, explaining his actions. To this end, I also pass the great seal.'

'Thank you your Right Honourable, thank you,' I reply with such relief. An outcome that I hope, will go some way to restoring the servants' confidence in the legal system that King Charles was so adamant to protect, costing him his life, by refusing to enter into discussion during the mock trial, as he described.

The corridor is completely void of all my comrades, those who put their whole lives on the line for me, raising their heads above the parapet for what they believed in. I make my way to leave the building, contemplating how William Lilly's prediction was so wrong this time, perhaps all his readings are flawed in this way. Brome didn't put up a bitter fight to declare his innocence, instead, he is content in the fact that he'd done nothing improper. I push open the heavy sculptured wooden door leading on to the street. The sunshine rushes inside as fresh air touches my skin. In the distance, I see my dear companions grouped together. How can I ever thank them?

'Madam. How did we do?' asks Elizabeth Ball with eyes bright and inquisitive. I hold aloft the documentation smiling, to which there is an almighty cheer from each and everyone.

'Can I thank you with all my heart. This document I hold in my hand, would not have been possible to achieve without your bravery. For that, the court protects your leases and employment. Margery Bower throws her arms tight around me. 'Well done Marm.'

'Mrs Bower,' I whisper in her ear, not wanting to bring down the mood, 'this still doesn't mean I have custody of my daughter. What will that poor child think of her mother who left her behind?'

'Now, come on Madam. Diana is well cared for, a good girl. She may not fully understand why you left her father; and in some ways that is good, but one day she will understand, I promise. One day.'

'I hope so, Mrs Bower,' and she is probably right. Something I must try to accept.

'Please everyone,' I announce. 'Can I at least offer you something to eat at my home, before your journey back to Holton?'

'That is kind of you Marm,' says George Ball, 'though we won't trouble you. We'd quite like to remove ourselves from the hustle and smoke here in the city, if you don't mind. We wanted to be with you when the verdict was read today, that's all. Hoping we could make a difference.'

I put my arms around his small, weak shoulders, where his arthritis is so severe, to show him that I fervently respect his wishes.

'Does anyone know where is Mary Hurles?' I shout, realising I haven't yet seen her.

'Gone back to work at the big house Marm', says Margery Bower. 'She couldn't wait. A little strict I think,' she explains, stepping into one of the carriages that stands in convoy.

One by one they find their seats. I wave goodbye as the wheels turn, aware this is probably the last time I shall see them, having now severed ties with Holton House. I watch as they take the bend, completely out of sight, before making my retreat away from the court rooms. The streets are busy with strangers all going about their business, allowing me space to lay down my thoughts to impress upon my mind like the parchment records I leave sealed; filled with horrific events of the past.

Nevertheless, a sadness of what has become does prevail. I embarked upon a journey with my husband who did love me, if not for a brief moment. We delighted in our third anniversary at Sandwell Hall, full of hope and tenderness. We wept together on losing our baby James we wept tears of joy to welcome our first born into the world. The war was his undoing. No. I should rephrase that. The war was both our undoing. With my spirit left untethered I cast the most tangled web of deceit to help my king. Unleashing traits within myself, even I had no idea I possessed. On Brome's return from exile, I was unable to release myself on his command being buried so deeply inside the labyrinth to which I had become embroiled. The die had already been cast when we left the sweet scented periwinkles and sweet smelling honeysuckles swaying in the formal gardens of Sandwell Hall; forcing me to negotiate my own path which I navigated towards a quiet despair.

CHAPTER THIRTY THREE

Letting Go
1659

I push the robust wheeled chair that supports my mother's frail, failing frame, closer to the window that overlooks the grand gardens at her home on the Guildford Park Estate.

'Is that position more suited to you, Mama?'

'Yes, darling. Oh Jane, you do look cadaverous.'

'I can't possible look as bad as all that,' I reply.

'You do Jane. Where did all your vitality disappear? All that joy for life which no one could tether?'

I plump up her pillows from behind trying to reassure her that I am in control of my life, omitting to tell her, that in truth, Brome has so far failed to make any payments of alimony, continuing to claim his innocence, hanging on to me like a festering carbuncle that refuses to heal.

'Oh Jane, if I could turn back the clocks.'

'Yes, mother, if only that were possible...' I stop what I'm saying, allowing her to voice her thoughts, not wanting to miss one second of what I know is soon to be her final words.

'...I would turn them back to the day your stepfather requested you to the front room to meet those dreadful people to whom he gave you away.'

'Me too Mama.' Though we both know neither of us were in a position to halt that tide. I put my arms around her shoulders. She holds my hands firmly.

'But then, I wouldn't have had my beautiful children.'

'No, darling, quite true,' she says tapping my hand before reaching to move away the wispy curls that hang around my face.

'Did you ride here today, Jane? You certainly look as if you did.'

We both start to giggle, remembering how I always refused to ride side saddle believing it would hinder my stride. How, on returning from a whirlwind ride, I would enter the house, quite bedraggled.

A knock at her bedchamber door halts our dreaming.

'Pardon Marm,' says Margaret. 'Diana, Anne and Elizabeth have arrived. Shall I show them in?'

'Shall we let them in Jane? Or do we want a moment longer to be alone?' my mother asks.

I would love to spend more time alone with her, but of course, it will not be possible to hold back the torrent of Diana and Anne's strong will.

'We shouldn't keep them waiting Mama.'

'You are quite right my little one,' she says letting go of my hand, trying to sit up a little straighter as Anne struts into the room.

'Jane, Why are you already here?' enquires Anne. 'Mother, you said two o'clock. We are here at two o'clock.'

Anne begins to take charge, moving me out of her way to readjust the pillows behind my mother that were already perfectly plump.

'No one is late. Jane is not early,' explains my mother. 'You are all here at the time I requested to see you.'

'Jane would never be early,' mutters Diana as she takes her seat before my mother.

'Now, now, Diana. We don't want any harsh talk from you today,' answers my mother, trying to appease her flock, as she has always done.

I fetch a chair for Elizabeth who looks even more frail and pale than usual, who I believe, everyday walks through life with a broken heart. A heart of an angel, that shattered into tiny pieces when her beloved William, who fought inexhaustibly to retrieve power in England for Prince Charles, died of horrific injuries sustained at the Battle of Worcester, eight years ago. A war, that has bludgeoned a trail of devastation, destroying any love that reigned before its uprising. It didn't matter to her that William dedicated all his wealth to his brother James' children, to ease the guilt he carried for his brother's execution two months after King Charles received the axe, leaving her without subsistence. Though it does quite clearly matter that her marriage to Thomas Dalmahoy, which she entered in 1655, does not provide her with the love she once knew, making life, it would seem, insufferable. Elizabeth makes no attempt to reassure us as to why she looks so unwell; clearly too weak to hide the pallid malaise.

'Girls.' calls my mother, painfully weak, but insisting on bringing a semblance of order. 'My one desire is for you not to squabble between yourselves when I leave this earth. Therefore, today, I shall announce my intentions.'

'We won't fight mother, I promise,' says Diana, as she moves forward to place her hand on my mother's knee, no doubt I'm sure, hoping for a fortune.

Diana, has I'm afraid acquired a taste for gambling at the card tables amongst her aristocratic circle of friends for which she has shown not one ounce of flair or skill, accruing quite an unimaginable debt.

'Now.' begins my mother, wanting to get back to business. 'I shall leave each of you one thousand and five hundred pounds. Elizabeth, as the eldest Maxwell, you will inherit this house and the Guildford Estate, where you will reside with your husband at my demise.'

'Diana,' my mother continues. 'The money you borrowed to satisfy the outstanding debts, we shall now forget. Though I do pray you will refrain yourself from such a pointless addiction and instead discover a pastime less harmful to your financial status, to fill your void.'

Diana shows her gratitude to my mother rather awkwardly, aware of her undoing. It's shameful how the rich squander their money, whilst the poor work relentlessly as labourers and servants, meeting our needs. My mother also announces that until I am more settled, in a more improved health, my inheritance will be placed in trust. Whilst I would like to question my mother's reasoning for such a suggestion, I don't trouble her, instead make my own deduction that she is safeguarding against Brome having power over my share.

'Girls, that will have to be all for I am very weak. Please call Margaret to help me to my bed?' she requests.

Nobody does as she says, instead, as a little family once more, we take turns to show our gratitude by helping to make her comfortable, tidying her room, leaving open the drapes so she can gaze at the garden from her bed.

'Would you leave me now girls please. Remember, always be kind and helpful to one another.'

In unison, we agree to uphold her wishes, though reluctantly start to move away at her behest. I kiss my mother on her forehead and take her hand. She squeezes it firmly, which speaks to me without the need for another word. At the door, I take a lingering look at her because I now accept these visits are dwindling away from us.

Margaret stands close by in the corridor to greet us as we leave my mother's bedchamber making sure, as always, that we are coping with the situation.

'Oh Margaret. Why is life so cruel?'

'I wish I knew that young Jane, but I fear it is something we shall never have the answer to.'

I smile at her, putting my arm around her shoulder. She has always been there for us. Grown up with us, devoting her whole life to the Maxwell and Ryder family. Never marrying or having children of her own. What will she do when my mother has passed? Maybe retire or remain in the household at the Guildford Estate with the newcomers.

As Elizabeth leaves the bedchamber, I offer her my arm to walk to the hallway.

'Sit down Elizabeth, just for a moment while we wait

for Anne and Diana. You will need all your strength for when you are the Lady of this vast estate,' hoping to see a glimmer of life in her eyes.

'Jane, thank you. I don't feel at all well. I don't know why?'

'When you get home, ask Mr Dalmahoy to call the doctor, to prescribe something to ease your troubles.'

She smiles at me with a hollowness. I wonder if when William died, he took her soul with him. Gone is the little lady who danced full of hope at the Court Masque; she who enthused all her selfless charm upon us.

Anne and Diana enter the hall wiping their tears.

'Jane, please share the carriage with us back to London,' requests Diana. 'I want us all to be together.'

'Thank you Diana, I'd like that.'

The journey is silent. Each of us deep in thoughts of lives lived and lost. A quietness that runs deep through the years of troubles that are behind us, and yet to come. The pretty clothes we wore, when bunched together to escape the plague, now replaced with the blackness of mourning from which we are unable to take flight in quite the same way. Time hasn't made us stronger, for it chipped away at our innocence leaving us weak, less hopeful, seeing life now, for what it really is. Our childhood was designed to protect us, but it gave us an interlude from the horrors that we are expected to endure. The baby house we played and the wooden horse we galloped, prepared us for nothing that we saw. We are each more sluggish, weighed down by our lives resting heavy upon us, unable to shake off those paths we led. Footsteps taken that remain for all eternity; each of us now broken by the passage of time.

As we enter Holborn, I take hold of Elizabeth's weak hand in mine, so she knows I am there for her and prepare myself to leave the carriage, so as not to delay my sisters with my fumbling, clumsiness.

'Do you want to come inside to see Sarah and William? They'd love to see you all?'

'No thank you,' replies Anne, responding for everyone.

'I shall see you soon. Love to you all. Thank you.'

With my heavy heart I enter the house, knowing that in a matter of days or weeks, my life will be a whole lot more empty without my dear mother.

* * *

What I didn't fully anticipate on the day we left my mother's side, was to lose my beautiful sister, Elizabeth, within a month of my mother's passing. Elizabeth had an uncontrollable fever that would not subside, though I remain convinced she died of a broken heart. We buried my mother in August, and Elizabeth in September. I could do nothing to save either of them and I'm left feeling wretched and helpless. All I can hope, is that my mother is reunited with my father, William Ryder and stepfather, James Maxwell, where they will be happy once more. They will be looking after their daughter Elizabeth too, who I am sure by now, will have found William, her true love.

The squabbling, that my mother so wanted to avoid, is being acted out with Diana insisting that Guildford Park, that passed to Elizabeth's second husband, Thomas Dalmahoy, after her death, should in part at least, go to her or to Elizabeth's children. For once, I have to agree with Diana, but I am too weary to take on that battle, leaving her and Anne to fight with the courts. My grieving still continues for my son, and now my mother and sister. Whilst, the separation from my daughter Diana is miserable, wrenching at my entire being; twisting inside my guts like a screw of iron. My distress is further ignited by Brome's constant claims to profess his innocence, having not yet paid one penny of the alimony he was ordered to commit. William Lilly was correct in his prediction, something I was convinced he had figured so wrongly on the day we left court in high spirits at our success.

I do however, detect some promise for our monarch

to return, a glimmer of hope is starting to emerge. Often I read illicit pamphlets, where talk is that the tide is turning in favour of something pro-royalist as years gone by. Though I have no intention of raising my hopes of a restored Stuart monarch, not until I witness the crown descend its rightful owner, which I imagine, will never happen in my lifetime.

My dreaming is disturbed with Sarah's footsteps approaching the sitting room. Tucking the papers I am reading beneath my seat, replacing with a religious tract.

'Jane, you will ruin your eyes with all that reading,' she says, going about her evening duties; closing the curtains, lighting the candles. If only she knew I was keeping banned literature in the house, threatening her position with the authorities. Though, most often I try to burn after reading, so I feel we are quite safe.

'It takes my mind off my sadness, Sarah. You understand don't you?'

'You always look so troubled after reading. I think it's too much for you. Why don't you work your tapestry and needlepoint, like you used to? You loved that. It's good for you. Not all this reading.'

'Yes, I could do my needlepoint,' I reply, hoping to give the impression that I have not given up on everything I once loved.

As she leaves the room, she halts at the door. 'Some

good news at least though, Jane. You would have to agree with that,' she says, seeming rather pleased with herself, stopping in her tracks.

'What is that Sarah? I could do with some good news.'

'All this talk that we might soon have a king again.'

'Where did you hear that?'

'That's what they say at the butchers and the bakers. But of course, we're not scholars like you, so we've probably got it wrong. Sure we have too.'

Shocked to hear that rumours are gaining momentum outside the elite, I turn my head, to engage her further.

'Imagine though Jane, if we did have a king again and you could go to the royal court like you once did. You'd like that, I know you would,' she says, starting a minuet and walking around the room as if holding a partner in dance, making me giggle.

I'm also smiling at her source of information; simply hearsay, rather than facts, is enough for Sarah to believe. Seriously though, I am uplifted by what she says, for if chatter of this kind has started amongst the traders, then a restoration could be true. News does indeed travel up and down the country this way attaching itself to any movable goods. Maybe it will happen. Maybe.

387

CHAPTER THIRTY FOUR

Long Live The King
23 April 1661

I lift my head off my knees with a jolt to find myself seated, scrunched up on the path. A gentleman walks past me, I draw in my feet, he doffs his cap. A monkey, twisting and dancing on its leash turns to look at me as his master strides off in the distance.

A feathered hat falls at my feet. A young Baker's boy runs to fetch it.

'Pardon Madam. I threw too high.'

'No harm done, young man.'

'Can I help you to your feet Marm?'

'Yes I think perhaps you can, thank you.'

'I thought I'd see the king today, but he didn't come down this way,' says the boy.

'Not to worry. You have plenty of time for that, the

king is here to stay.'

'I've never seen a king of England before. Have you, Marm?'

'Yes, my boy, I did, a long time ago, before you were born, I suspect.'

'Hackneys are starting to run again. If you've had enough of waiting, I could fetch one for you?'

'Yes please if you will. I should be getting home.'

The young boy, of about twelve years old, halts a nearby carriage for which I am rather grateful. The drive back to Holborn displays signs that the crowds are starting to clear but the colours still remain. Maypole ribbons flutter, though have stopped their spinning. Cheers can be heard, perhaps the party has begun.

'Holborn Marm,' shouts the driver as he comes around to open the carriage door.

'Thank you.'

'Unless Marm, you've changed your mind.'

'Why would I change my mind?'

'I remember you from years back. I took you to Ironmonger Lane, after you had me take you in the opposite direction first.'

'Are you sure that was me?' I'm sorry, I don't remember you.'

'Why would you Marm, you were awfully preoccupied back then.'

'Yes, I probably was too,' because in those days, I had a purpose in life. People needed me. I was useful.

I hand the driver the fare and make my way towards the house. What an extraordinary day. Yet, I don't quite know what I've achieved. I neither raised a cheer for the king nor saw him crowned or orbed. If the royal carriage passed by, then I missed him.

Coming closer to the house I see Sarah standing on the door step, gesturing for me to hurry along, something I am less keen to do in my old age, but I make an effort, if only because her whole face is smiling; her eyes gleaming with excitement.

'What is it Sarah?'

'Miss, please, come quickly. Someone is here to see you.'

I stand in the hallway to take off my cloak, willing her to give me a name so I can prepare myself.

'To see me, Sarah who is it?' I whisper.

'Please go into the sitting room. I shall bring in refreshments.'

Following her instructions, I start to open the door slowly, aware I've succumbed to Sarah's excitement, as my heart beats strongly. Still holding tightly to the handle, I see, standing in the middle of the room, with her back to me my beautiful daughter, Diana. She turns slowly to face me.

'Hello Mama.'

I rush towards her with open arms burying my head in her shoulder, holding her tightly, praying this is not an illusion; an image of that I have wished everyday to be a reality.

'Mama, how will you ever forgive me?'

'My dear, there is nothing to forgive. My darling girl,' I say, stroking her cheek, looking into her pretty eyes.'

We take a seat next to each other on the couch by the window.

'I must explain Mama.'

'I am certain there is no need.'

'Mary Hurles has told me everything. She explained why you left my father. Why you couldn't stay with me at the house. Why you left me with Katherine Allen. That my brother's demise was not your fault. Why, when we were small, you left Brome junior and me for days on end. She told me how brave you were in trying to help save the king from imprisonment.'

'I wanted to tell you myself Diana, but it was so difficult after I left Holton House. I never wanted to hurt you.'

'Can you forgive me for believing you had wronged me, Mama?'

'You have done nothing wrong to forgive. With you being here, everything today, is as it should be.'

'You have to believe me,' says Diana, still looking awfully upset. 'I asked my father all these questions and he said...'

I place my fingers on her lips to signal that she doesn't have to explain and to be quite honest, I definitely do not wish to hear Brome's version of my life.

Sarah comes into the room with a large tray of refreshments. Diana quickly moves to help guide her safely to the table. I look at my daughter, all grown up. A young lady. A proud, thoughtful lady.

London came alive again today and with my daughter by my side, I believe I can come alive again too.

The End

EPILOGUE

J ane Whorwood spent the remainder of her life fighting for alimony payment; defeated by Brome Whorwood's death, five months before her own passing in September 1684. Her efforts were futile, leaving an estate worth forty pounds.

In death, Brome and Jane were reunited. Buried alongside each other in Brome Chapel, at St Bartholomew's Church, Holton. In 1697, they were joined by Katherine Allen, being the mother of Thomas, heir to the Whorwood estate, at Brome Whorwood's bequest.

Despite Jane's troubles, she outlived all her sisters, with Elizabeth passing in 1659, Diana in 1675 and Anne in 1683. Her daughter, Diana, lived until 1701, married, leaving no issue.

Bibliography

Primary source

The National Archives: Lord Chamberlain's Department, LC5/180

The National Archives: Lord Chamberlain's Department, LC5/196

The National Archives: Office of Works Accounts, WORK 5

Printed Primary source

Ashmole, E., The Institution, Laws and Ceremonies of the Most Noble Order of the Garter (London, 1672)

Ashburnham, J., A Narrative by John Ashburnham (London, 1830)

Berkley, J., Memoirs of Sir John Berkley (London, 1699)

Burnet, G., The Memoirs of the Lives and Actions of James and William Dukes of Hamilton (Oxford, 1852)

Clark, A., The Life and Times of Anthony Wood 1632-1695 (Oxford, 1891)

Michelle Hockley

Calendar State Papers Domestic:Charles I (London, 1858-1897)

Calendar of State Papers Domestic: Interregnum (London,1875-1886)

Journal of the House of Commons: Volume 1-9 (London, 1802)

Journal of the House of Lords: Volume 3-14 (London, 1767-1830)

Secondary Source

Aylmer, G.E., The King's Servants: The Civil Service of Charles I (London, 1974)

Baker, J.H., An introduction to English Legal History (Butterworths, 1990)

Colvin, H., History of the King's Works, 6 vols. (London, 1982)

Cressy, D., Bonfires & Bells (Sutton, 2004)

Firebrace, C.,Honest Harry: The Biography of Sir Henry Firebrace 1619-1691 (London, 1932)

Fox, John., The King's Smuggler: Jane Whorwood Secret Agent to Charles I (The History Press, 2010)

Hockley, M., Charles I's Escape from Hampton Court Palace (HRP, 1999)

Before Spring Came Summer

Sharpe, K., The Personal Rule of Charles I (Yale, 1992)
Strong, R., Art and Power (Boydell, 1999)
Smuts, R.M., The Stuart Court and Europe (Cambridge, 1996)

Acknowledgement

Dr. Sara Wolfson; Dr. Sarah K Poynting;
Dr. Nadine Akkerman

Front cover

Carstian Luyckx, Still Life with Silver & Gilt Pot, c1650

About the Author

Michelle Hockley combines her musical aptitude with her love for language, to enthuse life into her characters and the scenes in which they find themselves.

After a successful career in Television and on London's West End stage, Michelle went on to read History at Durham University, where her love for facts, debate, analysis and investigation for the truth, flourished. Subsequently, her thesis was published by Historic Royal Palaces and she triumphed in her role as Senior Early Modern Record Specialist at The National Archives, and a fusion of her talents was brought to the fore where a musicality is always present in her writing combined with an honesty for her cast.

Her debut novel, *Before Spring Came Summer*, is an enchanting piece, influenced by facts, set in the seventeenth century, following the life of Jane Whorwood, who wrestles with events of the day as well as those presented to her by the society in which her life is lived.

With Michelle's novels, you won't only get a story, you will also get a moment.

20259344R00241

Printed in Great Britain
by Amazon